Jackrabbit
A *Just Cause Universe* Novel

Ian Thomas Healy

Local Hero Press Edition

Jackrabbit: A Just Cause Universe Novel
Published by Local Hero Press

1st Printing
Local Hero Press: trade paperback, April 1, 2014
Printed in the United States of America

ISBN-13: 9781971445052

Cover art by Jeff Hebert
Book design by Ian Thomas Healy

All rabbit images are public domain from http://openclipart.org.

Books by Local Hero Press

The *Just Cause Universe*

Just Cause
The Archmage
Day of the Destroyer
Deep Six
Jackrabbit
Champion
Castles
The Lion and the Five Deadly Serpents
Tusks
The Neighborhood Watch
Jackrabbit: Big In Japan
Arena
Hero Academy
The Path
Cinco de Mayo
Search and Rescue
Rooftops
Plague
Soldiers of Fortune
Just Cause Universe Compendium
Destroyer of Earth
Flint and Steel
The Club
Jackrabbit: Rinse and Repeat
Posse
Extinction Event
Rain Must Fall

Pariah of Verigo

Pariah's Moon
Pariah's War

Three Flavors of Tacos

The Guitarist
Making the Cut
The Scene Stealers

Collections

Airship Lies
High Contrast
The Good Fight
The Good Fight 3: Sidekicks
The Good Fight 4: Homefront
The Good Fight 5: The Golden Age
Muddy Creek Tales
Caped

Other Novels

Assassin
Blood on the Ice
Funeral Games
Hope and Undead Elvis
Horde
The Murder Squad (2026)
Roast Wyvern (and Other Recipes)
Starf*cker
Strings
The Oilman's Daughter
Troubleshooters

Nonfiction

Action! Writing Better Action Using Cinematic Techniques

Acknowledgements

Writing a book for me has always been a team effort. First and foremost, I must thank my dearest friend and foremost editor Allison Dickson, who always manages to find time to help bring out the best in my work. Kate Jenkins was also instrumental in helping to bring Jackrabbit and his friends to life in this book. I'm grateful to Shewanda Pugh for always having a friendly ear ready for me despite being two time zones away. I can't say enough nice things about Jeff Hebert's art and the phenomenal covers he keeps creating for me. Special thanks to Drew Hayes for stepping in to write the introduction to this book.

I'm especially indebted to my family for putting up with my writerly shenanigans (and believe me, there are a lot!), and for their support when I indulge in this vice of writing.

Last but not least, I have to thank you, the fans. Without your continuing interest, I would find it much harder to keep writing more tales of the *Just Cause Universe*.

Introduction
Drew Hayes

For the last decade or so, there has been a curious emphasis on making superheroes more realistic. What was once the territory of high-flying adventure and pulp intrigue has become laden with demands for authenticity and realism. From the cinema, to the comics, to independent artists, even I've been guilty of this in my own works. With so much weight behind this movement, it's easy to forget where superhero stories originated from.

Superhero stories were, in their original incarnations, charmingly straightforward. They weren't tales of moral ambiguity or over-violent grit; they were colorful adventures that paid no more than a passing nod to realism. Heck, the first real superhero didn't put any more effort into a secret identity than some hair gel and a pair of glasses. Somewhere along the way, however, we forgot that superhero stories aren't always meant to mirror the real world; they're meant to showcase a place all their own. They're supposed to be fun, dammit, first and foremost.

Ian Thomas Healy's *Jackrabbit* is a tale right back in the tones and styles of the old-school stories. The emphasis is on the enjoyable tale of title-named protagonist. It's a story that doesn't waste time trying to placate the real world with half-spun explanations of how super powers work. Instead, it dives right into the action; hopping out of the gate with homespun costumes and constant banter. From the mythical pantheon of all-but-forgotten gods to the easy-to-loathe inhuman villains, *Jackrabbit* is a throwback to the classic tales that birthed the original superhero genre. It does not strive to make you question what you think you know about a superheroes; its only demand is that you surrender yourself to comedic entertainment and get lost in a more enjoyable world where the good guys wear bright outfits (but not tails) and the villains are properly wicked.

Jackrabbit is, in true form to the tradition, outright and unapologetic fun. It captures the heart and adrenaline that many modern stories lack, so quit listening to me blather on and turn the page already!

Prologue: Gods' Home

One thing that the world's religions have never considered is the possibility that they are *all* correct. And after all that goofiness in Ancient Greece when the gods were messing around with mortals, having children with them, turning them into animals, turning them into animals and *then* having children with them, and generally acting like a bunch of irresponsible teenagers, they pretty much stopped hanging around on Earth and instead kept to their own convenient little pocket dimension, which they called Gods' Home.

Imagine the nicest resort possible. The suites are lavish and well-appointed, from the four-dollar bottles of water to the mints on the pillows, sheets of the finest silk, fireplaces, mini-bars, carpeting so deep you could get lost in it, a view overlooking Paradise, and room service from waiters with just the right amount of snooty attitude. Downstairs is the Main Hall, where most of the gods hang out. That's where you would find Jehovah and Allah playing a game of Five-Card Draw that's been going on for a couple thousand years now. There's quite a crowd watching them, mostly retired Greek and Roman gods and goddesses, and a couple of half-snake and half-bird Aztec demigods who don't understand why the game doesn't involve more beheadings.

Other gods amuse themselves with different games of chance, or just hang around the pool outside where it's sunny and eighty-five degrees every single day. Every night there's live music and all the *dim sum* anyone could want. The Flying Spaghetti Monster, a new resident in Gods' Home, is usually found here by the poolside bar, sucking down margaritas with Cthulhu and a god from a long-dead Sumerian squid cult.

Beyond the pool, the grounds of the resort stretch out for many miles in all directions. Go far enough, and you'll find that every kind of terrain is represented, from the veldt preferred by gods like Anansi the Spider or Itherther the Buffalo, to the desert of Mangar-kunjer-kunja the Lizard, to the jungles belonging to the various South American and southeast Asian deities like Chasca Coyllur and Ulilang Kaluluwa. If you look hard enough, you can even find a stretch of icy waste frequented by the animal gods of the Eskimos and vacationing Asgardians.

Some gods just hang around looking for trouble because, well, you're a god; where else are you gonna go?

Leporidus, the legendary God of Rabbits, fell into this latter category.

He was neither fearsome nor powerful. In fact, he looked pretty much like any other rabbit one might find frequenting the lady rabbits' hutches or warrens. He might have been a bit larger, a bit fatter, and his ears were a bit longer, but beneath his brown and gray-ticked fur lurked one of the most devious minds ever to spring forth from the primordial philosophy that birthed gods. After enjoying a brief surge of interest a millennium ago in North American indigenous tribes, he was living out his immortal retirement in Gods' Home. He chose to spend it sitting by the pool every day, soaking up the sun with his friend Anurus, the God of Frogs, and watching other gods.

"I was talking to Poseidon," said Leporidus, giving one ear a languorous scratch. "He was telling me about this weird new guy he saw yesterday."

Anurus croaked deep in his throat from his perch at the pool's edge. The corpulent frog was as fat as an amphibian could manage and still be somewhat mobile. His slimy skin shone in every color of the rainbow, including a few that hadn't yet been invented on Earth. When he filled his vocal sac, his croak could shiver mountains. At least, that was what he'd told Leporidus, who'd never witnessed it firsthand. Leporidus rather suspected that Anurus couldn't shiver a fly from its perch, but was canny enough not to mention it. "Weird guy? Someone new?" asked the God of Frogs.

Anytime a new god arrived in Gods' Home, there was much interested discussion among the denizens, for it happened less and less often as humanity replaced their religious faith with other substitutes like the internet, reality television, and the NFL. Leporidus wasn't bothered by it. After all, nobody had worshipped him in a thousand years. But he knew it was a subject of much discussion at the gaming tables indoors. The sudden appearance of the Flying Spaghetti Monster had caused such an upheaval that several of the Elder Gods had stomped away, secluding themselves for months. What one man started as a joke had become a bona fide religion.

Leporidus and Anurus thought it was hilarious.

"Maybe. Poseidon's just about seen it all," said Leporidus. The barrel-chested sea god had been in the hot tub for several hundred years, surrounded by nymphs and mermaids, and was considered to be one of the best-informed of all the deities in Gods' Home.

"Maybe we ought to go look for ourselves." Anurus set down a frozen concoction that he'd said was a grasshopper margarita. "It'd be a nice change from sitting here."

"Tired of my company after a thousand years?" Leporidus grinned and whistled through his large front teeth, a trick he'd picked up from fierce Castorus, the brown-furred Beaver God.

"No, but you know . . . Different things don't happen often here. It's always interesting."

Leporidus stood and shook out his luxurious fur. "Just what I was thinking. Hop to it, old buddy."

"Never heard *that* one before," grunted Anurus. Nevertheless, he bounced alongside his friend as they climbed the steps toward Poseidon's party.

You could always tell how powerful a god *really* was by the company he kept. Poseidon had retained Thor, the Thunder God, as his head bodyguard.

The muscle-bound god slapped his hammer into his palm over and over as Leporidus and Anurus approached. "This is a private party," he grated at them. "Invitation only."

"Oh," said Leporidus. "And here I've been invited and all. *Stop by and see me sometime,* said Poseidon to me. *Come and party with me,* he said."

"When?" Thor shook *Mjölnir* at them, making thunder rumble behind the distant mountains.

Leporidus smiled. "Even Poseidon has to take a leak once in awhile. You ever seen anyone drink as much as him? Sometimes I think Bacchus would go out of business if not for him. Anyway, I bumped into him in the can and he said for us to come by sometime."

A tiny bolt of lightning leaped between Thor's furrowed brows. "You said that yesterday."

"It was an open invitation," said Leporidus. "Hey, look . . . Loki's trying to sneak in!"

Thor spun around and roared in fury. "Where? That sneaky little bastard . . ."

While the Thunder God searched in vain for his arch-enemy, Leporidus and Anurus hurried past him. "Odin should have quit while he was ahead," said Leporidus, referring to Thor's father. "That one was dropped on his head one too many times as a child."

Poseidon, as usual, was surrounded by beautiful naked women. Leporidus and Anurus, being animalistic gods, only had the slightest passing interest in the human or even demihuman form. Leporidus, though, could appreciate Poseidon's love of the finer things in life, and few things were finer than the nymph giving the bearded god a shoulder massage with the Balm of Forbidden Trees. "Greetings to you, friend Poseidon," said the cheerful God of Rabbits.

"What do you want, Leporidus?" Poseidon gazed down on the two smaller deities with the malevolence of storm clouds in his gray eyes. "I thought I told you yesterday to piss off. Thor was supposed to keep you out."

Leporidus snorted. "Please. That half-wit couldn't find his own hammer if it wasn't hanging between his legs and constantly banging into his manhood."

Pina colada foam blew through Poseidon's mustache as he laughed in spite of himself. "Oh, dear me." He wiped coconut from his beard. "I should cast you down from here, but that was funny." He raised a magnanimous hand. "I grant you a reprieve from my anger."

"How kind of you, Posie. Hey, Toots, I'd love a drink. Something with carrots in it?" Leporidus poked a nymph with his paw on her ample behind.

Poseidon drained the last of his drink. "And another drink for me. A prickly pear margarita, I think." He looked at Leporidus. "Why are you here?"

"Oh. We wanted to ask you about that new guy you told me you saw."

Poseidon smoothed down his mustache. "He was an insect. Animalistic, like you fellows. Not humanoid. Lurking around the dark corners of Dionysus's." Dionysus's was a bar in Gods' Home, like Bacchus' Place, but not nearly as savory, especially with that annoying possessive *S* after the apostrophe that Leporidus was damn sure didn't belong there.

Dionysus insisted, though, and in the end, gods weren't supposed to get involved in each others' business. Well, not much, anyway.

"An insect god?" Anurus sounded interested and maybe a little bit hungry. "They're not common."

"No, and this guy was quite odd, even for an insect."

"Interesting. What were you doing in Dionysus's?" Leporidus scratched behind his ear.

"That's none of your—hey, what is that you're doing?" said Poseidon. "Fleas? Are you putting *fleas* in my water?" His ire rose like a storm surge.

"No," said Leporidus, backing away. "Honestly, I don't have fleas . . ."

"*Get away from here!*" Poseidon's roar shook the foundations of the pool, sending whitecaps and breakers in all directions.

Leporidus and Anurus glanced at each other and then ran for it. They didn't stop until they were safe, ensconced beneath a hedge some distance away from the pool.

"I think maybe we ought to stay away from coastal areas for awhile," murmured Anurus. "And inland lakes, just to be safe."

"I think I want to go see this weird new insect god," said Leporidus. "This place has been so dull for the past few hundred years. I could use a fresh perspective not tainted by two-thousand-year-old dogma."

"I could use a fresh dragonfly sandwich with some crispy French flies on the side."

"That's repulsive."

"I can't help it. I love bugs. They're delicious."

"You ought to find plenty where we're going. Especially if we tour the kitchen. I hear Hygieia won't even go near the place."

"You're not exactly raising my confidence," said Anurus, shivering at the thought of what sort of mess would keep away the Goddess of Cleanliness.

The two friends loped through the fields and forests, skirting around the main hotel, heading for the seedy backwoods shack known as Dionysus's.

As usual, the neon sign had a couple of unlit letters and therefore read *Di-n-sus's*. Anurus looked at the splintery wooden walls with distaste while Leporidus was disenchanted with the stinking fens around the building. From somewhere beyond the bar, in the deepest part of the forest, they could smell the tang of burning wood from Dionysus's stills.

"Phew," said Anurus. "This was a stupid idea. Let's go back to the pool."

"No way," said Leporidus. "We've come this far. I want to see the weird insect god."

"Rabbits." Anurus made the word sound dirty and rolled his eyes.

They crossed the creaking bridge over the fetid swamp stream and entered the bar. It was dim inside, lit by naked overhead bulbs. By the look of it, Dionysus seemed to have acquired his décor from the backwoods of Arkansas—splintery wooden floor with sawdust spread across unrecognizable stains, sputtering neon signs advertising mostly Sumerian brands of beer, and a single ceiling fan with greasy, dust-coated blades that didn't move the air so much as slide through it. Dionysus himself slouched behind the bar, sullen and drunk, a jug of his best moonshine sitting beside him.

"Ho, barkeep!" called Leporidus in his most cheerful voice, trying not to taste the thick, stagnant air that seemed to coat everything.

Dionysus emitted a long, grating belch.

"Nice," muttered Anurus.

"What ye want?" asked Dionysus.

"Oh, nothing much, really." Leporidus examined the bar's only other inhabitant out of the corner of his eye. "Two pints of your White Lightning and a spot at the bar to drink them."

Without another word, Dionysus plopped two chipped bowls in front of them. They were filled with a cloudy liquid that promised numerous hallucinations and hangovers galore.

Leporidus gave up his subterfuge and looked over at the insect god. He couldn't identify the creature's origin. It had a long body, short legs, and long antennae that wiggled constantly. Its head shone in the dim lighting, almost a perfect reflector, but the body was a flat black with traces of red in the chitin.

"Greetings, strange one," said Leporidus. "I haven't seen you around here before. Been in town long?"

The insect made a chittering noise at them, instead of speaking properly like a god ought to. Leporidus marveled that he could understand the sound at all.

"I have arrived recently," said the creature.

"I am Leporidus, the Rabbit God. My bulbous-eyed and charming companion is Anurus, the God of Frogs."

The stranger didn't respond.

Leporidus tried again. "And so I don't have to just call you *the dude with the antennae*, if we were to call you by name, what would it be?"

"Blattodeus."

"Charming name." Leporidus thought it sounded like someone being sick. He tried his White Lightning and determined that more than a sip might kill him in spite of his godhood. "What do you call your flock? Those who worship you?"

"Soon to be victorious."

"That's kind of a mouthful. I'd think you'd want to call them something that rolls a little more trippingly off the tongue. Blattodites. Oh, I see what you mean. That doesn't work at all. What are you expecting them to be victorious over?"

"The world of Man."

Anurus gasped and Leporidus waved a paw at him to get him to shut up. "Your people are going to take over Man's world? Nice try. The Rules don't allow it. Don't you remember your Ancient History? It's been tried."

"Where others have failed, I will succeed. It is inevitable."

Anurus gasped again and poked Leporidus in the back, frantic.

The Rabbit God sighed. "What?"

"He's not from around here," said Anurus.

"Well, duh. I can see that."

"No, I mean he's *really* not from around here. Don't just *look* at him. *See* him."

Leporidus focused the total of his mind on the stranger, bringing to bear the superb senses possessed by the divine. Then he gasped too. Blattodeus wasn't a *human* god at all!

Dozens of millennia ago, when the First Gods had walked Gods' Home, they laid down the Rules. Gods' Home was only for the gods created by Mankind. That was deemed both appropriate and proper, as only two other species in Man's world even had the slightest concept of Higher Beings. Animals simply didn't create gods.

Except some other race had done just that: those who created Blattodeus. The insect was a god created by non-humans, and therefore an impossibility in Gods' Home. Leporidus slurped down the rest of his drink to steady himself, feeling its fire coat his insides much in the same way as a nice, refreshing glass of magma would. "You . . . you shouldn't be here!"

"It matters not. Soon my people shall rule the Earth, and therefore I shall rule here." Blattodeus dropped to all sixes and scuttled out of Dionysus's bar.

"Not if I c'n help it, short, shquat, and fugly." Leporidus felt drunk and dangerous.

"What can you do?" whispered Anurus. "The Rules say no god may interfere directly with another."

"Rules don't . . . don't apply to him. He'sh not even a human god."

"Still, you can't do anything to him here in Gods' Home. Whether or not he is bound by the Rules, *you* still are. Hey, are you drunk?"

"Course I'm not. I'm a frickin' *god*. I don't get drunk. I'll find a Herald."

Anurus burst out laughing. "A *Herald?* You've got to be kidding! How is that even possible?"

"I didn't opt out." Leporidus let out a juicy belch that peeled varnish from the bar and told himself the room wasn't really spinning and there was only one frog sitting beside him, not three.

"What, you mean that huge pile of forms when we became gods? I just signed the short form," said Anurus in wonderment.

"I read 'em all. Took a hunnerd years." Leporidus giggled. "An' I took ev'ry option. No short cuts f'r this li'l . . . li'l bunny."

Anurus croaked long and loud. The windows in the bar all rattled with sympathetic vibrations. "Wow. A Herald. Like Jesus. Or Mohammed. Nobody's going to believe that the God of Rabbits has his own Herald."

"I wouldn't b'lieve it m'self," Lepidorus slid off the stool onto the floor and slipped in a pile of sawdust. "But somebody's gotta do somethin'. Can't let a stupid an'mal god take over th' world."

"*We're* animal gods." Anurus supported his intoxicated friend as they left the bar.

"Created by *humans*," said the Rabbit God. "That fella . . . Blassomus or whatev'r. He was cree . . . crate . . . cretate . . . borned by *animals*. Prolly *insects*." Leporidus swayed close to the edge of the wooden bridge and only by kicking with his powerful hind legs could Anurus keep them both from tumbling into the brackish water.

"Where are you going to find a Herald in this day and age? Nobody's got any faith anymore."

"Already got one in mind." Leporidus decided that walking presented far too much effort and plopped to the ground. "Kid's perfect for th' job."

"Oh?"

"C'mon . . . I'll show you."

One

"I'm breaking up with you!"

Jackson "Jay" Jones blinked as every book in his locker tumbled down to the floor, the last one knocking the Super Big Gulp out of his hand and dumping Mountain Dew all over the black Nike Air Griffeys with the red trim that he'd saved up for all summer. "What?" He turned to see his apparently former girlfriend standing in the hall with her arms crossed over her purple letter jacket.

Shari Washington tossed her mass of stylish braids that Jay suspected were extensions. She'd brought two of her white cheerleader friends with her and their sniffs of disdain were choreographed in perfect unison. "You're a shitty boyfriend."

Jay wished he'd had more time to prepare for this sudden breakup. They'd been dating for a couple of months, and he hadn't seen any signs of her discontent. He couldn't manage a better retort than "No I'm not!" Without a stronger position, he knew he'd have to run with it. "I'm a good boyfriend. Hell, I'm a *great* boyfriend. I've got my own car and everything."

"Weak, dude," said a passing kid with a trombone case. Jay could have facepalmed; he was getting dissed by a *band geek*?

Shari was unmoved. "You don't play sports. You work at a stupid dance studio, and your best friend is a fag. I can do better. Have a nice life, loser."

"Loser," repeated the other two cheerleaders. All three spun on their heels and flounced down the hall. The crowd of students parted like the Red Sea, leaving Jay standing in shock with soda soaking into his socks.

"She totally owned you, dude," said the ginger-headed freshman two lockers down from him.

Jay couldn't believe it. He was a junior, which was practically the same as being a senior, and a lowly freshman was talking smack at him. He'd have smarted off a reply if the kid hadn't been almost a foot taller and a good hundred pounds heavier. The youngster looked down at him with a mixture of pity and contempt. Mostly contempt.

"You suck so hard," said the kid, and loped off to his first class.

Jay blinked again and the freshman was replaced by Mr. Pillsbury, the basketball coach. Being tall, fat, white, and jolly ensured that Pillsbury would be called Doughboy by every student until the day he retired. "Look at you, Jones, you're a mess. What you need is some physical activity to take your mind off that floozy. Women are nothing but trouble anyway. I've got three ex-wives and am working on a fourth, so believe me when I say I know what I'm talking about."

Jay blinked. "What?"

"Basketball, bub. It's in your genes. You should be out there on the court with the other kids, not mooning around with your nose in a notebook. There'll be plenty of time for that after the NBA. You want to go to college, right? You come see me and we'll start applying for scholarships. They love to give underprivileged black kids like you scholarships. But you'll have to play ball first. You do the work, you reap the rewards. That's the way it works in the world, Jones."

"Underprivileged? But I'm not—"

Doughboy wasn't having any of it. He smiled and clapped Jay on the back. "Come see me after school and we'll get you signed up for the team." He looked down. "And you should probably change your shoes. Shame, too. Those look expensive." He winked. "And good for basketball."

Jay shook his head to clear away Doughboy's cheerfully innocent racism. He looked down at his feet, which felt like they were encased in wet concrete from the soda. His books had soaked up plenty of the sticky beverage and he doubted he'd be able to pry them off the floor.

A tingle on the back of his neck made him look back and there she was: Creepy White Girl. He didn't know her name, didn't know a thing about her except that she'd spent all of last year staring at him from behind those big-ass glasses every time he saw her. Her straight black hair was always held back by a headband and she wore odd dresses that looked like something out of a sitcom from the '50s. And there she was, staring at him again. It made him twitchy. He didn't know what she saw in him, but he saw nothing in her. Even now, when he'd just become single, and been made a fool of in front of the entire school, he wasn't desperate enough to think of her as the Creepy White Girl Who Might Want To Hook Up.

"Hey, punk, where's your boyfriend?" A couple of football players in their own letter jackets stood and surveyed him like he was a tackling dummy. "We heard that Shari finally dumped your sorry ass. Guess you better stick with your *boy*friend." They laughed like a couple of hicks with hayseeds stuck in their teeth, slapping each other's backs as they walked away.

Right on cue, Bunny appeared. Bunny's real name was Bainbridge, but he'd been Bunny since first moving to the neighborhood when they were both in second grade. It was still September and hot as hell outside, but Bunny wore tight black stretch jeans under a double-breasted navy blue jacket and gold lamé shirt. His hair was perfectly done up in twists. He looked cool enough that butter wouldn't melt in his mouth, as Jay's mom liked to say. Bunny offered a gracious smile. "Jay honey, you've absolutely ruined those shoes. Ruined them!"

The first warning bell rang and students started to dissipate from the hall. A quick glance over his shoulder confirmed to Jay that even Creepy White Girl had disappeared. He bent down to pick up his textbooks. All of their covers had soaked through, and half of his algebra book stayed stuck to the floor where it had hit. Bunny helped him collect his things, doing the best he could not to actually touch any of the sticky, wet books, and all the while fretting about Jay's footwear.

"I've got some spare flats in my locker, but I don't think they'd fit those gunboats you call feet. What on Earth happened to you today, Jay? You're usually so self-assured."

"Shari dumped me."

"Oh. Oh my." Bunny looked sadly at Jay. "I'll kick her ass for this."

In spite of himself, Jay snickered at the thought of the diminutive Bunny taking on Shari in a no-holds-barred cage battle. Poor Bunny would find himself outmatched by the feisty cheerleader. She'd have him begging for mercy in seconds. He sighed and peeled off his shoes and socks. He'd have to see if his mom would be able to salvage the expensive Nikes after she got back from her business trip to Toledo. "Ah, screw it. It's Friday and I no longer have plans tonight. I'm ditching," he said.

Bunny looked up at him, concern in his big brown eyes. "You sure that's such a good idea, Jay honey?"

Jay nodded and held out his phone to Bunny. "Call the office for me? Pretend to be my mom? Tell them I'm sick."

Bunny took the phone and did a credible if overly-dramatic impression of Jay's mom and excused him for the day. Then he made kissy-lips and photographed himself with the phone, then checked himself out in the picture. He handed the phone back to Jay and sighed. "Dear God, if I don't get some moisturizer I'm going to spontaneously combust right here in the hallway. Are you going to be all right?"

"Yeah, Bunny. Thanks."

"You could always switch teams, you know. I'd welcome you with open arms."

"I don't doubt it." Jay laughed. It was their running joke. Jay knew Bunny lusted after him, and Bunny knew it was a fruitless venture to try. "What about you, Bunny? You're already late for class and the Hall Monitor will be along any moment."

Bunny gave him a sly smile. "Girlfriend, *please*." He sashayed off down the hall, disappearing through a door just as the Hall Monitor walked through the intersection. Jay tensed, but the teacher's aide stuck with patrol duty never looked his direction.

Jay padded barefoot through the halls to the nearest exit. It was supposed to sound an alarm when opened during school hours, but Jay knew the teachers who smoked had disabled it so they could duck outside for a quick butt. He looked down at the metal grate in front of the door, which was supposed to be used for scraping mud off shoes before entering the building but instead had become a catchall for ashes and filters. The edges of the grate looked sharp enough to lacerate his feet to the bone. Beyond it lay hot pavement growing soft in the morning sun, then half a gravelly parking lot until he got to his truck.

He wished he could just jump over it all.

He sighed. His feet were already filthy from the Mountain Dew and treading the venerable halls of Bayview High. If he cut them on something, he might die of a sudden infection, which he thought might be a kindness rather than having to return to school tomorrow and face the traditional Gauntlet of Mocking and Hazing. But that would mean letting Shari win, and he couldn't let her know how much she'd really hurt him. He hadn't been *that* bad a boyfriend. Sure, he'd missed the first football game because he'd had to take his mom to the airport. And he'd had to break a date because Bunny had a meltdown in a Starbucks over a caramel macchiato that *didn't have enough pumps of caramel in it, Jay honey, and my life is over, do you hear me?* And he'd forgotten their one month anniversary.

He slapped his forehead with the realization. "Shit. I *am* a shitty boyfriend," he said aloud.

He rooted through the trash barrel beside the door until he found two empty Super Big Gulp cups. They were sticky and smelly inside, but they'd at least get him across the lot. Or maybe he could cut across the lawn. The soft green carpet was only a few feet away and called to him in an inviting way. His eyes dropped to the sign set at the edge of the field.

Keep Off The Grass!

Jay snorted. Grass was part of nature. It was *meant* to be walked upon, not admired from a distance. He looked at the cups in his hands and weighed the risk of being busted by someone on the faculty for daring to cross the field. Gazing back at the direct route to the parking lot, it looked more and more like pavement the temperature of lava and a gravel parking lot filled with chips of broken glass.

"Screw it." He threw the cups aside and jumped for the grass.

The grass welcomed his bare feet with its cushiony soothing touch.

"That's not so bad," he said.

Then the sprinklers turned on.

"You're kidding, right?" asked Anurus, incredulous at Leporidus's selection of the seemingly hapless human youth. "He doesn't look anything like a Herald."

"There's potential for greatness within him," said the Rabbit God.

"There's potential for needing a bath, but I don't think Hygieia would go near him either."

"You're hilarious." Leporidus combed out his fur with fastidious attention to detail.

"Why not his friend instead? He seems so organized and detail-oriented. He'd be the perfect Company Man, you know?"

"I don't want a perfect Company Man. Look what happened to Jesus. He got nailed to a cross for telling people to be nice to each other."

"Still, though, you could probably do a lot better if you took some time to look around."

"He'll do, Anurus. He'll do quite nicely. When I get through with him, he'll be a true Herald."

"We're going to have to go down there now, aren't we?" Anurus sounded resigned.

"You can stay here if you want."

"Are you kidding? I wouldn't miss this for the world."

Two

Jay was heading for the beach in his rusty, beat-up Toyota truck when his phone rang. He nearly shut it off without answering it, but then he saw it was his mother.

"Hi, Mom," he said, looking for a place to pull off the road. Conversations with her always made him need to pace and wave his arms.

"Jay, why are you answering your phone? Aren't you in school?"

A roadside stand appeared around a corner and Jay whipped his truck onto the sandy shoulder and shut down the engine. The stand might have once been a trailer, but it sat on four naked rims with shreds of rotten rubber hanging from them. The faded, peeling sign on the roof said *Droogs*, which meant nothing to Jay. He looked at the digital clock stuck to his dash by a piece of double-sided foam tape. It wasn't yet 10 AM. But his mom was in Toledo. That was three hours later. Maybe she'd forget. "It's lunch, Mom."

"Oh? Are you having lunch at a roadside stand?" Jay winced at his mother's preternatural hearing. Bunny often said she must be a parahuman, like the heroes of Just Cause or the Lucky Seven, but Jay knew better. She just had that uncanny Mom Radar that was right more often than it was wrong.

"No, uh, it's that Timmy Taco Truck that always parks by the school. Mmmm . . . tacos, right?"

"You better not be ditching, Mr. Jones. And if you are, you'd better not have gotten Bunny involved."

"No, Mom, he's in class. I mean, he's got class while I'm at lunch. I'm *A* Lunch and he's *B* Lunch."

"I'm trying to close a big deal here, Jay. This one is for your college fund. You do still want to go to college, don't you?"

"Yeah, Mom." Jay stuck his filthy feet into a pair of beach flip-flops he kept behind the seat and walked over to the stand. He figured he'd find a secluded section of beach someplace and watch the ocean for awhile to see if its rhythms might help him unwind his shoulders that were rock-hard from tension. The only other patrons of the stand had arrived on a tricked-out touring motorcycle. The tall lanky man and his pretty auburn-haired companion wore riding leathers with plenty of chrome zippers. They looked at him with mild interest as they sipped on milkshakes.

"Let me say some words to you, Jay. Tell me if you've heard them before. *Range Rover. Trip to Italy. Boob job.* These are all things I'm not getting because you want to go to college."

"I know, Mom."

"And if you decide to throw that away because you'd rather skip school when I'm out of town, I can promise you that your college fund will pay for all those things. All of them, Jay. You're going to have to learn to play basketball and get a scholarship, because you'll have paid for your mom's perky new boobs."

"God, Mom, really? Could we not talk about this right now, please?"

The biker slipped the counterman some money and shot a wry smile at Jay. "Hang in there, buddy," he said. "Don't let her get the upper hand."

"Shush," said the woman.

The counterman put a tall paper cup with a straw poking out of it down in front of Jay. "I didn't order that," he whispered, covering the phone's mouthpiece and looking with caution at the frothy white liquid within.

"They did," said the counterman, tilting his head toward the couple as they climbed back onto the bike.

"Milk?" Jay looked over at the couple.

"It does a body good." The biker winked at him. The back of his jacket read *BORN TO KICK ASS*.

"So let's have it, Jay."

"Have what?"

"Your grades. How are they?" Her disapproving tone made Jay feel like throwing himself out into the passing traffic. He checked to see if there were any semi trucks or even a bus approaching. Nothing but a bearded dude on a scooter, which wouldn't even remotely approach a lethal impact.

"Doing good, Mom. I got an 83 on my algebra test on Wednesday, and Mrs. Nipple—I mean *Niblett*—said my book review of *Watership Down* was really good." Jay picked up the glass of milk, looking at it in the light.

"83? Don't you dare bullshit me, Jay. I close deals with professional liars, and you're nowhere near as good as them."

"83, Mom, honest."

"You better have a B in that class by the time I get back on Tuesday, Jay, or you're grounded. That means you buckle down and study instead of spending your evenings with that cheerleader. And if you're sleeping with her and I find out about it, you're going to find out why some animals eat their young." She hung up, without giving him a chance to tell her that he and the cheerleader were no more.

"Sounds like you got yourself a world of trouble, kid," said the counterman.

Jay sighed and looked down at the milk. "My mom's a corporate shark. Kind of hard to please."

The counterman snorted. "Women. Nothin' but trouble. You gonna order anything else?"

"No." Jay glanced at the suspicious stains on the counterman's apron.

"Then I'm closed." The man yanked on a cord and a heavy wooden shutter lowered from the ceiling to seal off the back of the stand from the counter. Jay heard the click of the lock and then silence.

He spotted an arrow-shaped, faded wooden sign indicating a beach was only a quarter mile to the west along a side road. Taking the milk so he'd have *something* to drink in his teenage solitude, he got back into his truck and turned onto the road. Sure enough, the paved road became gravel and then sand. There was no parking lot, but room to pull over to the side and park along the entry road.

Beach was a charitable description of the narrow strip of sand, cluttered with a couple large pieces of driftwood and rocks. It resembled a private beach that hadn't been maintained in years. At least it wasn't full of trash like so many of them were, thought Jay as he found a comfortable rock to lean his back against. He kicked off his flip-flops, sipped at the cool, refreshing milk, and stared off at the Golden Gate Bridge towers in the distance without really looking at them. The milk a little sweet. He wondered if maybe the counterman had mixed something into it. Jay wasn't an accomplished, or even an experienced drinker, and he might not know alcohol by taste. Maybe it was just good milk.

A sour belch worked its way up his throat. Maybe it was a little more than just good milk. If there was booze mixed into it, he ought to go find a drive-through somewhere so he wasn't drinking on an empty stomach. But dammit, he'd gone to all the trouble to ditch, to lie to his mom, and to find a place to think away his sorrows about getting dumped. If the milk was doped up, so be it. He drank some more.

Shitty boyfriend. Why had Shari really broken things off? That thought spun around and around in his mind. "What the hell is your problem, girl?" he mumbled aloud. "I'm not *that* shitty." He drank more milk and wished he had some cookies to go with it. "Kiss my black ass . . . You never had it so good." He sighed and lowered the cup.

"It's about time you put that down that cup," said a voice. "I couldn't decide which you're trying to do first, drink yourself to death or bore me to death."

Jay jumped. He hadn't heard anyone approach. He looked around, trying to find the source of the voice.

"Down here, pal." Jay's eyes dropped to see a nondescript brown and gray rabbit sitting several feet away, staring at him. "Yeah, I'm the rabbit." It hopped forward a few inches. "And yes, I'm talking to you."

Jay poured out the rest of his milk on the sand.

The rabbit wrinkled its nose. "Can we talk?"

"What is this, some kind of joke?" Jay stood up, looking around for . . . well, he didn't know exactly what he was seeking. "Who's doing this?"

The rabbit hopped closer. "It's just me, I'm afraid. Oh, and my associate over there, who thinks this is a foolish idea." The rabbit nodded its head back toward the rock where a fat multicolored frog sat, shaking its head.

Jay bent down to take a closer look at the rabbit. He reached for it, but it sprang away.

"Easy there, big fella. Let's establish a few ground rules before we get into the touchy-feely part. I . . ." The rabbit paused for dramatic effect. " . . .am Leporidus, the God of Rabbits."

Jay burst out laughing. "I've got to be dreaming. Any minute now I'm going to wake up and find out I got roofied at a roadside stand. I hope my pants aren't around my ankles with someone going all medieval on my ass."

The rabbit said nothing, but gave off an exasperated vibe, insofar as a rabbit was capable of such things.

"All right, Mr. Talking Rabbit God, what can I do for you?" Jay made a valiant effort to sound dignified, but had to choke off a giggle.

"Skeptics," croaked the frog from the mossy bank. "Gotta love them."

Jay's eyes widened. "Oh, the frog talks too! I am never touching milk again, swear to God."

The rabbit stomped forward on its fuzzy feet, all flashing eyes and fury. "Dude, shut up for a minute. This is important. And swear to *me* if you're going to swear to anyone. We don't have time for any of your mortal foolishness."

The rabbit's tone was so earnest that Jay sat up. "All right. I'll play along. What's so important that the only talking rabbit in the world has to come to me for?"

"Jay Jones, I, Leporidus, God of the Rabbits, have selected you to be my Herald in the approaching Time of Need."

"I'm your what for the which?"

Leporidus sighed. "Look, it's a lot more impressive when Jehovah appears as a column of flame and burns a bush and uses His James Earl Jones voice, but I don't do that, all right? I'm a rabbit. This is as good as I can do."

"And you want me to be a champion? A champion of what? I was never very good at sports. I know . . . I'm the only black kid who can't shoot a basketball. I've heard it all before."

"Not *a* champion. *The* Herald. *My* Herald."

"Right." Jay scrunched up his face in confusion.

"I'll try and explain," said Leporidus. "I met this guy back in Gods' Home—that's where we gods hang out—but there are these Rules about who can do what . . ."

Jay blinked and managed to get out a "huh?"

The rabbit stopped. "I guess the explanation is pretty confusing."

"I think you bluescreened his hard drive." Anurus hopped over next to Leporidus.

"Huh?" repeated Jay.

"Computer jargon," said Anurus. "It's all the rage among the younger gods."

"All right," said Leporidus. "Try and stay with me here, Jay."

Jay nodded, trying to convince that the two talking animals before him weren't just puppets or robots or some kind of elaborate joke being played upon him.

"There's a bad god, an insect god, who's going to use his followers to take over your world. I'm the only one who knows about it, and you're the only one who can stop him."

"Why you?"

"The Big Guys—Jehovah, Allah, Shiva—they already used up their Herald clauses ages ago. There are only a few of us minor gods who can even select one, and I don't have time to conduct interviews to find out who else is out there."

"And why me?"

"Right place in the right time," said Leporidus. "Now, as I said, there is an insect god who is trying to take over the world. I can't oppose him directly. That's against the Rules. But he's not a human god, so he can bypass those Rules."

"I thought you said he was an insect god. He's a human? Like me?"

"No," said Anurus. "I don't believe we've been properly introduced."

"I'm sorry, my associate Anurus, the God of Frogs. Anurus, this is Jackson Jones, who will be my Herald."

"Call me Jay, and I haven't agreed to being your Herald, whatever that means," said Jay.

"You have no choice."

"We'll see about that. What about this bad god guy? Is he human?"

"No." Anurus's croak was dignified. "Humans create gods. But not this one. He was created by insects."

"A god created by insects who wants to take over the world," repeated Jay.

"Yes, that's it exactly." Leporidus worked his rabbit mouth into a semblance of a grin.

Jay raised his hands. "Okay, it was funny, but now it's just gotten stupid. I'm leaving." He stood up.

"*STAY, MORTAL! I HAVE NOT FINISHED WITH THEE YET!*" Leporidus roared in a stentorian voice. Overhead, lightning blasted from the clear sky to cleave a nearby tree into two smoldering halves. The blast of thunder echoed across the beach and blew Jay off his feet.

"Holy shit!" he cried.

"Gah," said Leporidus. "I hate doing that. You don't have any tonic water in your truck, do you?"

"N-no!"

"Pity. I've quite a taste for the stuff. Now do I have your undivided attention?"

Jay nodded, eyes wide and staring

"I require a Herald who can take the fight to the insect god's minions when they rise up. Out of all the humans in the world, I have determined you best fit my needs. Therefore, I am bestowing unto you such powers as I am able."

"Powers?" asked Jay. "What kind of powers?"

"I thought that went well, don't you?" Leporidus asked Anurus as they watched Jay leave down the road.

"The thunder and lightning was a little over the top," said the frog.

The Rabbit God shrugged his furry shoulders. "Sometimes when you need a mule to follow you, you have to hit him across the head with a two-by-four to first get his attention."

"Where'd you hear that?"

"Brighty, the Burro God."

"You made that up."

"Nope, completely honest."

"Seriously, you need to hang around a better class of god," said Anurus.

An idea occurred to Leporidus. "You're absolutely right, Anurus."

"Hey, where are you going?"

Three

The insistent beeping of his alarm clock woke Jay from a sound sleep. For some odd reason, he'd been dreaming of rabbits. But why had he set an alarm? It was Saturday. No school. Of that much, he was certain. He must have set it by accident. Not a problem; he reached out to shut it off.

His arm felt odd—thick and heavy, as if he'd slept on it. It wasn't tingling or anything so he paid it no mind. The alarm clock shut off with a crunching sound. That was odd enough for him to crack open an eye. He'd somehow managed to crush the alarm clock into several plastic shards. He groaned. Stupid piece of cheap, made-in-China crap. He sat up and reached for the pieces.

Then he stopped and stared at himself.

The arm extending from his shoulder didn't look like it belonged to him. *His* arms were a bit thin from his low-impact occupation of being a slacker student. *This* arm was bulging with muscles that looked like an athlete's. And not just any athlete either; they were the kind of muscles that grew through years of hard work and good diet. The kind of muscles that won awards and made girls and basketball coaches go all creamy.

"What the hell?" he muttered. Both his arms seemed to have grown in the night. As he looked

31

further, he saw his scrawny chest had been layered over with huge slabs of pectoral muscle, and below that was an honest-to-God six-pack. His legs . . . his legs swelled with muscles as hard as rocks with definition that would make sculptors envious. What had happened to him? He sprang to his feet.

Unprepared for the strength in his legs, he not only cleared the bed but hit the ceiling hard enough to rattle his brain around inside his skull, as if it wasn't already reeling enough from the unusual changes in his body. "*Ow!* What the hell?" he shouted. How had he done that? The pain subsided so fast that he wondered if he'd imagined it, but then he looked up. There was a rounded crater in the ceiling, with cracking plaster and dust falling from it like snow. "No way. No way did that just happen." But when he brushed at his hair, more plaster dust fell from it. Head spinning, he staggered into the bathroom on legs that didn't feel like they belonged to him.

He could do nothing but stare in amazement at his muscular physique in the full-length mirror hanging on the door. When he flexed his arms and the muscles rearranged themselves like Smartcars parking. They creaked with power. He shook his head in disbelief. "I'm dreaming, right? Something in that milk and I'm having a really . . . bad . . ." His eyes wandered across the great meaty slabs of his pecs and a six-pack abdomen that looked like a tray of dinner rolls. "Daaaaamn."

"Nice, huh?" said a familiar voice. He turned to see Leporidus sitting atop the toilet.

"You!"

"Me," said the Rabbit God.

"Am I dreaming?"

"Nope."

"Wait, you mean this is real? I look like a linebacker or something. I feel . . . I feel *amazing*. Did you do this?"

Jay waved at himself, astonished at the play of the muscles around his limbs.

"Like I said, I would bestow powers upon you. So what do you think?"

"Well, I'm big. Is that a power? But I don't feel muscle-bound or anything. I think I could wipe my own ass. I've seen bodybuilders that couldn't. Actually, I feel really flexible." He bent down to touch his toes. No problem. His hips felt loose and relaxed. He raised one leg straight up until it pointed at the ceiling while he balanced on the tiptoes of his other foot. "Dude," he whispered in awe of himself. "What else is there?"

Leporidus winced at the vision of what a sculptor might have called *Jay Unbound*. "For starters, why don't you put some clothes on?"

Dressing proved to be a surprising challenge. Most of his clothing fit the boy he used to be instead of the giant he'd become. He finally took an old t-shirt and ripped off the sleeves, figuring that would be sufficient, but when he forced his gargantuan shoulders through the holes, the fabric tore all the way down the sides. "Seriously?"

Rummaging through his closet for *anything* that might be large enough to fit into, he happened across an old Halloween costume. In sixth grade, he had gone as Juice from Just Cause. The gray tank top with the yellow lightning bolt was made of Lycra or Spandex or something. He remembered it had hung on him like a curtain. "Why the hell not?"

The stretchy fabric smelled musty from spending the last five years in the bottom of one of his drawers, but the shirt held together. Unfortunately, it stopped at his midriff, making him look more like the calendar boys Bunny liked to ogle than a superhero. But it was better than nothing. Stretchy would be the way to go. He found some bike shorts and tugged them up over his columnar thighs, bouncing around the bedroom as he fought to get them around his waist.

At last, dressed, he took a few ginger steps and waited to see if the clothing would fly off him. When it didn't, he looked at the Rabbit God in triumph. "Okay, Bugs, now what?"

"It's Leporidus," said the rabbit. "Try and remember it, as I am your God."

"I'll never remember that," said Jay. "I'll call you Leo for now." He tugged at his underwear; the bike shorts were giving him the most amazing wedgie ever. Superheroes must go commando all the time, he decided, twisting his hips as he walked to try to dislodge the stubborn boxer briefs.

"Leo," said Leporidus with a hint of disgust. "Eighteen hundred years a god and now I'm *Leo*. I tell you, it's a good thing the world needs a Herald."

"Yeah, about that," said Jay as he collected his wallet, keys, and cell phone. "What exactly am I supposed to do? Pockets . . . I don't have any pockets . . ." He spotted his mom's fanny pack. It would be better than nothing. At least it was red instead of pink. He held his breath and cinched it around his waist, adjusting the straps as far out as he could. Again, he waited to see if it would fly off. Again, he grinned when it didn't.

"I'm working on that. Or rather, Anurus is."

"Meaning you don't know?"

"Meaning we're working on it."

Jay thought it over. When it came to plans and schemes, nobody was better than Bunny. He was Jay's best friend, and it wouldn't be right not to involve him in something of such magnitude. Besides, if he didn't, and Bunny ever found out, he'd be furious. Jay pulled out his phone and called his friend. "Hey, dude, you busy?"

"Not especially," said Bunny. "I just finished my morning ballet class. What's going on? You're not usually up this early."

"Special occasion," said Jay. "Why don't you meet me at . . ." He paused as he tried to think of a suitable location.

"The beach," said Leporidus. "I like to live dangerously."

"What do you mean?"

"I pissed off Poseidon recently. He has a long memory and a short fuse."

"Great. I was really hoping to drown today."

"Jay honey, who are you talking to and where are we meeting?"

"I'll explain when we get there. China Beach."

"Sounds dreamy."

Jay looked around as he went out to his truck with Leporidus riding in his breast pocket. The Rabbit God had shrank himself down to the size of a guinea pig, his head sticking out and ears standing up straight. Nobody was watching; even old Mrs. Peavey wasn't out in her customary position of neighborhood watchperson. Jay bent down and grabbed onto the frame hooks under his truck's front bumper.

He flexed his legs and back and lifted the end of the truck several inches off the ground without the slightest effort. He grinned and set it back down. "Neat."

"You ain't seen nothin' yet," said Leporidus.

Jay squeezed himself into the driver's seat, banging his head on the door post because it was so much closer than he remembered it. Fortunately the weather was nice and he could hang one arm out the window. Otherwise, he would have had to drive leaning to the right just to get his new shoulders inside the truck. He'd need a new car if he stayed this size.

It was still two weeks before Spring Break, so China Beach was quiet but for a few locals. Bunny had already arrived and was burrowing into the trunk of his car, a little Volkswagen Rabbit convertible. Jay parked next to it and climbed out.

"Bunny," he said, trying to sound casual.

Bunny stood up, saw Jay, and his mouth dropped open. "Oh. My. God," he said. "Jay honey, you look fantastic. Absolutely delicious. What happened to you?"

"I met a god while drinking milk from a roadside stand yesterday."

"You met God while drinking roadside milk? Jay, are you sure it was milk?"

"No, not *the* God. *A* god. This one, in fact. Leo, say hello to, um, Bainbridge." Jay held out the Rabbit God in the palm of his hand.

Bunny shrieked in delight. "You got a pet! Oh, and he's darling!" He bubbled with enthusiasm, reaching out to stroke the soft fur. "Leo's a lovely name."

"Thank you," said the Rabbit God. "But it's Leporidus, actually. It's a pleasure to meet you, Bainbridge."

Bunny took the talking rabbit in stride, as if such things were commonplace to him. "Oh, charmed, I'm sure. Please, call me Bunny. Everyone else does. So you're a god? I'll bet you meet the most interesting people in your line of work."

Leporidus looked up at Jay. "Is he always like this?"

"Most of the time," said Jay. "Nothing fazes him. He's totally fearless and stuff."

"So you're responsible for turning my best friend into someone I'm going to have a very hard time keeping my hands off of." Bunny laughed. "Do you take requests? I've been trying to build a decent ass for three years now."

"It's not just the looks," said Jay, flexing his muscles and hearing threads give way on his t-shirt. "They're functional, too. Watch." He bent down and tilted his truck up to shoulder-level for a moment.

Bunny gasped and his fingertips flew to his lips. "He made you into a superhero!"

"A superhero? You mean like in Just Cause?" Just Cause was the world's premier superhero team, loaded with legendary parahumans. Jay hadn't considered that he might belong among them with his newfound abilities. The idea wasn't an unpleasant one. Maybe Shari would take him back if he was a superhero.

"What else can you do besides heavy lifting?" asked Bunny as he reached out to touch Jay's newly muscular arm and squealed under his breath when he did.

"I don't know." Jay looked down at Leporidus. "What else can I do?"

The Rabbit God found something very interesting to look at on the ground below. "Oh, you know, the usual. You're strong and tough. That's kind of standard for Heralds like you. And, of course, you have the, uh, the unique power of rabbits to draw upon."

Jay raised an eyebrow. "Unique power of rabbits?"

"You can, you know . . . jump. And cavort. And frolic." Rabbits didn't blush, but Leporidus sounded as embarrassed as a jock asked to solve a math problem on the blackboard.

"I can jump?" Jay sounded shocked. "You're a freakin' *god* and all you gave me is the power to *jump*?"

"And cavort and frolic," said Bunny. "You should start dancing for us at the school. It's killing Spence that he can't find a decent *prima danseur* who can do a real *grande jeté*." Spence was Bunny's on-again-off-again boyfriend from a rival high school. Bunny liked to say that if anyone in the world had ever been born to be a ballerina, it was Spence. Jay had never met him, even though they all worked at the same place. Bunny talked about him enough that Jay imagined him to be some great, bronze Apollo.

"I don't think you understand," said Leporidus.

"I'm your Herald, whatever that means, and I can jump? Well, shit. Now I've got something to save the world with. I'll be the envy of everyone on the track team. *Jackson Jones, the Human Jackrabbit.*"

"Fine, hotshot. Jump for us." Leporidus combed his claws down his ears and nodded toward the Pacific in the distance. "See how far you can go."

Jay glared. "Whatever." He bent down, flexed his legs, and sprang into the air.

Powerful leg muscles uncoiled with thousands of pounds per square inch, sending Jay flying up and out into the air, much, *much* further than he'd expected. It was like he'd bought a first-class seat on a rocket, or a roller coaster going up the first hill after the big drop. He yelled in surprise and elation as he hurtled along a lengthy parabolic arc. The trees and sand gave way to water and at last he splashed down into several feet of the cold Pacific. Water went up his nose, bringing him back to reality.

He flailed in the water until he managed to make it back to shore. Once there, shivering and dripping wet, he crouched and launched himself into the air again back toward Bunny and Leporidus. He judged the distance better, but still overshot them and twisted somehow in mid-air until he was flying ass-first, head down. His whoop of thrill turned into an *eek* of fear as he crashed into the branches of a tree. "Ow! Ow! Son of a—*Ow!*" he yelped as he banged down from branch to branch, finally belly-flopping down into the sand.

He hurt. All over. He wondered if he'd broken something besides just his pride. But even as he lay there in the sand, his body seemed to mend itself in short order until the pain was just a dull memory.

Feet in expensive leather sandals appeared before him and he squinted up into Bunny's amused face. "All right," said Jay. "I can jump."

Bunny giggled. "You're going to have to work on your landings, though. Your clothes . . ."

Jay looked down and realized that his makeshift outfit hadn't survived the encounter with the tree. "Hey, quit looking, you perv!"

Leporidus pushed his face into the ground and put his paws over his eyes.

Four

With a sturdier outfit Bunny borrowed from the dance studio, Jay embarked upon further experimentation of his abilities. With coaching from Leporidus, and kibitzing from Bunny, he discovered that he could spring the distance of a football field, give or take a few yards, and could reach the top of a ten-story building. This last test they performed in an alley downtown. When he thudded onto the alley pavement, Jay startled a nearby homeless man, who yelled at him in a drunken, incomprehensible dialect. "Hey, goddammit," he slurred. "Whazza shibboleth an' Imma gitchoor azathoth, ya baster!"

"Oh, uh, I'm sorry, mister."

"Thissiz malley!" shouted the man. "Gedda fuggout!" He threw a trash can lid with impressive aim, considering his eyes didn't point in the same direction. The lid bounced off Jay's shoulder, surprising him more than it hurt.

"Hey, man, what the hell?" yelled Jay.

"Imma meshoo up, punkass!" A barrage of missiles followed the trash can lid. Bottles, cans, chunks of pavement, and for some reason, rotting vegetables flew with deadly accuracy from the homeless man's hands to Jay's head and body. He decided that a balls-out retreat was in order, and sprang out of the alley to where Bunny and Leporidus waited with Bunny's car.

"Start it up, Bunny, quick!" cried Jay.

Bunny shrieked as he saw the man pursuing Jay, flinging all manner of detritus and foaming at the mouth. He made a credible leap of his own into the driver's seat and made the tires of his Cabriolet chirp as he pulled away from the curb.

"Bunny! Wait!" Jay ducked to avoid what looked like a flung chicken carcass from the screaming man. He jumped, angling himself by instinct, and came down right in the Rabbit's passenger seat. Pain shot through his buttocks. "Ow! My ass!"

Leporidus hopped onto the center console from the back seat. "You'll want to always land on your feet. You're optimized for that. If you smash down on your side or back, you're just as likely to die as anyone else."

"What, you can't make me invulnerable to that?"

"Every Herald must have his or her vulnerabilities. It's written in the Rules."

"I swear I can hear the capital letters when you talk." Jay wished he could rub the soreness out of his ass but the way he'd gotten his oversized body wedged into the seat, he knew he wasn't going anywhere until Bunny parked the car. They'd taken it because at least with the top down, Jay could sort of make himself fit inside it.

"You'll have to learn how to perform aerobatics—tumbling, gymnastics, that sort of thing." Bunny had been almost frothing at the mouth with excitement nonstop since Jay had first demonstrated his powers. "I've been trying to get you into classes at the school for years. Now you have no reason not to start. Oh, and I have an idea for your costume, Jackrabbit."

"Costume?" Jay planted his face into his palm. He wished Bunny had gotten the superpowers, not him. Bunny had a much better mindset for being a superhero.

"Well . . . of course!" Bunny sounded scandalized, as if the idea of not wearing a costume was pure sacrilege. "You can't be a superhero without a costume."

"Yeah? Watch me." said Jay. "I'm not going to dress up like those derps from Just Cause. Powers don't make me a superhero. I'm just a high school kid who's a little behind on my grades. Besides, I need to call Shari."

"Oh you did *not* just say that." Bunny whipped the car around a tight corner as if to illustrate his point. "That girl is bad news, Jay honey. Kick that bitch to the curb. You can do so much better than that."

"Jealous?" said Jay.

"Yes, dammit. I can't believe you'd go back to that skank." Bunny sniffed. "I know you're not gay, and believe me it's a crime against all that's right in the world, but it doesn't change the fact that I love you, man, and it breaks my heart to see you getting played like this."

"Bunny, please!" Jay sounded pained. He looked down at Leporidus. "You see what I have to put up with here?"

"I think he's right," said the Rabbit God from Jay's lap.

"What do you know about it? You can't even tell me what I'm supposed to do as your Herald. For a god, you're lamesauce."

"I told you . . . we're working on it. Now be nice. I'm your boss."

"Whatever."

Bunny dropped Jay off at his truck. "Oh my God, I'm totally late for intermediate class. Spence is going to kill me for leaving him alone with all those little girls! Say something nice about me at the funeral." He threw his car into reverse and screeched out of the lot.

Leporidus hopped down to the ground. "I'm off too. God stuff to do. I'll check in later." He vanished in a puff of air and cottontail.

Jay drove back to his home, lost in thoughts of being a superhero. Costumes? Fighting crime? He'd rather be playing Halo or surfing what porn he could get to around the filters his mom had installed. He wasn't hero material. He knew nothing about law enforcement. He was a junior, dammit, and he had a future to think about.

He couldn't be jumping off at every opportunity to stop purse snatchers and muggers and still make his grades.

He wasn't sold on the whole saving-the-world thing. Any doubts he'd had that Leporidus was somehow a practical joke had been laid to rest when Jay jumped three hundred feet into the Pacific Ocean. But for a god, the rabbit seemed freakin' uninformed. It was like the Rabbit God was as much in the dark as Jay felt most of the time. Maybe the only difference between them was a matter of scale. Jay had to worry about his grades, salvaging what was left of his reputation at school, and getting his mom off his back. Leporidus had to worry about saving the world while following the gods' Rules, and didn't know how to accomplish it.

Besides, what was his mother going to think when she saw her son bulging out of his clothes? Never mind that she'd have to spend money on a new wardrobe for him. Never mind that she wasn't the biggest fan of superheroes in general anyway. No, she'd be most angry that he had been ditching school and lied to her about it. He'd have to do something academic to make sure he got back onto her good side before he went any further onto the bad one.

Thinking of school made him realize that he'd still have to walk into the building on Monday morning. There wouldn't be any way he could hide the sudden changes in his body. It was bad enough being targeted as a nerd and loser, but now he could throw *freak* into the mix as well. He'd have every student and teacher thinking he'd taken some kind of *über*-steroids, and if he let it out that he'd become a parahuman, he might as well give up on any chance of having a life in school. He wouldn't be allowed to defend himself against any kind of teasing or bullying, because of the laws that stopped parahumans from using abilities on unpowered people. He wouldn't even have to do anything and he could be blamed for whatever anyone wanted to pin on him.

"Shit," he said aloud. "I'm screwed."

Jay didn't bother turning on any lights, and left his curtains drawn. He had a current events essay due on Monday and he was going to sit in the dark and write it instead of cavorting and frolicking. One good, positive accomplishment would have to suffice for the time being. He opened his laptop and woke it from *Standby* mode. Maybe staring at a blank screen would help him come up with subject matter for the essay. He needed a subject to latch onto; something unique and interesting.

The idea hit him like a shovel upside the head. He could write about himself. Well, not *himself* . . . his alter ego, the superhero, the Herald of Rabbits. Well, he amended, maybe he wouldn't go that far. He had to try and keep it halfway cool at least, and nobody would buy the Herald bit. What was it Bunny had called him?

Jackrabbit.

Okay, he could work with that. He typed the words *Enter The Jackrabbit* across the top of the page and looked at them for awhile, then followed with *The Parahuman in Post-Modern America.* That was good, he thought. That would get his Civics instructor's juices flowing. Now he just needed to come up with some filler for the essay itself.

Somebody knocked at his door. Glad for the distraction, he stood and cracked his head against the kitchen light. He winced and rubbed the sore spot as he walked through the house to the front door. It would take him more than a day to get used to his new height.

Shari stood outside on his porch, her cocoa skin bronze under the yellow porch light, looking upset and nervous. "Hi, Jay."

He froze, not knowing what to say. This went against the rules of the game. You got dumped, you got ignored. At least, that was how it was supposed to work. "Uh, hi."

"Can I come in? Can we talk?"

Jay pushed the door open wide and walked back inside. Shari followed him.

"Jay, I felt bad about dumping you the way I did. I want to tell you why I did . . . Are you okay? You look swollen or something."

"I'm fine."

Shari paced back and forth, unwilling to sit down and compose herself. Jay was fine with that. Let her be uncomfortable after the way she'd humiliated him. "I wanted to you to be my boyfriend. I really did, but something—someone—came up."

"A better boyfriend than me?" The acidity in Jay's tone could have etched copper.

"You weren't my first," said Shari. "You know that."

"So?" Shari had taken Jay's virginity on their third date. When he'd asked if he was her first, she'd laughed and said not to worry about it. He hadn't at the time. There hadn't ever been another time after that.

"There was a boy back in eighth grade. We were really close. We were going to date all through high school and everything. But his family moved to Africa for his dad's work. He didn't have email or anything. I thought he was gone forever."

Jay shook his head. He could see where this was going. "And now he's back."

"He Facebooked me Thursday night. His family moved back into town. He's going to Hayes now."

Rutherford B. Hayes High was Bayview's crosstown rival. Jay had never been full of school spirit, but now he had a good reason to hate on Hayes. "He's gone for three years and then friends you and you dump me just like that?"

Tears formed in Shari's eyes. "Jay, you're a nice guy, but let's face it. You and I weren't ever going to last. I'm a cheerleader, and you're kind of a nobody."

"So why'd you even go out with me in the first place?"

Shari shrugged. "You were really nice the way you asked. But I loved Mark. I still do. I can't just throw him away." She wouldn't meet Jay's gaze.

"You're just throwing *me* away." Jay felt like punching a wall, but was afraid that if he did, he'd knock a hole right through it with his new strength.

"Look, I'm sorry, Jay. This is just how it has to be. You're a nice guy. I'm sure you'll find some girl who's better suited for you than me."

"Yeah," he said. "Whatever."

"See you around, Jay." Shari left the bungalow. The door banged shut behind her.

Jay flopped onto the couch in the dimness of his living room. What was he supposed to do now? The living room suddenly felt cold and alien to him, and he knew he had to get out. He needed to feel some nighttime air on his face. He took a couple steps toward the door and then stopped. He'd been ready to go jumping willy-nilly about town, just bouncing around the area. But people were going to freak out about having a black boy dropping out of the sky next to them, even in this day and age.

There were several superheroes working throughout California. Most were concentrated around Los Angeles, but from time to time, a hero would pass through San Francisco in pursuit of a villain or to visit sick kids in a hospital or something. The upshot of all this was if Jay wore some sort of costume, he would attract less attention than if he were cavorting and frolicking around in his civvies.

He pulled out his cell phone and called Bunny. "Hey, Bunny."

"Jay honey, how are you?"

"You said something earlier about a costume," said Jay. "That still an option?"

"Of course it is. But what's wrong? You sound awful."

"Tell you when I get there."

"I'm hanging out in the costume shop at the studio."

"Okay." He hung up and tucked the phone back into the pocket of his shorts. The costume shop meant Bunny was taking a little private time with Spence, who was a senior at Hayes.

The costume shop was in the basement beneath the dance studio where they all worked. Spence and Bunny taught classes and Jay kept the facilities clean and maintained. It never failed to astonish him just how stinky little ballerinas could be. No matter how hard he mopped the floor in the main dance studio, it still smelled like feet. Because Spence mostly did one-on-one instruction and worked with a community theater, Jay hadn't actually met him before, but Bunny always had nice things to say about the him—that is, when Spence wasn't being a *total bitch*, in Bunny's words.

The studio was forty-five minutes away in typical traffic. Jay knew he could beat that on foot. He slipped a do-rag over his head and tied a bandana around his mouth in a makeshift mask. It wasn't much of a costume, but it would have to do. He left his wallet behind, slipping a twenty dollar bill into his pocket instead. He didn't want to carry any identification in case he was stopped for jumping too high or something. The law was complicated when it came to parahumans and usage of their abilities. He debated leaving his cell phone—his lifeline to the modern world—then decided that he didn't care much about the modern world at the moment. The phone stayed on the nightstand by his wallet. He clipped his key ring to the loop inside his shorts, hoping it wouldn't work its way loose.

The sun was only a hint of reddish gold at the edge of the Bay. He stepped into his tiny back yard and looked around. None of his neighbors were hanging around in their own yards. Even Mrs. Peavey was indoors, watching her nighttime reality shows. Good enough. He launched himself into the dusk.

He grew accustomed to traveling by leaps and bounds in short order. It was exhilarating, springing into the sky and feeling the cooling air rush past him while the landscape spun beneath him. He grew comfortable with the ground rushing up to meet him. It became a pattern for him. *Flex, leap, fly, twist, land, repeat.*

He more or less followed the main thoroughfares, as he didn't want to chance dropping into darkness and landing on something or someone he shouldn't. Whenever he touched down, people shrieked and pointed, then whistled and yelled after him when he launched again. Some cheered. Once he heard a popping sound and wondered if someone had taken a shot at him. He glanced back to see if anyone was pointing anything at him. When he turned back to prepare for his next landing, he found himself heading straight into the side of a box truck that hadn't been crossing the distant intersection when he jumped.

He had a moment of pure, blind, panic, and thrust his feet ahead of him to try and absorb the impact. He struck the truck with a resounding *THUD*. He spotted the horrified face of the driver staring out the window at him. Jay flexed his legs. "Howdy," he said, and pushed against the truck to flip across the intersection.

"Wow!" called a couple of kids on skateboards who couldn't have been more than ten years old.

Jay flashed them a thumbs-up, which they returned in kind. "Uh, stay in school," he said, spouting the first adult-type wisdom that came to his mind. He bounded up to the roof of a nearby building to get his bearings. His heart was pounding, but more with excitement than exertion. He didn't feel the least bit tired. It was different, looking at the city from a higher vantage point. *That* stretch of lights had to be the highway, and *that* one had to be the road he would take if he were driving, which meant the dance studio was over *there*.

Immediate thoughts of Shari forgotten, he whooped and jumped again, heading for his destination.

Five

Jay knocked on the door to the costume shop, breathless but cheerful after his exciting jaunt across town.

Bunny opened the door, wearing a dressing gown and his face covered in blue mud. "Jay honey! Come on in. We're doing facials. Want one? Your skin certainly does."

"No, that's all right," said Jay. "I'm not worried about my face right now."

"You ought to. Your whole T-zone is oily and your cheeks are dry," said Bunny.

"Not now, Bunny. Can I get a glass of water? I just jumped over here and, well, my legs aren't tired at all."

Bunny giggled and rushed off to the minifridge. The boys had turned the costume shop into a makeshift hangout, with Bunny and Spence's decorating sensibilities tempered by Jay's blue-collar chic. Colorful scarves attached to the walls and rafters helped to hide the unfinished ceiling. A TV was tucked into one corner amid boxes of fabric swatches and bling. The carpet was thick and littered with bits of thread and fuzz of every color imaginable. The street-level windows at the top of the basement let in some daylight, but Jay had put up some stick-on tinting to make the shop a little more private. He and Bunny had salvaged a couch from a garage sale and then one weekend while Jay was helping his mom, the other two boys had recovered it with a luxurious burgundy velour.

Jay kept the costume shop hangout a secret. It was hard enough for his tender high school reputation that he worked at a ballet studio, but if anyone found out that he hung around in the sultry boudoir beneath it, well, he might as well start wearing a dress to school.

Another blue-faced boy peeked out of the bathroom, his hair pinned up in plastic hair claws. "Well, hello there, sailor," he said. "I'm Spence." He was fair-skinned and blonde with dark roots, and he was as muscular as Jay had expected. Ballet, as Bunny so often said, wasn't for wimps and weaklings.

Jay nodded. "Hi Spence. I'm Bunny's straight friend Jay. Pleased to meet you at last."

Spence's face fell. "Oh, really? Damn. What a waste. Are you *straight* straight or just giving lip service to straight?" He pouted like it was for an audition.

"I like chicks, not dudes. Sorry, bro."

"I told you," said Bunny, returning from the fridge. "He's not interested. But as a fag stag there's none better." He handed Jay a bottle of Perrier water and opened one for himself.

"Thanks, Bunny."

"While you were on your way over, I told Spence about your new powers. He's very excited to work with you. *Very* excited." Bunny whipped out his cell phone, which was covered with faux diamond bling, and checked the time. "We've got about fifteen minutes before the goop has to come off. That should be enough time for measurements. Spence is the costumer for the ballet company. You won't find anyone better to outfit you in something stylish, sexy, and functional."

Spence bowed from the waist. "I'm not all that, really." He belted a red silk kimono around his waist and came into the main room. "Let's talk about what you want to convey while I work. Strip down to your shorts."

Not all dudes could have done it without blinking in the presence of two lustful gay boys, but Jay didn't hesitate and peeled off his clothing. Spence's eyes nearly popped from his skull as he drank in Jay's muscle definition. "Oh, dear me," he said. "Bunny, you didn't tell me he was *gorgeous*. It's going to be a pleasure working with you, Jay."

"Yeah, okay." Jay shot a pleading look that said *help me* at Bunny, but Bunny sat on the couch with his legs crossed like a prim secretary, and began to attend to his nails with a metal file.

Spence pulled a measuring tape and sketchpad from the pocket of his robe. He handed the pad and a pen to Bunny and then approached Jay with a hungry glint in his eye. "Take down some numbers, please."

Bunny set down his file, and held his pen at the ready.

"How tall are you, Jay? Arms out at your sides, please."

"Six-four, unless that changed with everything else."

Bunny looked up at him, estimating. "No, you're not any taller."

Spence stretched the tape around Jay's chest. "What are you thinking of calling yourself? What kind of image do you want to project? Bunny, chest is forty-eight inches." Bunny made a note.

"I thought I'd call myself *Jackrabbit*, since my powers are, um, rabbit-related."

"That's lovely. You'll want a lot of freedom of movement, I'm sure." Spence moved the tape again. "Waist, thirty-six inches. That's all? God, that's absolutely *obscene*. Bunny told me a bit about your jumping. You're also stronger than a normal human?"

"Yeah, some."

"You probably don't want a lot of bulky armor or anything. If you're in a battle, you'll use your quick movements to avoid being hit. Hips, forty-four inches. Baby's got back."

"Are you looking at my ass?"

"Oh dear me, yes. Yes I am. Guilty as charged. It's a lovely ass, if you don't mind me saying. Pardon my, um, reach." Spence looped the tape up over Jay's shoulder and through his crotch. "Girth, seventy and a half inches. I have some color swatches over for you to look at. Do you want a mask?"

"I don't know. I mean, it's going to be hard enough to hide all these muscles come Monday at school. People are going to figure it out anyway."

"Well, you should think it over. It might help to keep all those nasty supervillains from coming after you during your lunch period. Inseam, forty-one inches." Spence continued to take measurements and read them off until Bunny announced that it was time to remove their masks.

"Make yourself at home, Jay honey," said Bunny. "We won't be ten minutes."

While the two young men ran back to the bathroom, giggling and whispering, Jay wandered over to the couch, found the remote, and flipped on the television.

" . . .And it looks like San Francisco may have a new parahuman. Several witnesses reported seeing a man leaping from buildings and across streets." The newscaster was one of the perky ones who could deliver news of mass fatalities without losing her surgically-constructed smile.

"Daaaaaamn!" whispered Jay.

The broadcast cut to a shot of the driver whose truck he'd bounced off. "He just come out of nowhere," said the man around a mouthful of toothpick. "He didn't hurt nothin', but darn near gave me a heart attack."

The scene cut again, this time to the two kids he'd greeted. "He was cool!" said one.

"Yeah, cool! And he jumped right up there onto that building!" cried the other.

Jay put his hands on his cheeks, eyes wide in surprise. "Shit, I'm famous."

"Let's hope this new jumping-jack will be one of the good guys," said the newscaster. "Now here's Rusty with the weather."

Jay shut off the television as Bunny and Spence returned with their faces cleaned of mud. "Okay, I decided I definitely want a mask. And something that covers me from head to toe if you can do it. The less people see of the real me, the better."

Spence whipped out his sketchpad and rattled off a design. "I'm thinking something in a single, solid color. You don't want a grim, night-time avenger look, so black is out. White will get filthy in just a few minutes of leaping tall buildings in a single bound. How do you feel about a nice brown?"

Jay looked at his own skin tone, what he might have termed a *nice brown*. "I don't know. You're the costume expert, not me. Isn't it going to make me look naked, though?"

"How is that a bad thing, chocolate sauce? Brown will show off your body contours very nicely, in both artificial and natural lighting, plus it'll hide the dirt." Spence spun around the pad to show Jay. "What do you think of this?"

"Oh, that's simply darling!" said Bunny.

Leotard. Ears. Pixie boots. And a puffy *cottontail*. "I can't wear that! I'm not going to be a superhero who looks like a *Playboy* Bunny!" Jay rolled his eyes.

"What's wrong with that?" Spence started a new sketch. "Did you like anything about it?"

Jay shrugged. "I guess the ears were all right. I mean, I might as well look like a rabbit. Leo would approve of that."

"Who's Leo?" asked Spence.

"That's a really long story," said Jay. "And let me just say absolutely no tail on the costume."

"Oh, come on," cried Spence. "I'm creating art here. You have to give me something to work with."

"I said you could keep the ears, but no tail. I'm nobody's pin-up."

"Says you," grumbled Spence. "How about this one?"

"That one's even worse. It looks like I'm naked."

"No, you don't get it. This a single-piece bodysuit with an integrated hood and full-face mask. Head to toe, like you requested. A lovely, warm brown all over. With ears," said Spence.

"Isn't that kind of boring?" asked Bunny. "Where's the panache? Where are the bangles and baubles?" He held up his phone for display. "Where's the bling?"

"Nothing like that here," said Spence. "The panache isn't in the outfit; it's in the man wearing it. This is a costume that says *I'm not afraid of anything*. It calls attention to all the right parts. First and foremost the attitude." He flicked a finger against his drawing.

Jay considered the illustration. It would hide him as well as anything. He could see himself bouncing around the city in a getup like that. People would see it and think *rabbit* without having to stretch their minds. It was almost clownish the way the mask covered the face, leaving only the lips and eyes uncovered. He tried to make sense of Spence's scribbles in the margins, but they were in some kind of bizarre costumier's shorthand. "I think I like that," he said.

"Wonderful." Spence trotted into the back room, returning a moment later with a handful of color swatches. He riffled through them, discarding those of the wrong color or material, until he had only two left. "The suit will be bi-layered," he said. "This will be the interior material. It's soft, hypo-allergenic, and will help your skin to breathe. It will also wick away perspiration so you don't have unsightly stains on the outer layer."

"Is that a problem?" asked Jay.

Spence looked aghast. "I've been designing ballet costumes since I was ten years old. You wouldn't believe how much ballerinas sweat, and these skin-tight costumes show everything."

"Oh. Okay."

"The inner layer also will house the framework for the ear supports, eye shields in the cowl, and a cup."

"A cup?"

"Every superhero should wear a cup. You only need to get kicked in the *cojones* once to realize that."

"Oh. What are eye shields?"

"Superheroes should have white eyes without pupils. And they should also have eye protection from dust, flying debris, and other nonesuch. I'm going to use the lenses from safety glasses. They'll look clear to you, but when light shines on them, they'll appear white to anyone else."

"Ooooh . . ." said Bunny. "That'll look so cool."

Spence continued. "This outer layer will be sheer and give the appearance of fine fur, like suede or velour. Rubber-soled boots will be incorporated here, and texture pads on your palms and fingers so you can hold things. Football players use them."

"How long will it take you to whip all this up? And how much am I going to owe you when you're done?" Jay had begun to feel creeping doubts, afraid the price would be far more than he could pay.

"I have most of what I need in the costume shop." Spence pointed to a corner of his apartment that was crammed full of bolts of cloth, bangles, swatches, and costume racks. "And what I don't have, Bunny can get for me at the all-night boutique around the corner. With a cinnamon triple latte and DVDs of *Cats* and *Rent*, I should be able to finish it by morning."

"Seriously?" Jay's eyes widened. "You're that good?"

"Oh, you have *no* idea," said Bunny, then blushed.

"I'll tell you what . . ." Spence eyed Jay. "You refer any other superheroes you run across to me with their costume issues, and yours is free."

Bunny raised an eyebrow. "Going to branch out, Spence, love?"

Spence smiled. "Dear Bunny, the theater will always be my life, but a livelihood it isn't. I could build a reputation on someone like Jay, here. Imagine if I wound up with an exclusive contract to design for one of the big groups like the Lucky Seven or Just Cause!"

"Don't you figure they've got in-house costumiers?" Bunny pulled on some jeans.

"Yeah, well, they suck. Have you seen that horrid outfit they've got Doublecharge wearing? It's all the worst bits of the Seventies and Eighties together in one leotard." Spence was defiant. "So what do you say, Jay? Deal?"

Jay extended his hand. "You bet."

Spence grinned and fluttered his eyelashes. "I may just swoon." He pulled a slim cell phone from his robe. "Mom? I've got a costume emergency here at the studio. Don't wait up for me." He sighed and rolled his eyes while his mother said something. "My shipment didn't arrive for the Monday night show so I've got to make seventeen flower-themed costumes or else those poor little girls are all going to need therapy." Another pause. "Yes, mom, I'll have something to eat. Yes, I'll stay here. No, I won't hunt down any rough trade. I love you too."

"Rough trade?" Bunny raised an eyebrow at Spence and folded his arms. "Just what have you been up to while I've been away, you coy bitch?"

"Oh, dear. My mom thinks that because I'm gay, I'm always on the prowl. She means well, but she just doesn't get it." Spence rolled his eyes.

"Dude, that's just how moms are." Jay shuddered. "I don't even want to think about what mine would say if she found out about this whole jumping superhero thing."

Spence cracked his knuckles. "Bunny, call ahead to Starbucks and tell them to warm up the espresso machine. It's going to be a long night."

Six

"Rise and shine, Jay honey." Bunny sounded tired but cheerfully bubbly as ever.

Jay rubbed his eyes and sat up from the couch on which he'd fallen asleep. He yawned and squinted at Bunny. "What are you wearing?"

Bunny wore a sleeveless black leotard, pink tights with a puffball tail, and a headband with rabbit ears. It was the first costume Spence had designed. Jay blinked. It was even worse when modeled in person than on the page.

Bunny twirled for him. "Do you like it? I thought I'd be your sidekick."

"A sidekick?"

"Jackrabbit and the Bunny. Isn't that divine?"

"No." Jay stood up. His heavy new muscles rearranged themselves into fighting shape. "Any coffee?"

Bunny drew his finger across his throat. "Ix-nay on the offee-kay." He nodded toward the corner where Spence hunched over a small sewing table. The veins in his eyes looked like they belonged on a road map. He was making last-minute adjustments on the costume with fingers that shook from exhaustion and too much caffeine.

"Poor baby," whispered Bunny. "He's had four lattes since midnight. I had to go to the twenty-four hour Starbucks three times for him. He's going to need to sleep for the next two days just to recuperate."

"I'm fine." Spence sounded so grouchy that his characteristic lisp had disappeared. "Tell the pretty boy to come over here and get dressed, and to do it slow so I can watch."

Jay looked at Bunny, who shrugged and twitched his tail. "All right, here I am." He took the costume from Spence and looked it over carefully. "It looks okay to me. How do I put it on?"

Spence showed him the long Velcro panel that covered the opening in the costume's back. He climbed into it and slipped his feet into the incorporated boots. It was neat how they hugged his calves and cushioned his feet. The soles were pliant enough that he could flex them with his toes. "What are these, ninja boots or something?"

"Dance boots," said Spence.

Jay shrugged his shoulders into the suit and pulled the cowl over his head, adjusting it until he could see easily through the eye-holes. He sealed the back panel and shook his head to see how the ears felt. They waggled without losing their arch or flopping forward over his eyes. The cup in his crotch felt funny, but he knew it would be better in every way than getting kneed in the balls by some overeager purse-snatcher or shoplifter.

A pressing need made him think of a question he hadn't considered. "Hey, uh . . ." He cleared his throat. "How do I take a leak in this thing?"

"There's a Velcro fly," said Spence. "But if you need to have a sit-down, you're going to have to take it off."

"Note to self . . . avoid Mexican food." Jay grinned.

"Oh, wow," said Bunny. "The mask shows off your facial expressions. That's fantastic."

"Well, how do I look?" Jay turned around for them.

"I'd do you," said Spence.

"Spencer, please." Bunny play-slapped his boyfriend. "Besides, I saw him first."

"Okay, you guys are starting to freak me out a little. I'm going to change and then find some breakfast." Jay twisted around to reach for the back panel, marveling at his flexibility despite the huge muscles.

Bunny reached out and stopped him. "What's your hurry, Jay honey? Aren't you going to take the model out for a test-drive? You haven't even looked at yourself yet." He spun Jay around to face the tri-angled mirror at one end of the costume shop.

Jay had to admit, Spence did very good work. He was a vision in shimmering brown, every muscle's contour standing out in sharp relief. The costume rose seamlessly from toes to scalp, looking more like a layer of skin than clothing. The eyes, as promised, were white, and the mask clung to his face, moving with him. Jay made some experimental faces and the mask reflected them. With only his mouth exposed, his identity was well-hidden. He reached up and tweaked the wire-frame ears that perched over his head a more rakish tilt.

"Daaaaamn," he said. "I do look good." An idea occurred to him. "Spence?"

Spence had collapsed into a chair, snoring hard enough to make the nearby clothes hangers rattle in sympathetic vibration. Bunny took an opera cloak from a rack and spread it over Spence's shoulders. "Poor guy. He worked himself silly all night."

"Did he happen to give me any pockets?"

Bunny nodded. "Left front, but I wouldn't keep much in it. You put your keys in there, it's going to look like you have a tumor."

Jay took the twenty from his pants, and slipped it into his costume pocket. "I'll be back."

"Where are you going?"

"I already said. Breakfast. Thank Spence for me. I'll let him know if I have any problems with the suit when I get back."

Jay bounded up the steps from the costume shop six at a time to the exit door of the studio.

"Jay? I mean, Jackrabbit?"

Jay turned back, framed in the bright doorway, a rabbit in human form.

"You look great." Bunny gave him a sly smile. "Be careful out there, okay?"

"I'm a Herald," said Jay. "What could go wrong?"

He whooped and leaped into the sky.

It was a Sunday morning in Spring, and Jackrabbit was on his first patrol, in search of crime to vanquish, citizens to rescue, and a good bagel sandwich.

He bounced down the street, waving at paper boys and street vendors. A yuppie, perhaps a lawyer working the weekend, stopped in the middle of a crosswalk with his mouth hanging open as he stared at Jay, almost spilling his double half-caf with half and half as a bus was bearing down upon him.

"What the hell are you supposed to be?" asked the man as Jay landed next to him.

"Saving your life, and thanks for noticing." Jay grabbed the man and leaped out of the intersection just as the bus barreled through, brakes squealing. The paper coffee cup went flying.

"Hey, you spilled my coffee! I'll sue!"

"Thanks for flying *Jackrabbit Airlines*. No extra charge for being a grumpy bastard. We hope you enjoy the fact that you're not dead."

A couple of brothers, out early or still up from the night before, catcalled and whistled as he bounded on up the street, heading for a certain diner that made the best breakfast in town. Jay's grin stretched from ear to ear. He could get used to being a superhero. Having the suit on, the anonymity, made him feel free and alive, like he could say anything.

For variety's sake, he jumped to the rooftops and traveled along them for awhile. As he touched down on one building, he heard laughter and giggling from over the side and leaned over to look.

Two kids were busy tagging the wall of the building from the fire escape.

"Psssst!" Jay stage-whispered at them. "Look up here."

The two boys looked up at him.

"No, don't look," he said. "How can I sneak up on you if you look? Oh, wait. My bad." He flipped over the edge to drop onto the fire escape between them and surveyed their work. "You're no Turk 182, that's for sure. Sorry, boys. This just doesn't qualify as civic improvement."

He grabbed each one in an arm and leaped off the fire escape. They shrieked as they all dropped four stories to the alleyway below. Jay's powerful legs absorbed the landing without effort, and he marched the cowed boys around the corner to the front door. The building housed an antiques shop. Jay knocked.

An old woman unlocked the door. "I'm not quite open yet . . . is this some kind of publicity thing?" She looked at Jay with suspicion.

"No, ma'am. These two boys have graciously volunteered to spend the day assisting you around the shop as part of their dedication to a better community." He bent down, grabbed the boys by the fronts of their shirts, and grinned at them. "Haven't you?"

They both nodded, eyes wide.

"Well isn't that sweet?" said the proprietor. "As a matter of fact, I do have some heavy lifting for which I could use some young, strong backs. Thank you so much, Mister . . ."

Jay bowed. "Jackrabbit, ma'am. Always glad to help out." He bounced away.

As he neared the diner, he noticed flashing lights by Bayview High and diverted his course to investigate. Three police cars and a fire truck had parked beneath one side of the school with a crowd gathered around them. Everyone was looking up at a solitary figure perched on the edge of the decorative brick edifice atop the third floor.

Jackrabbit bounced down next to a policeman, whose attention was focused on the potential jumper above. "What have we got, Captain?" he asked.

"Sergeant," corrected the officer. "We have a jumper."

"Thanks for noticing." Jay grinned at his own joke, even if the officer didn't bat an eye. He leaped for the rooftop, not really paying attention to his angles.

"Hey!" The officer called after him.

For the second time since the acquisition of his powers, Jay misjudged a jump. He missed the rooftop and managed to catch hold of an outcropping adjacent to where the jumper was crouched.

"Whoa!" cried the young woman as Jay suddenly appeared in her view.

"Creepy White Girl," gasped Jay, surprised when he recognized her, no easy feat with her unfettered hair blowing in the breeze from the Bay and no glasses on her face. She didn't even have on one of those weird dresses. In a t-shirt and jeans, she looked almost, well, normal.

"What? Who are you?"

"Jackrabbit." Jay struggled to pull himself up onto the outcropping. "I'd shake hands, but I'm a little busy right now." He grunted as he strained for a better grip.

"What are you doing?"

"Trying to keep from falling. What are you doing?"

"I'm going to fly."

"Nice morning for it," said Jay. "Although I think the word you're looking for is *fall*, not *fly*. I may end up joining you there if I can't get up. Give a rabbit a hand?"

"Oh, oh no. I couldn't do that."

Jay managed to swing a leg up and around the outcropping and pulled himself up. "Well, I guess I managed okay. Thanks for noticing how heroic I am."

"Why are you dressed like that?" asked the girl.

"It's laundry day. One more day and I'll be naked," said Jay. "You really want to turn yourself into street pizza here? What's worth all this, anyway?"

"No, you don't understand. I'm going to fly."

Creepy White Girl seemed chipper for someone about to fling herself to her death. Jay felt a pang of guilt. He wondered if his avoidance of her was a contributing factor to the current situation. And he wondered what drugs she was on. "Flying sounds pretty tough. Why don't you start out a little smaller, like tap dancing or croquet?"

"What?"

He knew he had to think fast. "You've got to understand that there's a lot to life and you can't just throw it all away in one bad mistake. Think of all the movies you haven't seen yet and books you haven't read. Think of all the great TV shows you'll miss."

"I like *Survivor.*"

"Heck, think of all the *bad* TV shows you'll miss," said Jay, not missing a beat.

Creepy White Girl shrugged. "I don't know."

"Life's too precious for you to throw it away. You're special. I'm dressed like a giant rabbit and even I can see that." He realized he knew nothing about her beyond his nickname for her. "What's your name?"

"Kasey, but you don't understand, I'm going to *fly.*"

"Pleased to meet you, Kasey. I'm Jack. Jackrabbit." He extended his hand, over-balanced, and nearly slipped off his outcropping. "Whoops."

"Don't fall," she cautioned him.

"Good advice. You ought to take it too," he said. "Seriously, do you think it'll make you feel better?"

"Flying? Of course it will."

"Not *flying. Falling.* Like, to your death."

"What do you mean? I'm not going to fall to my death, Jackrabbit."

Jay leaned back, kicking up his feet and folding his hands behind his head. "It's not the fall I'm worried about. It's the sudden stop at the end."

Kasey stamped her foot. "I told you, I'm going to fly."

Jay sighed. "Kasey, this is kind of silly. What say we go back onto the roof and you can buy me a milkshake?" He wondered how she'd managed to get into the school on a Sunday.

"I don't know. I mean, I just met you and all."

Jay heard people moving around on the roof. He hoped that the cops or firefighters or negotiators or whoever would keep their distance and not spook the girl. He'd pushed so many of her buttons, he thought she might just be ready to give up her suicidal plans. He could tell their conversation had reached a critical stage and it was imperative that nobody interrupted them. "You have to buy me one."

"Why?"

He shrugged. "I don't have any pockets." He held his breath, hoping she'd take the offer.

A conflict raged across her face, which finally relaxed into a peaceful expression. "Sure, okay," she said at last.

A smile split Jay's face, tugging his mask at the corners of his mouth. "Great. I know just the place—"

Kasey jumped off the building into open air.

"Yikes!" Jay didn't even stop to think. He kicked off of his own outcropping, accelerating faster than she fell. He grabbed her in mid-air, shifted his grip on her, and landed on the ground with a jarring but non-fatal thud.

He set her down and she looked around, astonished that she still lived. "You all right?" asked Jay.

"Of course I am," she said.

The onlookers cheered like they were at a football game with the home team scoring the winning touchdown on a ninety-eight yard catch-and-run.

Paramedics mobbed around Kasey to make sure she wasn't harmed, while the police took up wary positions around Jay. He ignored them. "Kasey, I'll take a rain check on that milkshake if you don't mind."

"It's okay," she called over the crowd noise.

"Hey, who are you?" yelled a bystander.

"Jackrabbit, and thanks for noticing!" said Jay.

"You one of the good guys?" asked a cop.

"Nope. One of the *great* guys." Jay winked at him. He flexed his legs and bounced up and away, clearing entire city blocks with each leap, until he had put some serious distance between the excited crowd and himself.

He paused atop an office complex to catch his breath. He was thrilled with the way his morning had begun, so much so that he stood facing downtown and whooped with joy, arms outstretched as if he would embrace the entire city.

"You know how silly you look right now?" said a voice.

Jay turned to see Leporidus crouched by a rooftop air conditioner. "Oh, hello, Leo. I was wondering when you'd turn up."

"You know how I said I was still working on the saving-the-world thing?"

"Yeah?"

"Maybe you'd better find a television."

Seven

Nobody saw the Ship before its arrival.

One moment it wasn't there, and the next it was circling the world in a high polar orbit over the central Pacific. Gigantic in its proportions, the Ship was far larger than an aircraft carrier. It could even be seen by the naked eye, a dark oblong smudge in the sky. Every nation in the world went into high alert status as scientists realized the thing overhead was neither a figment of their imaginations nor a glitch in their computers.

The Ship orbited in silence, despite being bombarded with inquiries, introductions, and threats from every corner of the globe. Radio Shacks were bled dry of amateur radio equipment as every nutcase with an agenda wanted to be the one to whom the Ship first said hello.

Every news network ran footage of the Ship, shot by amateur and professional astronomers, civilian imaging satellites, and one short segment that had been leaked from United States Space Command before the military clamped down on all security breaches. They alternated the blurry, pixelated, and occasionally spectacular images with a parade of talking heads theorizing on the Ship's origins, its builders, its mission, and saying nothing over and over again in every permutation imaginable. Just Cause and its parent organization, the Parahuman Resources Agency, were unavailable for comment, and all the White House would say was that they were still assessing the situation.

Jay stood in the middle of the café where he'd intended to buy breakfast, staring at the television in amazement along with everyone else in the diner. Nobody seemed to care or even notice the young man dressed as a rabbit in their midst; there was real news on the television for the first time in, it seemed, years.

He felt a sudden weight on his shoulder and nearly jumped out of his skin. As it was, he narrowly missed getting his ears severed by a ceiling fan. The spectacle of aliens was so impressive that nobody reacted to Jay's leap of surprise. "Easy, my friend," said the Rabbit God, who'd appeared out of thin air.

"Hey, man," said a guy with a stubbly chin and a knit cap pulled down over his scraggly hair. "Did you know there's a rabbit on your shoulder?"

"No, he's where he belongs. There's a rabbit under his feet," said Jay.

"Huh?"

"Too metaphysical?" asked Jay.

"I don't care, but you're blockin' the teevee."

Jay obliged by shuffling to one side a little. He couldn't believe what he was seeing, but there it was as plain as the ears on his head: *aliens*. His ass sphincter was already tightening up in anticipation of unwanted probing. "So this is what you were talking about?" he asked Leporidus.

"I think so. Anurus said Blattodeus seemed very excited about something."

"Who? And who?"

"Anurus, the Frog God. You remember him, don't you? And Blattodeus, the insect god that doesn't belong in Gods' Home."

"Yeah, that all sounds real important, but these are freakin' *aliens*! Are they going to invade us and suck out our brains? Shove things up our butts?" He dropped his voice to a whisper. "I'm only seventeen! What am I supposed to do when aliens attack?"

"Hey, man," said the scraggly man again. "What the hell are you supposed to be, a giant cockroach?"

Jay's mouth fell open. "Cockroach?" He looked at himself in amazement. "Oh my God, how could you think that? I'm a rabbit. A Jackrabbit."

"Yeah, all right. Sure. You're a rabbit. Are you some kind of superhero or something?"

Jay looked around, not quite sure the man meant him. Maybe someone from the New Guard had stopped into the cafe for a quick bagel sandwich. "Me?"

"You're the only guy in here wearing a rabbit suit," said the man, whom Jay was beginning to suspect might be under the influence of something illicit. "You're going to save us all, right, man? That's what you do, right?"

"Save you?" Jay felt more like sinking into the floor than being a hero at that moment.

"Yeah," said a lady in a Disneyland hoodie. She pointed at him. "He'll protect us. That's what they do."

Jay looked from her to the scraggly man. More eyes turned toward him until everyone in the diner was staring at him, looks of worry mixed with hope across their faces. He glanced down at Leporidus on his shoulder, but the Rabbit God seemed content just to perch and let the scene play out. What could he, a mere high school student do in the face of what might well be the end of everything?

He could ease their minds. Of that much, he felt confident, and that confidence came out in his voice. "You bet that's what I do. Aliens? Please. I've been to Oakland. There's nothing a few space bugs could bring scarier than that."

Somebody whistled, and Jay could see people nodding in agreement.

"Good," said Leporidus in Jay's ear.

He took it as an endorsement to continue. "I'll take them on all by myself, and they'll learn to tremble at the very mention of the name *Jackrabbit*."

"Overdoing it a little now," said Leporidus.

The diner clientele ate it up like a platter of free sliders. Jay grinned and his ears stood up tall and proud. The people applauded, cheered, and a few of the braver souls slapped Jay's back, exhorting him to stomp all over those freakin' aliens who were gonna come and take their jobs, and might even be socialists to boot.

Jay's grin became a little pained. He glanced down at Leporidus again. "So what do I do?" he asked, quiet enough not to be heard over the applause. "I can't jump into space. Can I?"

"No," said Leporidus. "I've seen enough for now. Let's go." He shifted on Jay's shoulder.

"Just a minute." Jay stepped over to the counter and smiled at the waitress. "Hey, darling . . . I jumped all the way over here from the Bay, and I'm starving. You think I could get a bagel sandwich and a coffee to go? And a carrot juice for my friend here?" he added as an afterthought.

"No, really, I'm fine," said Leporidus.

The waitress glanced at him, then did a double take.

"Just ignore the talking rabbit," said Jay. "How about that sandwich? With everything on it?"

The waitress popped her gum. She turned and yelled toward the back. "Juan, give me a spare tire with everything for the weirdo in the rabbit suit here."

A man in a business suit poked Jay. "What're you super guys going to do about the aliens?" The man poked him again.

Jay's smile turned a little painful. "I'll bring it up at tonight's meeting in the clubhouse. I can't miss it, because it's my night to bring the cookies. I'm sure we'll figure something out. Oh!" An idea occurred to him.

"Aliens are bad." The man made like he was going to poke Jay once more.

Jay grabbed the man's finger. "Want to lose it?" he whispered in as threatening a tone as he could manage.

The man shook his head, wide-eyed.

"Then cut it out."

"Hey, Bunnyman, stop assaulting the other paying customers and collect your order." The waitress held up a paper bag and a doubled Styrofoam cup.

Jay gave her a smile and released the man's finger. He handed her his twenty dollar bill. "It's *Jackrabbit*. Keep the change."

The waitress raised an eyebrow at Jay's generosity, but she pocketed the money before the weirdo in the rabbit suit took it back.

Jay collected his food and shouldered his way out of the crowded diner. Behind him on the television, the President urged people to remain calm.

"So do you know anything about these guys?" he asked Leporidus as he started back toward Bunny's dance studio, careful to keep his thumb over the lid of the coffee cup so not to lose half of his drink with every bounce.

"Not a thing," admitted Leporidus.

"Then what are you doing here instead of working on that?" asked Jay.

"It seemed like a wise idea to check up on you. You know, to make sure you weren't thinking of doing anything silly."

"Like dressing up in a giant rabbit costume and playing superhero?"

"Exactly."

Jay paused atop a rooftop to eat his sandwich, a phenomenal creation consisting of eggs, bacon, sausage, tomato, a green chile pepper, cheese, mayonnaise, and Tabasco sauce. He brushed crumbs off his chest and drank his coffee. "I was actually thinking about joining one of the superhero teams.

After I write my essay, that is," he added, recalling his looming deadline.

"Why? Don't you have enough to worry about?"

"Thanks for the vote of confidence, Leo old pal. I'm only your Herald that's supposed to save the world, and I don't even know what I'm supposed to save it *from* except some insect god. I had normal problems last week before you came along, like acne and getting dumped by my girlfriend."

"You're about to have more of them." Leporidus looked over Jay's shoulder.

"Huh? What do you mean?"

"Company," said the Rabbit God, and vanished off Jay's shoulder.

Jay spun around. His eyes settled on a flying figure approaching from the west. He squinted, trying to make out details as he or she drew closer. What started as a winged blue blur resolved into a slender young woman in a bright blue gymnastics leotard over white tights. A scalloped cape with a feather pattern traced upon it in what looked like black marker sprouted from her shoulders, held by a ribbon. She had a blue balaclava over her head and face to hide her features, but she'd cut a hole in the back of it to let her raven-colored hair fly in the breeze like a crest. A pair of blue Converse high-tops completed the ensemble. It looked like the kind of superhero costume someone would put together on a spur of the moment. She waved at him as she circled overhead. He shrugged and waved back, motioning her to land by him.

She dropped gracefully to the rooftop a few yards away and smiled at him, her lips painted a bright and cheery blue beneath her balaclava. "Hi, I'm Bluebird."

"Jackrabbit. Nice to meet you." Jay hoped that Spence's mask design was cunning enough to hide his eyes as he checked her out. Nice figure, curves in the right places. He just hoped the balaclava didn't mean she was a butterface, as in *she's got a body to die for, but her face . . .*

"I know. I saw you earlier today. So should we, like, fight now or what?" she asked.

"Uh . . . what?"

She stepped toward him. "In the comics, whenever two superheroes meet for the first time, they fight each other because they don't realize they're heroes. Are you a hero? I am, although I'm kind of new at it. I like your costume. You look just like a rabbit, really, although I never saw one as tall or well-muscled as you until today. I made this costume myself. Do you like it? So far all I really know is that I can fly. What can you do?"

Jay's eyes widened. It was like facing a verbal machine gun. "Uh, I can jump real high. And I like your costume. And yes, I'm a hero. What are you doing here?" Too late, he realized the error of his ways in asking her a question.

"Oh, well, I was having a totally difficult morning. You know, like, high school drama type stuff. And then something wonderful happened and the next thing I know I was flying around the Bridge. Are you from around here? I've never been anywhere but here. Just plain old me in plain old San Fran. Anyway, I decided to skip studying for my algebra test and get a late breakfast and I was going to go to this one diner and, like, get a bagel sandwich and a milkshake. They're really good there—they put chilies and tomatoes on them. On the sandwiches, I mean, not the milkshakes. That would be yucky, like the creamed chipped beef they have in the cafeteria every other Thursday. Oh, is that your cup there? You must have been, then. Anyway, I saw you on the rooftop and, like, at first I thought you were naked because of the color of your costume and I thought to myself, what's a naked man doing hanging around on a rooftop. Since I'm a hero, I figured I should investigate, because that's what we're supposed to do. But then I recognized you and realized you're not naked, just wearing a very, um, tight costume that shows off everything. So I thought I'd, like, come and introduce myself. I'm Bluebird. Oh," she laughed. "I already said that. I get so turned around talking to people sometimes. You look kind of familiar. Do you go to Bayview?"

Jay blinked. "No, why would you think—"

"Do you think I talk too much? I almost never talk the rest of the time. I'm really, really shy. Oh. I'm sorry. Here and I don't even know you and I'm telling you all about my problems."

"That's all right," said Jay. "We costumed types ought to hang together. You know, form support groups, do twelve-stepping together. That sort of thing." She opened her mouth to reply and he held up a hand to forestall another vocal assault and battery. There was something about her that seemed familiar. "Are you a Herald too?"

"Oh, how funny you should ask me that! I was about to ask you the same thing. Yes, of course I'm a Herald. I didn't know there were any others. Sialia didn't mention it."

"Sialia is the . . . the Bluebird God?"

"Goddess, but yes."

"Did she create you in response to the insect god's plan?" asked Jay.

Bluebird cocked her head to one side. "Well, of course, silly. Why else would she strip herself of her divine powers?"

"What do you mean?" Jay felt he was in for another long-winded explanation and stretched out on the rooftop, hands folded behind his head, leaning against an air conditioner.

"Creating a Herald saps most of a god's powers, leaving them mostly useless for any other god-like activities like miracles or divine retribution or communing with mortals. It's because that power goes into *you*. Can I sit there with you? I've been, like, flying all morning and boy are my arms tired. I love that joke. I never get tired of saying it now that I can really fly." She plopped down next to him.

Jay was appalled. He didn't realize that Leporidus had given up his own godlike abilities to give Jay some minor superpowers of his own. He wondered if that was in the Rules that the Rabbit God had mentioned. If they were, it was a stupid rule. He'd complain, but had no idea where to begin. Maybe he'd sacrifice a goat or a bucket of chicken or something; whatever constituted acceptable format for complaints to the management of Gods' Home. "Wow," he said at last. "I didn't realize it took so much to make a Herald."

"I know," said Bluebird. "When Sialia came to me, we had a long discussion about it. Well," she admitted. "*I* had a long discussion. She mostly just listened. Anyway, I tried to talk her out of it. Surely she had a better candidate than me, I argued. But she wouldn't have any of it. And now I can fly like a, well, like a bluebird."

"Can you do anything else? Shoot death rays from your eyes? Pull an aircraft carrier into dry dock? Make a hundred copies of yourself?"

"No, I can't do anything useful like that. Most of my talents are wasted, like tying cherry stems into knots with my tongue, shaping balloon animals, or making toasted cheese sandwiches."

"Toasted cheese sandwiches?"

"I'll make you one. I guarantee you it'll be the best you've ever had."

Jay looked up into the sky. It was a clear day for San Francisco. High overhead in the clear blue sky, he could see a tiny dark smudge moving north. "Listen, I think that Ship thing has something to do with why we're here. I mean, why we're Heralds."

Bluebird shrugged. "What ship?"

"Haven't you been near a television or radio or anything today?"

"No. I've been flying," she said. "I didn't even bring my iPod with me. What if I, like, got hit by an airplane or a helicopter or something because I didn't hear it? My animals would starve without me. Well, probably not Buster. He's a scrappy one; he'd probably eat all the others. I've got two dogs, three cats, two cockatiels, and an iguana. Buster's the iguana. He's such a sweetheart, but he's got a real mean streak towards my warm-blooded pets."

Jay sighed. "There's an alien Ship orbiting the Earth. It showed up earlier this morning. It's . . . oh, hell. Come back to my, um, hideout and I'll show you what's going on. You can meet Bunny. He's my, um, sidekick."

"You have a sidekick? That's so cool! I wish I had one, although I don't know what I'd call one. There isn't really anything that goes naturally with *Bluebird*."

"Yeah," said Jay. "Shall we?" He stood, getting his bearings in the neighborhood, and oriented himself in the direction of the dance studio.

Bluebird nodded, likewise getting to her feet. Her wings extended and formed into the correct shape. "You're really good at this superhero thing, you know," she said. "You've already got, like, a hideout and a sidekick and a costume and everything. Have you got a cool car too? It would be really funny if you drove a Volkswagen Rabbit, although I guess that's not really that cool."

"Actually, now that you mention it . . . No, it's not really my car. It's Bunny's. Follow me." Jay bounded into the sky.

At first, Bluebird tried to glide downwards and climb upwards with him, pacing his jumps, but she soon tired of it and instead settled with level flight. They both found it difficult to maintain any kind of consistent conversation when one participant was bouncing in and out of the other's airspace, so they traveled in silence.

A police helicopter buzzed toward them as the pilot checked them out. Bluebird smiled and waved with all the skill of a professional parade float girl and flitted around the 'copter. Jay hoped it wouldn't follow them for very long, and was happy to see it veer away after a few minutes. The pilot must have decided the boy dressed as a rabbit and girl flying like a bluebird didn't present enough of an interesting situation to warrant questioning. Maybe in another town, it would, but it *was* San Francisco.

Jay was just fine with that. He had enough problems building up without the complications of a police inquiry.

Eight

"Your headquarters is in a dance studio? That's kind of weird," said Bluebird as Jay knocked on the costume shop door. "But I guess it's a good idea. I mean, who would think to look for a secret headquarters in a place like this? Usually they're in, like, the basements of mansions or the penthouses of high-rises or caves or abandoned mines or something. All I have is my bedroom in my parents' house, but I'm thinking about trying to find an inaccessible radio tower somewhere. Do you know about any in the area? I bet inaccessible radio towers are dirty places . . ."

Spence opened the door and smiled at Jay. He raised an eyebrow at Bluebird and invited them both inside. "Hello there, I'm Spence. I do superhero costumes. Welcome to the Rabbit Hole."

"Rabbit Hole? I love it! It sounds so, like, mysterious and clever and stuff. I'm Bluebird," she said, shaking his hand. "Do you really do costumes? I made my own. Do you like it? I just kind of threw it together from some stuff I had lying around my room. And this is my dad's. It's hot and itchy, but superheroes are supposed to, like, hide their identities, right?"

They descended to the shop to find a wide-eyed Bunny huddled on the couch with a massive bowl of popcorn, watching the coverage of the Ship.

"J—I mean, Jackrabbit!" cried Bunny. "Have you seen this? We're being invaded or something."

"Invaded?" asked Jay. "Did they do something while we were coming over here? Last I saw they were just orbiting."

Spence chewed on his knuckles. "Any minute now we're going to see giant spaceships flying overhead and sucking people off the streets and then anally probing them. Well, that last part might not be so bad, but the rest of it is just about scaring the pants off me!"

Bunny looked over, a little interest peeking through his fear. "Really?"

"Oh my God, you're *gay!* I *love* gay guys! We have to, like, go shopping and stuff!" Bluebird clapped her hands together.

"Look, I know it's scary and all," said Jay. "It's like a summer blockbuster movie or something, but this is why I—"

"*We,*" said Bluebird, interrupting.

"*We* were created," said Jay. "This is what we're supposed to stop."

"You guys don't need to worry. We're, like, Heralds, and we wouldn't have been made into Heralds if it wasn't to deal with a really serious problem. Space aliens are serious, aren't they? I mean, like, in the movies they're always eating people or laying eggs inside them or something, and I think that's just nasty. I wouldn't want anyone to lay eggs in me. Oh! I wonder if I can lay eggs? Maybe that's one of my superpowers. I'll have to ask Sialia. Although I don't know what I'd do with a bunch of eggs. Or how I'd get them out of my costume. I'd have to have a flap of some kind. I wonder if laying eggs feels like pooping? Because that would be really embarrassing if you were trying to lay an egg and made a turd instead."

Spence wiped his buttery fingers on a napkin and

placed a gentle finger over her lips and her prattle died away. "Well, I can't fight aliens, so I'm going to stick to what I know, and I know that costume is hideous. Let's have a look at you, darling." He directed her to the three-way mirror and had her posing this way and that while he took measurements and notes.

Jay leaned over and whispered to Bunny, "You think we'll have school tomorrow? I never did finish my Civics essay."

Bunny's phone beeped. He checked it. "District email alert," he said. "Classes will be in session tomorrow and regularly until further notice."

"Seriously?" Jay's ears drooped.

"Where's Leporidus?" asked Bunny. "Shouldn't he be telling you what you need to do next?"

"I don't know. He disappeared right before I met, uh, Bluebird. He's a god, you know. He's probably busy doing god things like smiting and changing physical laws and stuff."

"So what are you going to do?"

"I don't know. I'll talk it over with Bluebird. I don't exactly have a PowerPoint presentation for *How To Save The World*, you know?"

"Hey, you're not, like, making plans without me, are you?" called Bluebird from the corner, where she was stripping out of her costume. Jay realized that she wore nothing under it but a smile. He turned around, feeling his costume ears standing on end.

"Uh," he managed.

"Oh, it's all right," she said. "I'm not ashamed. I told you I was shy, but I'm feeling a lot more confidence since I learned how to fly. I'm going to have to get over being shy anyway, because there's a boy I'm going to ask out on Monday at school, because I'm not going to be afraid to anymore."

"That's fantastic," said Jay.

"Besides. *He's* gay, and *he's* gay . . ." she pointed to Spence and Bunny in turn. " . . .And *you're* much too much of a gentleman to peek, so I don't have anything to worry about. I'm really talking too much, aren't I? You can turn around now."

Jay faced her again. She was wrapped up in Spence's kimono. Her mask was off, and her face was familiar to both him and Bunny.

"*Creepy White Girl,*" they both said.

"My name's Kasey," she said. "But that's a funny nickname. I suppose I have been kind of creepy because I'm so shy and stare all the time in school. I'm feeling a lot better about myself now, though. Thanks to you, Mr. Jackrabbit, and your pep talk this morning. And Sialia giving me my powers."

"She's the Bluebird Goddess, right?"

"Oh yeah. She actually met me yesterday morning while I was walking to the pet store. You know that song *Mr. Bluebird on my shoulder*? She totally landed on my shoulder and started talking to me and telling me that she was going to make me a Herald. I thought I'd eaten some bad oatmeal or something." Kasey laughed. "And then this morning I woke up really early and discovered I had, like, superpowers. I was so excited I went and flew over to the school, just to see if I could do it. Then I had a long talk with Sialia and when we were done, there were people on the streets and somebody saw me and thought I was, like, going to kill myself. I didn't want to fly away with everyone looking, but I was going to have to if I wanted to get down off the school. Lucky for me, you showed up."

"Wait . . . You weren't going to kill yourself?" Jay felt like his whole body was scrunched up in concentration as he tried to follow Kasey's narrative thread.

Kasey laughed. "No, not at all! I never said I was going to *jump*. I said I was going to *fly*."

Jay slapped his hand over his face. He could feel his ears quivering like they were popped mattress springs.

"So when I saw you, I knew I needed, like, a superhero costume of my own, so I went home and made one out of my old gymnastics leo from junior high. It's a little tighter on me now, because my boobs are bigger, but I could still squeeze into it. Can you believe it?"

"Honey, you let Spence and Bunny worry about your wardrobe now," said Spence around a mouthful of pins.

Jay knew it wouldn't be right to hide from her anymore. Not now. He pulled his cowl forward. "Hey. It's me. Jay. I'm sorry I called you Creepy White Girl. I never actually knew your name before today."

Kasey's smile lit up the room like a floodlight. "That's okay. I knew yours. And you were so sweet to think you were saving my life the way you did. In fact, I'm going to nerve up right now and do something I've wanted to do for two years."

Jay's eyes widened as she pranced right over to him and planted a kiss right on his lips. It was a sweet, unexpected gesture, but it threatened to cause a very predictable response. Jay panicked as he felt the sudden pressure against his cup. "Hey, uh, listen. Maybe I should change back to my street clothes."

"I'm sure Spence here will need some time to work on my costume," said Kasey, "And I'll bet he has something around here I could wear that's more substantial than this lovely silk kimono. Then we could go and, like, get a bit of lunch." She rubbed her flat tummy. "Flying around all day is hungry work. Besides, we have to figure out how we're going to save the world, right?"

"All right," he said. "Give me a few minutes."

Fifteen minutes later, Jay and Kasey left the dance studio in Bunny's car. Jay had to borrow some clothes from Spence's wardrobe since the clothes he'd left home in weren't really suitable for going to a restaurant, and were too tight to drive the car comfortably. He'd tried to pick stuff that didn't make him look too much like a gay pirate, but the costume shop *was* for a dance studio, and selections had been pretty limited. He'd wound up in a pair of stretchy jeans that contoured to his legs like tights and a baggy cutoff *GLEE* sweatshirt.

Kasey giggled that Bunny's car really was in fact a Volkswagen Rabbit. She insisted on calling it the Jackrabbitmobile and made constant jokes about *reactor engaged* and *turbines to speed.*

"Oh, let's go eat there." She pointed to an upscale Mexican restaurant. "My treat. Maybe they have milkshakes, because I owe you one." She winked at him and he laughed.

He parked the tiny car and extricated himself from the cramped seat. They went inside and the hostess seated them. For being nearly one o'clock on a Sunday, the restaurant was close to empty.

"Quiet in here," said Jay. "I wonder if everyone's staying at home because of the Ship thing."

"I don't know. Maybe," said Kasey. "Or maybe the food here gives you the shits."

"Excuse me?" The waitress stood beside the table with her hands at her sides, as if she couldn't believe what she'd just heard.

"She said she's so hungry that she's making a lot of spit," said Jay, shooting a warning glance across the table at Kasey. Without her big black glasses, she looked a lot less like the Creepy White Girl he was used to and more like a Hawt White Girl, but her newfound confidence and propensity for babbling was going to get them both in trouble if she couldn't curb it.

"Huh," said the waitress. "What do you want to order, then?"

"Chile relleno plate and iced tea," said Jay. "Half and half green chile please."

"Taco salad and diet coke, please."

After the waitress left, Kasey leaned forward across the table so she could speak with more intimacy to Jay. The things the motion did to her boobs made it hard for him to concentrate. "So, uh, your goddess . . ."

"Her name is Sialia. She said there's a terrible danger coming to the world, one that only the Heralds can fight. Well, that's us, right? I bet it has something to do with that spaceship. Jay, my eyes are up here."

"Oh, uh, sorry." Jay felt his cheeks grow hot and he forced himself to keep his eyes on hers.

She giggled. "I know, they're a lot more spectacular than they were before. Of course, you're a lot bigger than you were too. I guess that's one of the good things about being a Herald."

"I think Bunny was right when he said it was an invasion. Why else would aliens come here?"

"I don't know. Maybe we've got like really good TV? Or they need, like, water or something? Maybe they want to eat us. That's an alien kind of thing, right? Like maybe we taste good or they don't have any food on their planet or something."

The waitress set their plates down and Kasey's monologue slowed as she ate a forkful of taco salad. The hostess escorted another couple past their table and Jay froze as he realized the girl was Shari. A bit of uneaten food tumbled from his fork to land beside his plate.

"Are you all right? You look like you saw a ghost," said Kasey around a mouthful of lettuce and grilled chicken.

Shari looked down and saw Jay staring at her open-mouthed. "Oh my God," she said. "Jay . . . I didn't expect to see you here."

"Likewise." He glared at her companion. He was of average height, chubby, had a scraggly beard, and wore glasses. This had to be the one she'd dumped him for. "Shari, aren't you going to introduce us?"

Shari swallowed. "Jay, this is Mark. He's my, uh, you know."

Mark extended his hand like an automaton. "Nice . . . to meet you . . . Jay."

Kasey turned and held out her own hand. "Wow, you talk kind of weird. Is that, like, the way you always say things? With all those pauses? Oh, I'm sorry, I'm being rude. I'm Kasey. We're just having some lunch. It's really good. Have you eaten here before?"

Mark looked down at Kasey's hand and shook it without the slightest bit of emotion. "No . . . we just stopped . . . on a whim . . . I talk . . . this way . . . because I do."

Kasey took a sip of her drink. "I had an uncle who had a lisp once. We used to laugh every time he said *San Francisco*. Well, it was very nice to meet the two of you, but I think you should leave now before Jay, like, breaks the table."

Jay realized he was holding the table's edge in a death grip. It was starting to crack under the inexorable pressure of his superhuman strength. He forced himself to release it. "Nice to see you again, Shari. And nice to meet you, Mark."

"I'm sorry, Jay. I didn't know you would be here." Shari looked embarrassed.

"Have . . . a nice day," grunted Mark.

The hostess whisked the two newcomers away to a table across the restaurant and out of view.

"Your friends seemed nice enough," said Kasey. "Although the guy looks like a stoner to me."

"Did you get that too? I'm glad it wasn't just me." Jay grinned at her. "And they're not my friends. Shari and I used to go out. But she dumped me to get back together with him."

Kasey finished her soda. "I know. I watch you, remember? She's cute in a slutty cheerleader kind of way. You guys don't really match, though. You seem too smart for her, and your skin tones clash. I mean, you're like rich chocolate sauce and she's sort of turd-colored." Her cheeks grew red. "Now me, though, I'm more like vanilla ice cream. Chocolate sauce goes great on me. I mean, like, on ice cream. You know what I mean. God, I feel like I'm talking too much. It's probably all the caffeine in this soda. I'll be awake all night at this rate, and there's nothing good to watch on Sunday nights. Most TV is pretty boring, though. Except *Survivor*. I like that show. I don't watch much television as a rule. I think it's a bad influence. What do you think we should do next?"

Jay was starting to get the hang of following Kasey's stream-of-consciousness dialogue, but sometimes it all backed up and all he could do was shrug and say "Huh?"

"About the Ship and saving the world and all that," said Kasey with as much patience as could be expected from a chatterbox like herself. "What do you think we should do? I kind of think we should go talk to somebody in charge, although I have no idea who that would be. I mean, like, shouldn't somebody be told about this threat and that we're supposed to be the ones to stop it? *Oh, eww!*" Kasey recoiled as a brave cockroach scuttled up onto the table.

Jay stood up. "Check, please."

The restaurant manager was nice in spite of being flustered. "I'm so sorry," he said. "All this craziness. I'm sure it came in from outside. I have a clean place. I want people to have a clean place to eat."

"Hey, don't worry about it, dude," said Jay. "Even with aliens up there, people still need a place to go get a taco salad."

"I only have one cook who showed up for work today," said the man. "Everyone stayed home or went to bars or whatever people do when they're afraid." He shuddered. "I'm sorry. I didn't know what else to do, so I came to work. Let me at least buy your lunch."

"It's okay, mister," said Kasey. "We promise we'll try to fix it. The alien thing, I mean." Jay gasped. Was Kasey going to give up their secret identities right there?

The manager laughed. "Fix it? What can you do? You're just a couple of kids."

Kasey smiled and squeezed his arm. "Trust us. We're, like, the good guys."

"Do you . . . Do you want to see the kitchen? See how clean we keep it?"

"No, that's okay. Just hang in there, bro," said Jay. "And, uh, put out some roach traps or something."

"Can I at least send something with you?"

Jay and Kasey looked at each other. She belched into her fist, quiet and ladylike. "Oh, no, I don't think I could eat anything right now."

They left the restaurant before the manager could get any more panicky. "Man, people are really scared," said Jay. "And I really can't blame them. I'm freaking out a little too. I mean, aliens, right?"

"He did have a good point, Jay, and like, so did you. Just because there are aliens up there doesn't mean everything stops. We should try to, you know, still live our lives. Let's go take care of your Civics essay and figure out how we'll save the world. I mean, we don't even know what those aliens want yet, right? Maybe they're friendly. And if they're not, what are we going to do when they're up in space and we're down here? I can't fly into space any more than you can, like, jump there. I'm sure Sialia and your Rabbit God whose name I can't remember have a plan, and as soon as they're ready, they'll let us know what it is. Until then, we can't let everything else fall apart."

"You're going to help me write my essay?" Jay squeezed himself behind the seat of Bunny's car.

"Well, duh! I mean, like, why not? We're partners, right? We've got to stick together, and if that means I help you with the Civics essay, then that's what I'm going to do."

"Are you in Civics too?"

"Jay, I sit like, right behind you."

"I'm sorry. I guess I never noticed."

"That's okay. That's how I know you've got a cute little mole on the back of your neck and that you like to tap your cheeks with your eraser when you're thinking. I, like, wrote my essay on Tuesday, so I can totally help you with yours. But Jay, I hope you're okay after, you know, seeing your ex just now. I mean, I know you're on the rebound and having another woman over to your house would be difficult, even if she does happen to be a Herald like you and is trying to save the world from some kind of space alien invasion . . ."

Jay burst out laughing. "All right, you made your point. Kasey, you have to pause and take a breath once in awhile. You're welcome to come over." They drove in silence for awhile as Jay threaded the Rabbit through streets that were empty of most traffic, heading for his mom's suburban bungalow. Midday Sunday traffic would normally be stop-and-go, but Jay had never seen the roads so deserted. The restaurant manager must have been right about how many people were staying at home, probably glued to the news networks or Twitter.

While waiting at a stoplight, the sound of breaking glass made them both turn to look. A group of kids had thrown a mailbox through the plate glass window of a toy store and were raiding the display of remote control vehicles and video games. The brazen theft in broad daylight astonished Jay. Nobody was stopping the kids. The only other vehicle on the street was a city bus that roared past them, running the red light.

"It's us," said Jay. "Nobody's going to stop them if we don't do it."

"What, you mean, be all superheroey on them?" asked Kasey. "But we're not in our costumes. We're just a couple of kids like them."

"We're a couple of kids, but not like them," said Jay. He shut off the car. "Hey!" he yelled. "Knock it off, you shits!"

"Yeah," called Kasey. "Somebody worked really hard to put up that display and everything, so you boys better, like, leave it alone!"

"Yeah? Or what?" said one of the boys. "There's five of us and two of you, and I ain't afraid of no girl. You better step off."

"What's wrong with you guys?" asked Jay. "This isn't the time to act like a bunch of assholes."

"Who you callin' an asshole, asshole?"

"I'm calling you one." Jay grinned and cracked his knuckles. "Asshole."

A police car skidded around the corner and squealed to a stop in front of the store. The five kids who were burgling it ran into an alley. Jay almost leaped after them but Kasey's hand on his arm stopped him. The harried-looking cop got out of his car. "Hold it right there, you two."

"We weren't doing it," said Kasey. "We saw the boys who broke the window and we were going to, like, stop them. I think it's totally a bad reflection on society that as soon as something weird happens, some people think that they can, like, do whatever they want. I wouldn't ever stoop so low as that. Would you? I mean, we have to still be good people, right? Because in weird times like this, that's all we have."

The officer blinked at Kasey. "All right, well, I guess I didn't see the two of you causing any damage. But you can't park your car here in the middle of the road like that. It's not safe."

Jay looked around at the deserted street. "Okay, officer, I'll move it. We were heading home to, um, study anyway."

"Good idea." The cop glanced upward. "Probably better to stay off the streets these days anyway."

Jay drove the rest of the way to his house, parked Bunny's car and shut off the ignition. "We'd better figure something out quick. I never really thought about how fragile our society could be in the face of danger."

"That sounded really, like, smart, Jay. You should write your essay on that."

Mrs. Peavey waved at them from her porch. Jay waved back. Her eyes grew large as she noticed the huge muscles straining under his clothes that she hadn't seen before. It was too much to hope that she'd miss such a detail. Being a busybody meant she kept tabs on everyone and everything in the neighborhood. "Jay, is that really you?" she called. "What on earth happened to you?"

"Oh, you know. I've been hitting the gym a lot recently," he said. "Well, I have to get to my homework now, Mrs. Peavey."

"Aren't you going to introduce your friend to me?" The elderly woman's tone switched to the sour, accusing one she used when she was being nosy.

"Mrs. Peavey, this is my . . . friend, Kasey. Kasey, Mrs. Peavey. She's been my neighbor since I was six."

"And a very good boy he was back then. Charmed, my dear." Mrs. Peavey shook Kasey's hand. "And how do you know Jay?"

"I'm a Hera-*ow*." Kasey winced as Jay stepped on her foot with one of his oversized gunboats.

"She's my tutor, Mrs. Peavey. You know, tutoring?"

"I see." Mrs. Peavey's tone was frosty. "I'd hate to

think you were doing anything *immoral*, Jay, especially with your mother out of town."

"Don't worry, Mrs. Peavey. She's my tutor. And nothing else. I've got an essay to write and she's going to help me."

"I see." Mrs. Peavey leaned back in her chair once more. "Well, good luck with it, Jay. It was lovely to meet you, Kasey. Stop by anytime."

"Thank you, Mrs. Peavey," they said as they headed inside Jay's bungalow.

Kasey looked around. "This is nice. It's clean. Has your mom been gone for a long time? I'm kind of a slob around my house and if I was left alone, I'd probably destroy the place in a couple days. I can't even cook except for the microwave."

Jay shrugged. "My mom taught me to cook on the grill, but that's about it. She says a man ought to know how to cook on a grill, so that's my job since my dad's gone."

"Where did he go? Oh, did he die? I'm sorry if he did."

"No, he's just not around. He and my mom split up when I was six. The checks came for a couple years but then stopped. I don't have any idea where he is now." Jay led Kasey into the kitchen where his laptop was set up. "I don't even really think about him."

"Is your mom nice? It looks like she's worked really hard to give you a nice place to live and everything."

"Yeah, she's great." Jay turned on his laptop.

"What's your essay going to be about?"

Jay read her the title: *Enter The Jackrabbit: The Parahuman in Post-Modern America.*

"Oh, that's good! So you're going to write an autobiographical account of what it's like to suddenly discover that you're a parahuman superhero with the charge of saving the world along with a couple of plucky gay sidekicks and, like, a partner named Bluebird who can fly?"

"So we're partners now?"

"Well, duh!"

"That's good to know." He began to type, first pecking out words one by one, then picking up speed as they began to flow. He tuned out the rest of the world as he wrote.

Eventually, he became aware of someone behind him. He looked up to see Kasey, reading over his shoulder as he wrote. Suddenly, he felt very self-conscious. "Um," he began, clearing his throat.

"Don't mind me," she said. "I'm just reading along. You write really good. But you don't ever come out and say that you're Jackrabbit, do you? It's kind of like Peter Parker saying he was taking pictures of Spider-Man when he really is Spider-Man. Except you don't sling webs, of course, and you're not a photographer. You should have someone, like, take pictures of you, though. You're really photogenic, especially in that costume. When you wear it, you look like you ought to be on a calendar, you know? Like a different picture of Jackrabbit for every month. In January you could be skiing. In February you could be ice-skating. In March you could be frolicking in the flowers."

"Frolicking in the flowers?" Jay laughed.

"That's what bunnies are supposed to do in the Spring," she said with defiance. "I made a list of the big superhero teams that we should contact and in what order. I think we should go meet them in person, too, because they might want us to demonstrate our powers." She waved a piece of paper at Jay.

"Are you high? They're all over the country. We can't just leave," said Jay.

"Why not?"

It occurred to him that he didn't really have a good answer to that. Nevertheless, he tried. "My essay is due. And my mom's coming home on Tuesday. If I'm in Denver or Chicago or something and she finds out, I'll be grounded until I'm thirty."

"You'll be fine. Hey, you're almost finished with your essay, but it's, like, kind of light on actual content, you know? Won't Jackrabbit need to do something to be worth writing about?"

"Oh, yeah. That's true. But traveling's expensive."

"I didn't think about that. I've got some money saved up. I was going to buy a car this summer, but I guess now I kind of don't need one. We could always fly standby. What if we left tonight and came back tomorrow? If you email your essay to Ms. Levinson, you could get away with missing a day."

"What about your folks? Aren't they even worried about you after your, um, this morning?"

"Sialia gave me my powers before the paramedics got my information. My folks don't know that was me, this morning. I'll just tell them I'm saving the world. They'll understand."

"You can tell your folks something like that? And they'll believe you?"

"Well, duh. Of course they would. I don't lie to my parents. And if I tell them I've got to save the world, they'll just tell me to be careful and to let them know if there's anything they can do to help. Can't you, like, tell your mom the truth?"

"Oh hell no."

"That's too bad, Jay. Here, let's look up some airfares. If we fly standby, I bet it's not too expensive. The New Guard is in L.A., Just Cause is in Denver, and the Lucky Seven are in Chicago. We should start with them, don't you think? They're like, the most legit."

"How are we going to buy airline tickets? We're minors." Jay felt like the weight of the world was crashing down upon him.

"Don't worry. My folks can get us the tickets. We just have to, like, be honest with them about why. They're very cool. They'll understand and help us out. We'll just need the money, is all."

Jay's eye fell on his car keys, sitting beside his laptop. His truck was in the driveway. He'd bought it with his own money, and he was attached to it. But he couldn't really fit inside it anymore with his new physique, and didn't need it so much to get around now that he could cavort and frolic. He had bigger fish to fry.

He had to save the world.

He grabbed his keys. "Come on, I got an idea."

Nine

The auto pawn shop had given Jay eight hundred dollars for his truck. He'd been offended at the first offer of five hundred and asked for three times that amount. The owner talked him down to accepting eight hundred and it still smarted when he signed the title and handed over the keys.

"I liked that truck," he said to Kasey as they walked out of the store.

"I like flying." She twirled around once in the air. Although the wings were on her costume, she seemed to retain aspects of them when not wearing it. In his peripheral vision, Jay thought he could see movement along her back where the wings would be, but nothing when he looked directly at her. "Let's go buy some tickets."

They purchased the tickets online, choosing Denver because it was the cheapest flight and had a round trip which would get them home by Monday evening. There were a lot fewer available flights than normal, which they figured was due to the airlines cutting down on the risk of having people in the air if something happened with the aliens. Then they split up. Kasey flew home to gather up an overnight bag and ask her parents for their help, while Jay ran over to Spence's to collect her costume.

"You're going to see Just Cause?" Bunny squealed in delight. "You have to tell me if Mastiff is really as big as he looks on TV."

"Bunny, I'm not going to check out another dude for you." Jay rolled his eyes.

"At least get me a picture of him." Bunny sniffed in mock disappointment, but his downcast face only lasted a moment. "Wait until you see her in this new costume," he said. "I mean, I wouldn't go straight for her, but you're going to have a hell of a time keeping your mind on your job." He winked at Jay.

Jay enjoyed the Sunday evening flight to Denver. He was the largest person in the row on a plane that wasn't even sold out, so he had plenty of elbow room, a benefit given his new larger stature. The flight attendants were friendly and even made the standard safety speeches entertaining and funny. The drink cart came by early and they gave out full cans of soda instead of the little toddler-sized ones. Kasey was an agreeable, if talkative, traveling companion. Jay learned more about her in the two and a half hour flight than he had about any single person in a year.

After landing, they carried their bags through the Denver Airport, which seemed like it should have been much busier than it was. People were afraid to travel, afraid to leave home even to come to work. The quiet made Jay nervous, but he found Kasey's chatter a calming influence. They paused by a bank of televisions to catch the latest news on the Ship. So far, nothing had changed. The Ship remained silent and impassive despite being bombarded by radio signals from every corner of the globe.

"Do you really think that's what we're supposed to stop?" asked Kasey.

"I suppose." Jay readjusted his bag over his shoulder. He was still feeling a little overwhelmed by how fast things had moved, but was determined to be superheroic, especially with the hot chick who'd talked him into this escapade. "But they don't seem to be much of a threat as long as they keep circling up there."

"I don't like it," said Kasey. "They're watching us, looking to see how we react to their presence, seeing where we are weak and where we are strong. It's like we're a wounded zebra and it's a lioness circling in for the kill. I know I said that I don't watch much television, but I watch *Animal Planet* a lot. That doesn't feel like entertainment to me, because I love animals. But blood makes me oogy, and if I was a vet, people would always be bringing in their dogs or cats that were hit by a car and I'd have to, like, go throw up in the back. It just wouldn't be very professional."

"No, probably not," said Jay. "Do you think we should call them first, or just show up?"

"Just Cause? Don't they have a 1-800 number? But I don't imagine you get anywhere calling it. It's probably like calling the cable company or the phone company. I've never understood how the phone company can be so bad at answering calls. I mean, it's the phone company, you know?"

Jay nodded. "All right, we'll just show up, then. I, uh, don't think we should change here in the airport. Let's find a map."

"Got that covered." Kasey pulled out her phone and fired up the GPS. They put their heads together so they could both see the tiny screen showing where Just Cause headquarters was located, along with the Hero Academy, where young parahumans were trained to become licensed superheroes under the tutelage of retired heroes of days gone by. Having located it, they decided it wasn't too far to travel to by jumping and flying, so they just needed a place to change.

Jay was all for using a gas station bathroom, but Kasey wouldn't hear of it. "Have you seen inside gas station bathrooms? They're nasty. I don't want to let any part of my clothing or my new costume—which I haven't even, like, seen yet, by the sway—touch the floor in one."

"So what do you want to do, then? Change here in the airport?"

"Oh God, no! That's just as bad. People get, like, airsick and stuff in bathrooms here, I bet."

Jay let out an exasperated sigh. "So should we go get a hotel room or something? I don't think any will rent to a couple of kids like us."

"Oh! That gives me a great idea," said Kasey.

Jay's smile became a bit pained.

"We could, like, ride to one of the hotels here around the airport and then go up and change on the roof. That wouldn't take very long and then we could, like, go see Just Cause. They're a big superhero organization. I'm sure they're open all night, right?"

"So you don't want to change in the privacy of a bathroom, but you're okay stripping down on the roof of a hotel?"

"Well, yeah. It's dark now, so nobody's going to see us. And I know you'll be a perfect gentleman, which you've been so far. I'll have you know I'm very good at reading people and I can tell already I have absolutely nothing to fear from you, right?"

Jay followed the thread of her monologue to the end and nodded. "I'm just here to save the world, Kasey, same as you."

"Well, that's settled then. I'm just going to call my folks and let them know we've arrived safely and we're going to go save the world in a little while." She thumbed numbers on her phone. Jay couldn't believe how she was able to just *talk* to her parents, like they were her friends or something. That made him feel guilty, because he hadn't talked to his own mom since the Ship's arrival. She must have been worried about him, and he was worried about her too. He pulled out his phone to call her and it rang in his hand.

It was his mom. He almost dropped it as he answered. "Hi, Mom."

"Hi, Jay. I'd have called you sooner but these companies wouldn't even cease their negotiations for a goddamn alien invasion. Are you doing okay? Have you burned down the house yet?"

"No, Mom. Everything's cool. Except for, you know, the aliens."

"I know. I'm trying to just get all my stuff handled out here so I can get home and be with you. Have they closed school or anything?"

"No, we still have classes tomorrow."

"Out here they've canceled schools and there are National Guard units patrolling the streets. People are looting, Jay. Looting! I've never seen this before."

"I saw some looters this afternoon back in, uh, downtown. A cop scared them off."

"I hope things don't get any worse. I haven't heard if Just Cause or the military is doing anything yet, but a lot of people are scared. I'm a little scared too, to tell the truth."

"I'm sorry, Mom. I'm sure everything will be all right."

"Listen, Jay, I need to talk to you about something. I have good news and bad news. The good news is you're going to college. The bad news is that it might have to be in Toledo."

"T-Toledo? Why?"

"Listen, there's a headhunter here trying to recruit me to work for . . . Well, for now let's call them Company B. They're the ones I came to meet with. They're offering a very attractive package."

"Wait, do you mean they want you to move? To Ohio?"

"Us, kiddo. Us."

"But Mom, that's not fair. All my friends are here."

"I know it's a big change, but this is our future. Not just mine. Not just yours. Ours."

"Mom, I don't want to go to Ohio. I've got to save the . . . I mean, I can't . . ."

"Jackson." It was rare for his mother to ever use his first name. "Look, I promise not to make any decision before I come home and we talk about it. They can give me that much time."

Jay sighed. "Okay, Mom."

"See you tomorrow night. I'll bring home something special for dinner. We'll watch a movie. Your choice. Be brave. If anything happens with, you know, the aliens, you go stay with Mrs. Peavey. She'll need someone to keep her company. She doesn't have any family, you know."

"I will, Mom. I promise."

"You take care of yourself too, kiddo. I love you."

"Love you too, Mom." He hung up.

Kasey closed her phone. "What's wrong? You look like your dog just died. Except you don't have a dog, do you? I didn't see one at your house."

"I don't have a dog. My mom might be taking a job in Ohio."

Kasey blinked. "Ohio? But that's all the way across the country."

"She said it's not a sure thing yet."

"I hope not." Kasey didn't meet his gaze. "Because we've still got to, like, save the world."

He tucked his phone away. "I'll worry about Ohio later. Let's pick a hotel."

They found a Marriott van and took it. The driver accepted their tips without comment or observation. The building was near the airport, and was hd with open-air decks on each floor. Jay and Kasey shouldered their bags and strolled around the back side of the building. Security lights illuminated the parking lot but it being a Sunday night with a potential alien invasion, not too many cars were parked there.

"Okay, let's go." Kasey flew straight up the side of the building like she was riding a wire.

"Hey, wait," Jay whisper-shouted. "At least make sure nobody's looking first!" He looked around and didn't see anyone. "Ah, the hell with it." He sprang into the air, hoping the building didn't have a rooftop pool that he might come down in. Unseen landing spots could prove to be a problem in his ongoing campaign to save the world.

He thudded down onto the crushed gravel and tar of the roof above the sixth floor. The rooftop was unlit and crisscrossed by HVAC pipes and dotted with air vents. A jet roared overhead on its way to the runways to the east. "Kasey?" he whispered.

"I'm here." He jumped several startled feet at the sound of her voice right beside him. "I was just making sure you weren't going to land on anything important. It would, like, suck if you came down on one of those." She pointed to an aluminum exhaust pipe sticking three feet out of the roof surface.

Visions of the most awkward impalement ever danced in the fringes of Jay's mind. "Thanks. I mean that."

Kasey's smile was hard to see in the darkness, but he could hear it in her voice. "Anytime. We're partners, right? We've got to look out for each other. Ohhh, what's *that*?"

Jay turned to follow her pointing hand. A great orange light was poking up from the distant fields. "Some kind of explosion?"

"No, there'd be some kind of big kaboom," said Kasey.

"Maybe it hasn't gotten here yet."

They waited for a minute to see if the ground would shake. In that minute, the orange dome pushed its way higher up the horizon and they could make out surface features on it.

"Oh, hell. It's the Moon." Jay slapped his forehead. "Epic fail."

Kasey laughed. "I've never seen a big orange one like that. It's pretty, though."

Transfixed, they watched the moonrise for a few minutes. As it passed away from the edge of the horizon, the Moon lost its apparent gargantuan size and its color brightened to the white with which Jay and Kasey were most familiar. "Wow," said Jay. "I wonder if it's like that all the time out here?"

"I don't know," said Kasey, "but now there's enough light to see what we're doing." She looked around. "This rooftop is kind of icky. I wish we'd found one with a pool or something."

"Somehow I don't think they designed it with superheroes in mind."

"Well, they should."

"Isn't this supposed to be, like, a business trip? Us saving the world?" Jay turned away from Kasey and opened his bag.

"Don't you figure your mom goes hot tubbing and clubbing and stuff while she's on her business trips?"

"I don't know. I never really thought about it. And thinking about my mom makes me think about Ohio, which sucks."

"Oh. I'm sorry. I hope you, like, don't end up having to go. Ohio sounds really, um, Midwestern."

He finished dressing in the Jackrabbit suit. "Are you done? Can I turn around and look yet?"

"Just finished. Oooh, I wonder what it looks like in the daytime! How do I look?"

He saw mostly the shadows of a helmet with a visor and some kind of cloak. "It's hard to see in the dark," said Jay. "Even the moonlight isn't that bright."

Kasey thrust her phone at him. "Here, take my picture with the flash so I can see it."

Jay raised the phone, let the camera do its magic self-adjusting, and snapped the picture. In the brief moment of the flash, he saw her in all her superheroic glory. Whether by design or by accident, she'd chosen a cliché heroic post with legs braced apart and hands on her hips. Her phone recreated the image on its screen.

"Oooh," she squealed. "I got spots in my eyes."

Jay's mouth dropped open as he looked at the picture of Kasey in her Spence-designed costume. Spence had given her a close-fitting helmet with a bird's beak visor, repainted it a much glossier blue, with the kind of sparkling detail normally reserved for custom motorcycle gas tanks. The bird's eyes on either side of the helmet were so detailed they seemed to have depth. He'd made a bodysuit of the same layered fabric as Jay's, but in ocean blue that darkened to black on her legs and arms. Instead of a simple cape of loose fabric, her cloak wings hung and extended from her shoulders, waist, and wrists, and were trimmed with blue feathers. Where Jay's suit employed a strategic athletic cup and supporter, Kasey's incorporated support for what Spence would have referred to as *the girls*.

She grabbed the phone to look, and then laughed and spun around in the air. Her wings spread outward like they were real instead of a costume accessory. Jay wondered if whatever divine power that made his costume's ears respond to his emotions made her wings move the same way. "So? What do you think?"

Jay realized his mouth was hanging open and he shut it with a snap. "Uh . . ." he said. "You look great."

She flipped her hair, caught in a blue-banded ponytail that emerged from a hole in the back of her helmet. "Well, duh! I don't care what anybody says, a good costume is important for a good superhero. You have to look good because it makes you feel better and more powerful. Let's go visit Just Cause. I bet they're going to freak out at us."

The trip would be about eight miles, as the Bluebird flew or the Jackrabbit bounced. They decided that a direct approach would be the best way to get the attention of the hero organization. In this case, the direct approach would be to arrive at the front gate of the compound and knock politely.

Wind raced down the side of the mountains, picking up speed as it crossed the plains to whip around the airport hotels. The stiff breeze was chilly; Jay would have to tell Spence he needed a suit for cooler temperatures. And maybe one for high summer too.

"Oh my God, it's so dry here." Kasey touched her lips with her gloved fingertips. "I'm going to need, like, an industrial-sized lip gloss just to survive."

Jay perched on the roof's edge and looked at the six floor drop beneath him. His brain screamed at him that he was crazy, that he was going to splatter himself across the parking lot, streaking gore across the rented Lexuses and Lincoln Town Cars below. But then Bluebird smiled and launched herself into the darkness, and he couldn't let her leave without him.

He sprang off the edge of the balcony. The parking lot rushed up at him. He angled his legs and they neatly absorbed the impact of his landing as he thudded down next to a couple of tourists in western attire, the man sporting a gigantic ten-gallon hat. "Howdy, pardner," drawled Jay. He flashed them his best grin, then flexed his legs and leaped after Kasey in great bounds.

Jay attempted to carry on a conversation with her at the zenith of every leap. "I was thinking that . . ." *BOUNCE* "they've got to be able . . ." *BOUNCE* "to track us on our . . ." *BOUNCE* "way in. At least we . . ." *BOUNCE* "will be expected."

"Hey," Kasey called after him as he dropped toward the ground. "This is a stupid way to talk," she added on his next arc. "We should get radios."

"Yeah." They needn't have worried about getting lost, even in the dark. The Just Cause compound gleamed like a diamond amid the darkness of the open fields, illuminated with stadium lighting. As they progressed west toward it, Jay explored different ways of jumping. He tried moving his body around in midair, twisting and flipping it in the moonlight, getting comfortable with moving around in three-dimensional space. Kasey laughed as he began striking odd poses along his arcs—arms folded behind his head, laying on his side, running and swimming in midair, and in a classic 'flying' pose. This last one carried him to the front gate of Just Cause headquarters.

He dropped down next to the guard shack as Kasey spiraled in from above. "Hi there," he said to the two uniformed security guards. "I'm little Jackrabbit from next door. Can Just Cause come out to play?"

"Wh-what?" asked the taller, mustachioed guard.

"I'll try again. We're from the Agency. Somebody here requested a couple of temps. You know, to do filing, data entry, save the world, that sort of thing."

"What my partner is trying to say," said Kasey, "is that we've come here to join Just Cause. So, like, call somebody in the main office and let them know Bluebird and Jackrabbit are here."

"I'm Jackrabbit and she's Bluebird, in case you weren't clear." Jay beamed. "We're the good guys."

The other guard, a short and portly fellow with octagonal glasses, picked up the shack phone and called in the visitors. He spoke for a few minutes and then looked up at Jay and Kasey.

"They're sending someone out to meet you."

Soon, two members of Just Cause exited the brightly-lit headquarters and approached them. Jay recognized the winged Native American, Desert Eagle, and Mastiff, the muscular youth in gray and brown who rode a heavy-duty ATV. Jay leaned over toward the guard with the mustache and whispered, "Are my ears straight?"

The guard, surprised, shook his head. "One's, uh, a little crooked."

Jay fiddled with it, failing to improve it in the least. He sighed. "Ever wake up with an ear you can't do a thing with? I'm having a bad ear day."

Mastiff stopped the ATV and stepped off it, staying back far enough to allow Desert Eagle enough room to drop lightly to the ground. Her feathered wings folded against her broad, muscular shoulders to hang behind her like a cape. She wasn't wearing her normal costume leathers or custom semiautomatic pistols; instead she was dressed in cutoff jeans and a special shirt that buttoned up the back. An ornate beaded headband held back her heavy black hair from her face, which was open and friendly.

"Hello, I'm Desert Eagle. This is Mastiff." She nodded her head toward the young man behind her. He was every bit as tall, and even more muscular than Jay. His brown mask left his blonde hair and stubbly chin uncovered. "How can we help you today?"

Kasey opened her mouth to reply but Jay was faster. "We're from the church of religious consciousness and we'd like to talk to you about the Rabbit and Bluebird Gods. No, not really. Well, sort of."

Mastiff snickered into the back of a glove. Desert Eagle raised an eyebrow. "Is this some kind of school prank?"

"We're here to join Just Cause," said Kasey. "We're brand new superheroes and we're supposed to save the world. At least, that's what Sialia—she's the Bluebird Goddess—and . . . and . . . I can't remember the name of the Rabbit God. But anyway, they, like, gave us our powers because there is an insect god, um, I don't remember his name either. Where was I? Oh yes . . . the insect god is going to use his minions—is that the right word?—to take over the world. And we think he's going to use that Ship thingie in orbit right now."

Desert Eagle's mouth dropped open. Mastiff's eyes watered as he stifled his giggles. Jay smiled at Desert Eagle and spun a finger by his ear to indicate that Kasey was crazy.

She punched him in the arm. "I'm not crazy. That's totally the truth."

Jay shrugged. "Yeah, but it sure sounds crazy. I wouldn't believe it if I was them."

"Hey—" said Desert Eagle.

Jay held up a hand. "Hang on. I think it's important that Bluebird and I clear the air here. She may be flighty and a bit featherbrained, but you have to admit that we've both got really, *really* stylish costumes and the powers to back them up."

"Hey!" Kasey sounded scandalized.

"And we've got a story to tell you and we think you ought to at least give us a chance to tell it to the entire team before you lock us up in Deep Six. We can't help that we look so darn good. We also can't help that we're supposed to stop an invasion of some sort. How about it, huh?"

Desert Eagle looked at Mastiff, who shrugged.

Kasey whispered at him, "I'm *not* featherbrained."

Interlude: Gods' Home

The pace of life in Gods' Home was less than frenzied. One might say it was lackadaisical. It wouldn't even be out of line to say it verged on the comatose. When you have individuals who have existed for thousands of years, there's no need for anyone to hurry anything, especially since novel events are few and far between. In the two thousand years since Jehovah and Allah began their card game, they have played but ten hands, splitting them evenly with no noticeable gains or losses in chips. Bacchus' pool party has been going on almost as long as any god can remember. Before the young Greek god took over, a Sumerian mastermind named Enki handled the distribution of spirits among the divine.

Is it any wonder that they were slow to respond when Blattodeus, the insect god, made his move?

Unlike his fellow supreme beings who were content to wait for their drinks to be refilled or for Vulcan to get the grill hot enough for the steaks, Leporidus hurried. In fact, he was pelting through the halls of Gods' Home in a panic, asking every god he encountered if they'd seen Anurus. Most of them apologized and said they had not. A few seemed surprised to know there even *was* a God of Frogs. Ares was downright rude about it, launching an expertly-timed kick at Leporidus's hindquarters and sending him careening into a waste bin.

"A curse on you and your ancestors." The Rabbit God shook off sandwich wrappers and sticky soda-coated straws. He scrambled down the stairs into the kitchens, past several of the minor gods of cooking, shouting for Anurus.

The two of them had worked up a plan. Anurus, often overlooked even at the best of times, would shadow Blattodeus to discover the rogue god's plan of action. He would give regular reports to Leporidus on the insect god's movements. Time passed at an indeterminate pace in Gods' Home, and Leporidus couldn't say with any certainty how long Anurus had been fulfilling his duty.

But he'd missed a scheduled meeting.

Then he missed another.

By the time the third appointment had passed by with still no sign of the Frog God, Leporidus dissolved into full-blown godly panic.

His greatest fear was that Blattodeus had somehow tumbled onto Anurus's stalking, and *done* something to him. Normally, gods couldn't harm other gods. It was proscribed in the Rules as a form of interference. Gods understood that the game was to be played in and *only* in the mortal realm, using mortals as the pawns. A legend among the gods, ancient even to those who were old when the first men gave them names, was of a war between gods in untold ages past.

One had chosen to rise above the others, to interfere with them in Gods' Home itself. A war was fought, not between mortal Heralds, but between gods. In one battle so many were slain that the effects spilled over onto the Earth itself and the fallout resulted in the extinction event which men identified as the end of the Reign of Dinosaurs. There were still parts of Gods' Home where no god dared go for fear of finding spirits of vengeful deities, lurking, waiting for their chance to rise up once more like the terrible lizards they had been. Before the Age of Mammals led to the new breed of gods, the Dinosaur Deities had reigned supreme for millions of years, and now all had vanished. A question which had remained unanswered and was a favorite topic of conversation over a few of Bacchus's mixers was *what happens to gods who die?*

Leporidus didn't believe Anurus was dead, but his doubts grew with each passing moment when he couldn't find the God of Frogs. Blattodeus was not a god created by men, and therefore he may not have been subject to the Rules as the other residents of Gods' Home were. If he had harmed or slain Anurus . . . Leporidus feared to think of the consequences among the mortals. Frogs were not highly regarded by men, but the sudden inexplicable extinction of the amphibians would nevertheless wreak havoc across the globe. And over the course of his long life, Leporidus had grown rather fond of the mortal world. He'd chosen to spend untold years filling out the long form for god-hood, instead of opting-out of all the inclusive rights therein, and by Gods' Home itself he was not going to throw away those rights by turning his back on Men now in the hour of their need.

Even if they didn't know it.

He ran around a corner and crashed into another god. The two tumbled across the floor and came to rest by a large potted fern. Leporidus realized it was Sialia, the Goddess of Bluebirds. He'd been meaning to find and speak to her about her Herald. He was uncomfortable with Jackrabbit's recent decisions; especially the one involving the Bluebird's Herald. He hadn't even known any other gods besides him had taken the time to fill out the appropriate pages permitting creation of Heralds.

"Leporidus, I've been looking for you," she said. "I've just come from the woods. I saw Blattodeus. He had Anurus staked out in a clearing."

"Staked out? Torture, here in Gods' Home? Son of a *bitch*." Leporidus took great pleasure in using the human expression of contempt. "We must see to him."

"There's more," said Sialia. "The insect god has called up an army."

"In the mortal lands? I expected as much," said Leporidus grimly. "I can only hope our Heralds fight hard; it is beyond our ability to help them now."

"Not just among the mortals," said Sialia urgently. "Here, in Gods' Home."

"*What?*" Leporidus couldn't believe his prodigious ears.

"He's drawn an army of insectile warriors out of the very ground," cried Sialia. "Even now they are converging upon us! Whatever shall we do?"

Leporidus heard the clicking of chitinous armor from up the hall and the hiss of voices spoken through sharp mandibles. "We run," he said. "Quickly, into the deepest part of the forest. We'll scratch out a hole and wait. Then we'll try to rescue Anurus."

"Then what?"

Leporidus sprinted for the woods, his feet flying so fast that they appeared as a fuzzy blur. Sialia paced him overhead, her wings beating like a hummingbird's. Leporidus spoke the phrase that many gods considered rude, if not downright blasphemous.

"We pray."

Ten

It was closer to morning by the time the Just Cause commander Doublecharge found time to meet with Jay and Kasey. Desert Eagle had set up the two teens with some snacks and beverages and let them wait in a comfortable lounge. They'd fallen asleep with Kasey resting her head on Jay's shoulder.

Six o'clock came much earlier in Colorado than it did in California, and waking proved to be a heroic challenge for both youngsters, even at the hands of Mastiff. "Come on, you two. Time to get up and go to work," he said.

"I think I need some coffee," said Kasey. "Ugh. And a toothbrush. And a hairbrush."

"I'd kill for a carrot smoothie," said Jay. He sensed one of his ears was kinked in an odd place. He tweaked it. It didn't get any better. "And I think I have bed ears."

"Get yourselves together," said Mastiff. "Fearless Leader Doublecharge wants to meet you in ten minutes."

Jay and Kasey stood up, working out the kinks from sleeping in chairs, and accepted coffee from the commissary with gratitude. Kasey was afraid that toothbrushes didn't seem to be forthcoming until Desert Eagle brought them a couple, which they put to good use.

As Jay brushed, he noticed that his teeth seemed, well, *bigger* than normal. Especially in the front. He spat foam into the sink below him and spread his lips wide into a grin. Yeah, there were a whole lot of big bright teeth there. "Lookin' good, kid," he told his reflection. He winked and noticed that somehow his mask completely duplicated the facial expression right down to the white cover over his eye narrowing. How was that even possible? It was a mask; it wasn't his face. Was it? Maybe the mask *was* the face of Jackrabbit, and Leporidus had seen to it that the mask and Jay's face were one and the same when required, thanks to his godly power.

At last, they were brought to Doublecharge's office. The experienced heroine had lines on her face under her black and white mask and was reviewing what looked like a handwritten report of their arrival at the compound. "Let me get this straight," she said. "You've been given your powers and charged by the gods to defend the Earth against an invasion?"

Jay gave her a toothy grin. "More or less."

"Look, I really don't have time for this," said Doublecharge. "I think it's great that the two of you want to help, and I'm sure I could find a place in our overall scheme for another flyer and, uh . . ."

"A jumper," said Jay. "With a great disposition to match. I'm a motivated team player, with great customer service and interpersonal communication skills. At least, that's what it says on my resume. How could you not hire this face?" He smirked and pointed at himself.

"But you look like you're underage to me, and I just don't see how I can recommend a change in our deployment to the President simply based on your stories. You can apply to attend the Hero Academy next semester. But for now, I'm afraid I'm going to have to ask you to—"

Doublecharge vanished right in front of them.

There was a crash behind them as a shocked technician dropped an expensive-sounding piece of equipment.

Jay and Kasey looked at each other in surprise. "Whoa," said Jay.

Kasey nodded. "Totally!"

"Hey, check that out." Jay pointed to the monitor that tracked parahumans across the country.

It was blank.

Doublecharge's radio, sitting untended on her desk, beeped. "Doublecharge? This is the Command Center, over."

Jay picked it up and pushed the *transmit* button. "This is Jumpin' Jack Rabbit on WRBT radio, reporting Doublecharge just disappeared." He smiled at Kasey. "I missed my calling. I should have been a DJ."

People flooded into the office: more technicians, people in military uniforms, including one with a lot of stripes on his shoulders who seemed very interested in Jackrabbit and Bluebird. Radio calls were coming in fast and furious, asking various parahumans to report in. Soon they became frantic, requesting *any Just Cause member or affiliate, please respond at once.*

The man with the stripes turned to Jay and Kasey. "I'm General Gershwin. I want the two of you to stay right where you are until we figure out what happened."

Jackrabbit snapped his heels together and gave a smart salute. "Yeth thir, General thir!"

Reports arrived from around the nation. Every American parahuman had vanished without a trace. An Air Force officer covered the mouthpiece of a phone and looked up at the General. "Sir? The White House has received information from the British Prime Minister that their National Superteam has disappeared. And so has Russia's Peacekeepers."

"So it's a worldwide phenomenon, then?" asked General Gershwin.

"Too early to say, sir, but it certainly seems that way."

The General rubbed his hand across his bald head. "So how does that explain the two of you?" he asked.

Jay and Kasey both shrugged.

"Come with me." Four armed guards fell in behind Jay and Kasey as the General escorted them to the Command Center.

The Center was as advanced and busy as anything Hollywood had recreated. A giant computer screen of the world filled one wall, filled with flashing icons and lines of varying color and thickness. Banks of monitoring stations formed a half-circle in front of the great screen, and a bank of large televisions stretched the length of the ceiling, each tuned to a different channel. People ran this way and that, yelling information at each other or whispering into telephones. Jay hadn't realized until now how connected Just Cause really was to the infrastructure of the United States military. The most striking thing about the Command Center wasn't the impressive technology. It was the dais at one end with several large chairs where Just Cause members could monitor events before being dispatched.

They were all empty.

"Sir, look!" called one of the junior officers. General Gershwin turned to see what was causing the excitement rippling throughout the Command Center.

All the cable channels being monitored were showing the same thing. The various talking heads had been replaced by a swirling gray mist. It wasn't static or snow; it was an image, and unpleasant shadows flitted through the thick fog, barely visible.

"What is that?" asked the General. "Where's it coming from?"

"I don't know, sir," said the officer. "We've lost the entire satellite system. Someone just yanked it right out from under us. I'm showing this on every channel."

Several people, including Kasey, shrieked as a large bug crawled across the screen image, obscuring it for a second with shiny chitin and wiggling antennae. Once it passed, everyone saw a figure standing amid the swirling mist. It stepped forward, details becoming clearer as it approached the transmitting camera.

The figure was a human man of indeterminate age or racial origin. He had darkly tanned skin and pale hair, albeit it formed into tight curls like Jay's. He wore a shiny black suit of articulated armor. When he spoke, only his lips moved; the rest of his face never moved in the least. "I . . . am the Supreme Leader . . . of the Elder Race. We . . . have returned . . . to reclaim our birthright . . . as rightful masters . . . of this world."

Jay snorted. "No points for original ideas, but you can't fault the method."

The Supreme Leader continued. "We have taken . . . all parahumans . . . prisoner. Our agents . . . already infest your world. You cannot . . . stop us. If you . . . still do not believe . . . in our power . . . allow me . . . a small demonstration."

Nothing happened immediately. General Gershwin looked around. "Did they do something?"

"Checking on that now, sir."

Jay leaned over and whispered to Kasey. "I bet this is our party."

"Oh, I'm sure it is," she said. "But, like, why didn't they take us when they took the other parahumans?"

"I don't know," said Jay

"Sir, I'm getting reports of massive numbers of traffic accidents and gridlock." The officer in charge looked up in surprise. "Sir, I think they somehow shut off every single traffic signal in the world."

General Gershwin looked surprised. "Interesting. And clever. If they can shut down our traffic infrastructure, they can likely do the same to more critical systems."

Jay flipped his ears. "More critical than traffic control? You ever been caught in rush hour on I-5?"

"Suppose they'd shut down the power grid. Or the air traffic control system. Or strategic defenses," said the General. "I'll take traffic jams over nuclear war."

"He probably doesn't even have to drive himself," Jay whispered to Kasey.

The Supreme Leader spoke again. "Now that you . . . have experienced a taste . . . of our power . . . we are prepared . . . to accept your surrender."

Kasey poked Jay in the ribs. He yelped and flinched and everyone stared at him. "Sorry," he gasped. "Ticklish. Don't *do* that."

Kasey said, "He talks like that dude we met in the restaurant the day before yesterday, don't you think? The one with your ex-GF, and I'm sorry to bring her up again, because I know how painful it probably is for you. But don't you remember how funny he talked? He had all these pauses in his speech too, just like this Supreme Leader guy. I wonder if maybe he's one of the agents. That would be a really strange coincidence. Anyway, it's just something I noticed. I'm a little thirsty. Do you think I could have a bottle of water? And maybe some lip balm? I'm all out." She made pouty lips. "I can feel them chapping."

"Lip balm? At a time like this?" General Gershwin sounded incredulous.

"She could have asked for a backpack nuke, and the keys to the space shuttle," said Jackrabbit with glee. "I'd say lip balm is a bargain at twice the price." He paused. "Say, could *I* have a backpack nuke and the keys to the—"

"Absolutely not!"

"I'll bring it back with a full tank."

"No!"

Jay kicked at the floor like a sullen toddler. "Man, I never get to have any fun."

"Lieutenant, get me the White House. Inform them that we have two members of Just Cause that were not taken for some reason, and that they may have some information," said Gershwin.

"Yes, sir."

"Technically we're not in Just Cause yet," began Kasey before Jay wrapped a large hand across her mouth.

"But that's only because Doublecharge vanished before she had a chance to offer it to us," said Jay. "And that's the truth. Uh, more or less."

An aide handed Kasey a glass of water. She rattled the ice cubes. "I *asked* for a bottle. But I suppose this will have to be good enough. It's important to drink enough water. Did you know you're supposed to drink half your body weight in ounces of water every day? It helps flush toxins out of your system."

A movement where none should have been caught Jay's attention. "Bluebird, can I borrow that for a minute?" Without waiting for an answer, he swiped the glass from her, dumped it out onto the floor amid her protests, and leaped several feet across the room to slap it down mouth-first on a tabletop. Numerous clacking sounds filled the air and he realized several soldiers had their rifles leveled at him.

"I was drinking that, you jerk!" cried Bluebird. "I'm still thirsty!"

"General," said Jay. "Check this out."

General Gershwin approached and bent down to look at what Jay had caught under the glass.

A frantic insect the length of a thumb ran about, beating against the glass with its feelers and feet. It wore some kind of complicated electronic device on its back that seemed to have been glued to its carapace. Tiny lights flashed on it, and the subtle sparkle was what had caught Jay's eye from across the room.

"What the hell is this?" asked the General.

"That's a Madagascar Hissing Cockroach," said the wide-eyed Lieutenant.

"How do you know that?" asked Kasey. "It just looks like a big ugly bug to me. I'd be afraid to squish something that size. I'd ruin my shoes."

"I wasn't aware you counted entomology among your expertise, Lieutenant," said the General.

The officer blushed. "It isn't. I went to an amusement park on furlough, and they had a promotion about free passes if you, um, sort of ate one."

General Gershwin turned a little green. "You didn't."

The Lieutenant's blush advanced from rosy pink to dangerous crimson. "It was a really good deal."

"You didn't eat more than one, did you?" asked Jay. The Lieutenant put his head in his hands. Jay slapped his forehead in disbelief. "Oh my. No wonder they want to invade us. They're rage invading because of Appetite McGoo over here."

"What's that thing it's wearing?" asked Kasey.

"We'll find out." The General looked bilious at the notion of eating anything with that many legs. "Somebody get me an exterminator."

Eleven

"All right," said General Gershwin. "While the lab people are examining the bug and the device it wore, I want some answers from the two of you." He, Jay, and Kasey were sequestered in Just Cause's conference room. The General's aide sat behind him, recording the interview with a webcam.

"All right," said Jay. "Just remember to ask your questions in the form of questions."

"I . . . what?"

Kasey covered her mouth so hide a snicker.

"Ask away, General. I have no secrets." Jay leaned back and put one large foot up on the table. Being in the rabbit costume made him feel witty and invincible, like a teenager squared.

"What's your name? Your real name?"

"Ah." Jay rubbed his chin. "Yeah, okay, I have a few secrets. But we'll do our best to give you the straight scoop on what's going on. At least, as much as anybody has bothered to tell us."

"Please."

Jay went on to tell an edited version of the events surrounding his becoming Jackrabbit. He left out any reference to Bunny, although he did mention Spence as *an expert in superhero costumes*. He hoped it might filter down to get Spence some more business. The only part he told exactly as he knew it was the story related to him by Leporidus about the insect god's intent to overthrow the world. Gershwin listened, impassive, not moving so much as a muscle in his face. Jay was impressed that anyone could have such a level of focus. Or perhaps the General's brain had short-circuited after one too many of the jokes Jay sprinkled throughout his narrative.

"And I guess that's about it," said Jay. "Unless you want to hear some songs? I do a great Journey . . . but I'll need a shower with good acoustics."

Gershwin shook his head. "Absolutely not. Now I'd like to hear your story, Miss, uh, Bluebird."

"Oh, you don't need to call me *Miss*. When I'm in costume, you can just call me Bluebird. Of course, you don't know what to call me when I'm not wearing it, but I have a secret identity too, you see. Anyways . . ." Kasey babbled on about her meeting with Sialia, the Bluebird Goddess. She also explained about her powers, the problems with her folks' water bill, how she met Jackrabbit, details of her last shopping expedition to Eddie Bauer, and identified all her pets by name.

As she babbled away, Gershwin's eyes transformed from impassive and suspicious to glazed over. At last he shook himself and cleared his throat.

"You expect me to tell the President that you were given powers by the Rabbit and Bluebird Gods and charged with the defense of the world against an insect god who's going to take over using his, uh, minions? Good God, they'll lock me away!"

Jay shrugged. "It's the best story I've got. At this point, anything else would sound far-fetched."

"And you can't substantiate this with anything concrete?" asked Gershwin.

Kasey fluttered her wings. "Well, aren't all the other parahumans in the world gone? And we're still here. Have you heard about any others? No. Why do you suppose that is? Maybe, like, we're somehow exempted or protected from whatever happened to others. Maybe we're the Chosen Ones of the Gods. So, face it, General Grumpypants!"

Jay slapped his forehead, making his ears quiver atop his head. "Oy. I don't believe you actually said that. Mostly because I wish I had first. Carry on." He waved a hand in a magnanimous gesture.

The General pinched the bridge of his nose and sighed. "All right. At the moment I'm choosing to believe your story, because I can't for the life of me figure out a better one either."

"See?" said Jay with a triumphant grin.

"Now I'm going to have to figure out how to boil this all down into politically-friendly language for the President. Heralds of the Gods or not, it doesn't tell me where our parahumans have gone, how to get them back, or how you're going to stop this invasion. Can't you call on your, uh, *sponsors* for some hints?"

Jay and Kasey looked at each other. This was a new idea. "We haven't read ahead in the textbook. They're supposed to cover that next week," he said. "The truth is, Generallissimo, they've always just sort of shown up whenever they felt like it."

"They are gods, after all. It's not like they're at our beck and call or anything," said Kasey.

A junior officer stuck her head into the room. "Sir? The etti . . . enti . . . the bug doctor wants to see you in the lab."

General Gershwin stood. "Come with me. The two of you probably ought to hear whatever she has to say. It might be useful to you somehow."

"I have to say, Your Generalship, you're taking this pretty well, all things considered," said Jay.

The General looked up at him. "Son, I've spent thirty years in the military, a lot of it around parahumans. Very little surprises me, but I do my best to remain a skeptic."

"And you certainly excel at that, sir," said Jay. "I'll have my boss put a good word in for you with the God of Suspicious Military Types."

Under escort by armed security guards, the trio walked through Just Cause headquarters to the sciences wing, where the captured cockroach had been brought.

The guards outside the entrance to the biological sciences lab came to sharp attention and saluted as the General passed. He waved at them in a preoccupied fashion and hurried into the lab. It was packed full of tables loaded with burners and test tubes, pipettes and centrifuges, microscopes and mass spectrometers. Computers and monitors were everywhere, each showing the same thing so a scientist working on a project could turn to whatever workstation was closest. A large tube-shaped device all wrapped up in white plastic and gleaming chrome dominated the floor. Cables snaked from it to the wall and Jay figured it was some kind of scanner like an MRI or something.

A slender woman with spiky blonde hair and horn-rim glasses looked up from a microscope. The lights sparkled off a tiny diamond stud in her nose. She straightened her lab coat and stepped over to introduce herself. "General Gershwin, I presume? I'm Doctor Tenenbaum."

The General shook her hand. "Jackrabbit and Bluebird," he said, motioning to the two heroes behind him.

"She's Bluebird, I'm Jackrabbit," said Jay. "In case the costumes didn't give it away."

"Pleasure to meet you both," said Dr. Tenenbaum. "Call me Trixie."

Kasey giggled. "Trixie? Seriously?"

The doctor smiled. "It's really Patricia, but I hate that name. So the two of you brought me this fascinating little beastie?"

Jay nodded. "What can you tell us about it?"

"Well, it certainly *looks* like a *Gromphadorhina portentosa*, but I'd say the similarities are only chitin-deep. That's a little entomologist humor."

"Very little," said Jay. "But thanks for making the effort. Maybe with a better-informed audience?"

Dr. Tenenbaum wasn't offended at all. "Tell me, Mr. Jackrabbit . . . how do you get a foot that large into your mouth?" She winked at him.

"With lots of butter and a crowbar," he said.

Kasey jabbed her elbow into his ribs. "Tell us more about the bug."

Dr. Tenenbaum took them over to the lab table where the insect in question had been immobilized under the giant imaging scanner. "Well, it's still a Madagascar Hissing Cockroach, but it has some fascinating differences. For example . . . it has a brain."

"Just between you and me, so do I," said Jay to General Gershwin. "I just don't like to brag about it. It makes me feel like I'm showing off."

"Ah, but normal cockroaches don't have them. They have nerve clusters spread throughout their bodies that act like a brain, but they have nothing resembling a central cortex." She pointed to a spot of dense tissue on the imaging screen. "This one does. I can't imagine how. Cockroaches stopped evolving in the early Cretaceous, before the dinosaurs died out."

"Why?" asked Kasey.

Dr. Tenenbaum shrugged. "They're at the top of their evolutionary niche. If it ain't broke, don't fix it. And cockroaches are, for all purposes, perfectly adapted to life here. There hasn't been any reason, any need for them to evolve further. That being said, however, if they were to evolve, it would be in the area of intelligence. Which seems to be what's happened here."

"So you're saying this one is smarter than the average cockroach. How smart is it then?" asked General Gershwin. "It was spying on us. It had some equipment glued onto its shell. Could it have been controlled somehow? Or acting autonomously?"

Dr. Tenenbaum looked down at the insect. "Cockroaches are amazing creatures. Their survival instincts are unparalleled, even among the so-called higher life forms. Put a cockroach and a human in any environment you like and the roach is likely to outlive the human." She pushed her glasses up her nose. "I can't say with any certainty about its level of intelligence, but it's likely far below even that of a reptile. There just isn't enough brain matter there to make a significant difference." A line appeared between her eyebrows and her forehead creased. "It is very dense tissue, though. Puzzling. My assistant should be here shortly. She's bringing some other roaches from my personal stock. I want to compare genetic patterns to see if I can isolate the genes responsible for this mutation."

"Personal stock?" asked Jay. "Some people have a wine cellar, you have a roach cellar?"

Dr. Tenenbaum smiled at him, clearly up for matching him witticism for witticism. "Yep. We just decanted a batch."

The door slid open. A woman in her late 30s, black hair gone prematurely gray, entered the lab carrying a large black case.

"In fact, here it is now. General Gershwin, Jackrabbit, Bluebird, my assistant, Jeanette Flores."

The woman extended her hand to them. "It's . . . a pleasure . . . to meet you. I brought . . . the other roaches . . . like you asked."

Jay and Kasey glanced at each other. They both recognized the unusual speech pattern. The General made eye contact with Jay and gave the smallest of nods. He, too, must have picked up on the woman's speech. "Nice to meet you as well, Ms. Flores. Been working with Trixie very long?"

"Only . . . a few months," she said. "I just . . . graduated."

"Congratulations. If you'll excuse me, I have an important telephone call to make." Gershwin headed for the door.

"I'm afraid . . . I can't allow that." Flores dropped her case and withdrew two weapons from the pockets of her coat.

"Oh, *hell* no!" Jay saw that her eyes were focused in two different directions, making her capable of aiming both weapons at the same time. One was pointed at the General, the other wavered between him and Kasey. The guns looked like they'd come straight out of a Hollywood science fiction epic, all shiny chrome and glittering plastic and LEDs. Instead of a barrel, each weapon terminated in a circular red lens.

"Move away . . . from the door," said Flores. "You three . . . back from . . . the scanner."

Hands raised, Jay, Kasey, and Dr. Tenenbaum stepped back. Jay's eyes never left the tip of the weapon, but he slipped his foot underneath the rollers of a high-legged stool, calculating angles instinctively in his head until he gave up and decided he'd just fake it.

"Jeanette? What are you doing?" Dr. Tenenbaum was aghast, her hands hanging helpless at her sides.

"What must . . . be done."

At that moment, General Gershwin yelled for help from the guards beyond the door.

Quick as a wink, Jay swung his leg to whip the stool at Flores. It struck her as she fired at Gershwin. A crackling beam of crimson spat from the end of the weapon. It missed Gershwin, but the stool hit her. A section of the wall turned white-hot and flashed into nothingness as Gershwin flung himself to the floor.

Jay grabbed Kasey and Dr. Tenenbaum and jumped up and over the imaging scanner. They landed in an awkward heap of arms, legs, and wings.

"Ouch," said Kasey. "Thanks, but ouch. I don't have any room to fly in here."

"What's going on?" cried Dr. Tenenbaum.

"She gets lasers? Seriously?" yelled Jay. "Hey, General, how come she gets them and we don't? That's so freakin' unfair!"

Automatic weapons chattered as the guards in the corridor opened up, firing from behind the cover of the door and through the hole in the wall. Flores did a funny tap dance across the floor as bullets stitched across her torso. Gershwin crawled to the door under cover of his troops' fire, yelling at them to "terminate that bitch!"

In spite of numerous smoking holes in her flesh, Flores flipped a switch on one gun with her thumb and instead of a narrow beam, a wide fan of energy spewed out. The General and his men dove for cover as she swept the beam from floor to ceiling. The beam was less destructive than before, only setting fires ablaze instead of incinerating whatever it struck.

"I think she's bulletproof." Kasey coughed as the lab filled with smoke.

"If you've got a secret Bluebird Sonic Attack of Death or something, now would be a great time to discover it," called Jay.

Dr. Tenenbaum lunged from behind the scanner, risking being hit by the troops that had again opened up on Flores. She released the captured roach from its containment and pulled it back to safety.

"Are you crazy, lady?" hollered Jay. "You're going to get yourself killed in the name of science!"

Tenenbaum dropped the roach into a Ziploc baggie then tucked it into her pocket and muttered "Now don't forget that's in there and *land* on it." Then she looked up at Jay. "This could be the most important thing ever discovered in the insect world. I'm not about to let it get blasted to smithereens by a bunch of overzealous soldiers."

Flores ignored the gunfire from the half-dozen guardsmen firing clip after clip at her. She turned her weapons on the imaging scanner, blasting chunks into ash. It would only be seconds before there wasn't any cover left in the room.

Jay bellowed over the chatter of guns firing. "Quit shooting, you trigger-happy morons! Not everybody in here is bulletproof!"

A moment later he heard the General's roar more or less parroting his, except with fewer niceties.

"Okay," said Jay to Kasey. "You take Dr. Tenenbaum out of here. I'll cover you."

"How are you going to cover us? Because, like, I can see almost every inch of you in that suit, and you're sure not carrying any guns."

Jay winked. "I've got my lucky rabbit's foot. What more do I need?"

"How can you joke at a time like this?" Kasey ducked as another chunk of the machine fizzed into nothingness.

"Would you prefer *oh God oh God we're all going to die*?"

Dr. Tenenbaum screamed, "Oh, God, we're all going to die!"

"Go," said Jay.

In spite of her slender build, Kasey lifted Dr. Tenenbaum like a child in her arms and kicked away from the wall, snapping her wings out in spite of the close quarters. She kept low to the floor, shielding the doctor as best she could. As Flores snapped around to fire at her, Jay sprang from behind the smoking ruin of the imaging machine. He flipped upside-down and planted his feet against the ceiling, then jumped toward the near wall, rolling in mid-air to land against it parallel to the floor. Having gained tremendous momentum in the two previous leaps, he flung himself across the room, spinning around and planting against Flores' head a solid roundhouse kick he didn't know he had in his repertoire of moves.

The force of his strike lifted her up and off the ground so hard and fast that she left her shoes behind. Her weapons tumbled loose from her grasp to shatter against lab furniture. Her body flew one way, and her head another.

Jay staggered his landing, surprised at how effective his kick had been. He was shocked that he'd knocked her head completely loose, especially after she'd resisted so many bullets.

What happened next would haunt his nightmares to the end of his days.

Instead of the gout of blood one might expect, a swarm of cockroaches flooded out of the ragged stump of her neck, scattering in every direction.

Twelve

"Don't let them get away," cried Jay as the roaches spread out across the lab, looking for dark nooks and crannies in which they could hide.

"You men, secure this room," cried the General. "The rest of you, fan out and capture any insects you can."

Dr. Tenenbaum shrieked as she realized her erstwhile assistant lay headless on the floor.

Kasey looked over and said, "Eww!"

Soldiers spread through the room, opening drawers and moving furniture to try and catch the nimble roaches. One by one, the insects scuttled and scurried into air vents and drains and eventually General Gershwin called off the search. "What the hell just happened?" he asked. "Why were those insects inside that woman? Was she a parahuman? An alien?"

Nobody had any immediate answers for him.

He ordered Just Cause headquarters under complete lockdown and detailed a unit to acquire a supply of anti-roach spray from a local retailer, then called Orkin and Terminix himself to requisition an army of professionals to come treat the Just Cause facilities. "From now on, no civilians are permitted to travel anywhere within the facility without a military guard present."

Jay raised his hand. "Uh, may I be excused? I'm a little upset. Accidental decapitation. Roaches. You know."

General Gershwin nodded. "Take some time, but don't leave the base." He turned to go, then looked back. "And thank you, Jackrabbit. I believe you saved my life."

"And you saved mine, Bluebird." Dr. Tenenbaum's hands still shook.

Kasey smiled. "We're superheroes. We're supposed to do stuff like that. Did you see how she was, like, totally bulletproof? And there wasn't any blood inside her either. Do you suppose she was even alive? I bet the bugs used her like a car or something."

The General stopped by the ruin of the door. "The aliens' Supreme Leader said something about his agents already being here on Earth."

"*Infest* was the exact word he used," said Jay, turning back from the door. He'd been thinking about going to go throw up in the bathroom and then finding a quiet place to curl up in a fetal position, but it sounded like things were going to be a lot more interesting in the General's presence. "Like roaches in a New York apartment."

General Gershwin's jaw dropped. "Cockroaches from outer space? I think I'd believe your story about being gods' Heralds first."

Dr. Tenenbaum pulled the captive roach from her lab coat pocket, looking at it. "It's not as far-fetched as you might think. Roaches have been around for more than three hundred million years. They were around before the dinosaurs went extinct. Who knows what they might have accomplished without the interference of mammalian evolution? What if they came to the prehistoric Earth aboard meteorites or comets? Or somehow managed to escape the Earth and travel elsewhere?"

General Gershwin snorted in disbelief. "Insects building spaceships?"

"I'm a scientist, General," said Dr. Tenenbaum. "And I'm looking at the facts as I've discovered them. This roach has a brain. That's completely unique to the species. It had advanced technology with it. And there were the roaches in . . . in Jeanette. And she used handheld weapons with power that we can't even create. Someone has to have invented those weapons, someone has to have taken the world's parahumans, and someone is in that Ship orbiting overhead. I don't know if they're intelligent roaches or something else, but there are too many clues for me to discount the theory as unsound."

The General sighed. "I have to brief the President. I'll tell him what I know. Doctor, I'd like you to accompany me, and then I'd like you to figure out a way to stop these critters more efficiently than shooting at them." He turned to his aide. "Get an autopsy performed on the victim right away. I want to know everything about her. And as for the two of you . . ." He looked over at Jay and Kasey. "Don't stray too far. I suspect there will be more people who want to speak to you."

Jay and Kasey left. "I need some fresh air," said Kasey.

"Yeah, totally," said Jay. "Hey, there's a door." They approached it, wary of the two soldiers on guard.

"Hi there," said Jay. "You boys wouldn't mind stepping aside and letting us out, would you?"

"Sir, we're under orders to keep the compound secure, sir. I'm sorry."

"But that couldn't possibly mean us," said Jay. "We're the good guys. You know, superheroes."

"I'm sorry, sir. We have our orders."

"Oh please?" said Kasey. "Look at us. We're animal-themed Heralds, right? We're outdoorsy types. There's no place for me to stretch my wings in here. We're just going to get some fresh air and fresh perspective on how to fix this whole problem." She launched into a tirade about how sunlight was imperative for every creature from animals all the way up to superheroes.

He felt his will weaken as she cajoled and coaxed. At that moment, Jay would have gladly stepped aside for her; he'd have let anyone with her through as well, up to and including Darth Vader, Osama Bin Laden, and the Wicked

Witch of the West. He realized that Bluebird had another power besides flight, and it was one of great subtlety.

The soldiers on duty glanced at each other and shrugged. "I guess it would be all right, ma'am." They stepped aside to let the two heroes pass.

Jay paused at the door. "Good work, son."

The soldier ignored him.

Jay hurried to catch up with Kasey. They found themselves in a large manicured field, bordered on two sides by Just Cause buildings. Beyond the eastern edge of the green grass they saw the wild prairie grasses and stunted trees that seemed to be more appropriate. He recalled that the team's facilities were located on federal land that had once been used for manufacturing chemical weapons. As cleanup of the grounds progressed, nature had reclaimed its own.

Kasey stretched her arms over her head, taking a deep breath and doing things to her costume that Jay found difficult to ignore. "Mmm . . . doesn't the sun feel good? I was never much of someone for being outside, but since I became Bluebird, I feel better when I'm outdoors."

"I was, uh, at the beach when the Rabbit God came to me."

"You were ditching that day, weren't you? I never saw you the rest of the day after that hussy of a cheerleader dumped you," said Kasey.

"Maybe."

"Drinking?"

"Uh . . . Just milk. Honest. At least, I think it was just milk." His ears drooped down.

"Milk? You don't seem the type, Jay. But I'll let it go for now. I don't want to judge you. I don't want to judge anybody right now. It's been a really weird morning so far."

"You got that right."

They walked across the greenbelt and tread carefully around prickly bushes and sticker weeds in the grasslands beyond.

"That was quite the Jedi Mind Trick you pulled on those two guards back there," said Jay.

Kasey tilted her helmet back to let the breeze catch her face. "It was, wasn't it? I have no idea what happened there. I just knew what I wanted and kept talking to them until they caved in. You know me, I can talk like nobody's business. I bet I could have, like, talked them into anything if I'd kept going."

"It was like some sort of hypnosis. Like you were, I don't know, weaving a spell with your words."

"Nerd. Total D 'n' D nerd."

"Nerds don't have my vertical leap."

Kasey laughed. Then she sobered. "I've never been very good at getting my point across to people because I'm so shy. That's one reason I talk so much now, I guess. I just keep throwing out words until something sticks. But it felt different this time. It felt almost like I was singing. I wasn't, was I?"

"No, but I understand what you mean. The song of the Bluebird," said Jay. "I bet that's another of your powers. Your goddess didn't tell you about that, did she?"

"No."

They found themselves following a trail made by animals through a grove of trees. "I've picked up some mad skills with angles and momentum." Jay held back a branch so it wouldn't slap Kasey in the face. "They just sort of come to me when I look at things." He glanced around the trees. "I could bounce through this entire grove from tree to tree and never touch the same one twice. It's like the lines are already drawn out for me. Kind of sucks that we already did geometry in math. I bet I could ace it now."

"Yeah, totally," said Kasey. "You've got another power, you know."

"I do?"

"I don't know what to call it though. You make people laugh. You make them forget themselves when you do."

"How is that a power?"

"Are you like that normally?"

"Well, no. Good point. So I'm master of the witty comeback. I don't see how that's a benefit."

"Maybe it isn't. But you can make a bad situation seem better when you joke about it. You could probably work someone into, like, a frenzy just by saying the right things at the right time."

"Trash talking as a superpower." He changed his voice to one of a husky, drunken redneck. "Mah mommah's proud'a me!"

They exited the grove of trees and found themselves on a small hill. "Oh, wow," said Kasey. "You can see everything."

To the west, they saw the massive peaks of the Rocky Mountains. Beneath them the towers of downtown Denver rose from the plains, giving way to the rest of the city. The muted browns, reds, greens, and purples of the mountains contrasted with the silvers and golds of the city.

"It's not the Bay in June," said Jay, "But yeah, definitely cool."

Kasey turned to look up at him. "Thank you, Jay"

"For what?"

"Saving my life back in the lab. Introducing me to Spence. Being a good sport about my jabbering." She stretched up on her tiptoes and kissed his cheek, a furious blush spreading across her cheeks.

"Bluebird . . . Kasey, I . . ."

Their eyes met, followed by their lips.

The little voice in the back of Jay's mind, the one which said this was wrong, was quashed by the taste of her lips and the mulberry scent of her skin.

She pushed his cowl back, twisting her fingers into his hair. Likewise, he pulled her helmet off, letting it fall to the ground. She reached up and pulled her ponytail free, shaking her hair loose like a cloud of chestnut-colored smoke. Her feather cloak made a soft blanket onto which they sank, their skin mingling like dark and white chocolate.

"You can touch my boobs," said Kasey in between kisses. "If you want."

"Awesome."

"Humans," grumbled Sialia. "Always thinking with their glands instead of their heads."

"Oh, I don't know," said Leporidus, full of good cheer. "Animals have been thinking with their glands for millions of years. It's a productive way to evolve."

"This isn't about evolution, it's about the survival of the mortals and their gods."

"I can't think of anything closer to survival than what they're doing." Leporidus grinned. "It's their way of cheating death."

"How is this going to help us rescue Anurus? Or recover Gods' Home from Blattodeus' soldiers?"

"It isn't." Leporidus kicked back in the hole he'd dug in the deep forest. "But it will strengthen their bond, and that strength will serve them well in the upcoming struggle to save their world."

"Oh, come on. That's not even the proper way to do it. They're just . . . what do you call it?" Sialia rolled her eyes.

"Making out." Leporidus looked away, embarrassed. "You can't fault them for creativity. Or flexibility."

Thirteen

Jay and Kasey watched the stars coming out, one by one, only marred by the regular landing lights of airplanes approaching and departing from the oddly-shaped airport further to the east. Jay lay on his back, his costume rolled up behind his head like a pillow. Kasey lay half on top of him, resting her head on his shoulder and her hand on his chest. She'd taken off her helmet while they were kissing and it lay beside her. They'd pulled the feather cloak around them to ward off the slight chill of the evening.

"You're awfully quiet," said Kasey. "I know that's not unusual for people around me, because even though I used to be really shy and quiet, like I told you before, but recently I tend to fill silence with the sound of my own voice. So tell me, Jay, what's going on in that devious mind of yours? I'll bet you're coming up with a plan to defeat the cockroaches altogether, aren't you?"

"Actually, I've got no idea how to defeat them. I was hoping you'd work that part out while I take care of the actual kicking-people-in-the-head part of the plan." He stuck up his foot underneath her feather cloak and wiggled his toes. "That's my specialty."

She punched him on the arm. "Silly goose," she said with a laugh. "I'm no planner. Duh!"

"That makes two of us. It's getting dark. You think we should head back? They might think we were captured like the other parahumans."

Kasey kissed him where his neck met his shoulder. "We could let them think that for a little while longer."

The idea had merit, given the response her words evoked, but he told himself there would be plenty of time for that later. "No, we ought to head back before they go and do something stupid."

"Like what?"

"I don't know. Nuke us from orbit? Military minds work on different wavelengths than normal peoples' do."

They dressed in their costumes again and headed for the Just Cause compound. Within minutes of them setting foot on the manicured lawn, dozens of soldiers rushed out of the surrounding buildings, weapons ready, and surrounded them.

"Easy, fellows." Jay held up his hands. "We're the good guys, remember? Check out the ears." He waggled them for good measure.

General Gershwin stomped across the grass. "Where the hell have you two been?"

Jay grinned at Kasey, who blushed. "Communing with Nature, your Generalship, sir. We were trying to contact our bosses for further orders, but it looks like we're on our own here." He bowed low, making his ears bob forward. "Jackrabbit and Bluebird at your service. How can we help?"

The look on the General's face suggested he knew *exactly* what they had been up to and didn't think very highly of it. "The autopsy on Dr. Tenebaum's assistant is complete," he said. "I think you'll be very interested in the results."

Jay noticed that a third army had moved into Just Cause headquarters besides the team's own security force and the U.S. Military; everywhere he looked he saw men and women in company uniforms, carrying backpack sprayers of insecticide, sticky traps, and bags of powder.

Dr. Tenenbaum saw them enter and hurried over to join them. "The problem with roaches is they're so good at hiding. We don't know how many of them are loose in the buildings. The best we can do is to try and make it impossible for them to move around."

"How are you holding up, what with your assistant losing her head and all?" asked Kasey.

"Pretty well, all things considered." Dr. Tenenbaum shrugged. "It hasn't really sunk in yet."

General Gershwin introduced them to a portly coroner named Sam Draper. He had bad skin, two days' beard growth, and needed a haircut. "How you doing?" he mumbled around a toothpick that rolled around his mouth like it was attached to the inside of his cheek. "You want to see the body?"

"Oh, uh, thanks but no thanks." Jay felt his stomach churn a bit. "We'll default to your expertise. Tell us all about it . . . and keep it clean, would you? I haven't eaten since this morning and would like to be able to enjoy my dinner." He looked at the General. "Speaking of which, what's a bunny got to do to get some *flayrah* around here, anyway?"

"*Flayrah*?" asked the General.

Jay rolled his eyes. "How about a nice fat carrot for starters?"

"There's some chow in the cafeteria," said General Gershwin. "And you're welcome to it once we're finished."

"Nothing like a good old-fashioned autopsy to really get the gastric juices flowing." Jackrabbit rolled his eyes upward as if to implore Leporidus to intervene.

"Ugh," said Kasey.

"All right then." Draper rolled the toothpick across his lower lip. "Long and short of it is, she's dead."

Jay turned to Kasey. "See? I told you so. People just don't live after getting their heads knocked off."

Kasey punched him on the shoulder, hitting the same spot she'd knuckled before.

"Ow, I'm going to have a bruise. I'm a delicate flower, you know."

"What I mean is that according to public records, Jeanette Flores died six months ago in a traffic accident. There's a Death Certificate on record in the Arapahoe County Coroner's office."

Jay raised an ear at that. "So who's lying on the slab in there with her head in a bucket?"

"That's the odd part. It's her. Dental records are an exact match."

"Is she, like, a clone or something?" asked Kasey.

"We just got a court order to exhume the body," said General Gershwin. "We'll settle it once and for all that the . . . *thing* in the morgue cannot be a reanimated human. That flies in the face of everything we know about science."

Jay's eyes widened. "Oh my God . . . she's a *pod person!* What's next? Naked space vampires? Donald Sutherland pointing at everyone and screaming?"

Draper rolled his eyes in conjunction with the toothpick. "There was significant artificial shoring of her internal structure that I can't remove. Every tool I tried on it either broke or bent."

"He showed some parts of it to me," said Dr. Tenenbaum. "I found what looked like miniaturized control stations throughout the torso and limbs. Each was optimized for, um, cockroaches."

"Wait," said Kasey. "You're saying that it's a robot?"

"No," said Draper. "More like a mech."

"What's a mech?" asked Kasey.

"A robot," said Jay. The others looked at him. "What? A dude can't be jumping around all the time. I do occasionally surf online. There's a lot on the internet that isn't porn." He paused. "Of course, there's a lot of porn, too. Not that I look for it. Sometimes it just, you know, pops up. Hmmm. Maybe that wasn't the best choice of words. Ow!"

Kasey dug her knuckles into Jay's shoulder again.

"Stop talking. Please," said Dr. Tenenbaum.

"Anyway," said Draper. "It looks like someone took the body of Jeanette Flores and turned it into a high-tech battlesuit for cockroaches. Probably her super-intelligent ones." He nodded at Dr. Tenenbaum.

An idea just hit Jay and he didn't like the sound of it at all. "Oy," he said, and smacked himself in the forehead.

"What's the matter?" asked Kasey.

"I just thought of something. You know how my, uh, you know that guy we saw back at the restaurant in San Francisco?" said Jay.

"Your ex-girlfriend's new boyfriend? Yes . . . I didn't like him."

"Me neither, but for different reasons. There was a roach on the table right after he left," said Jay.

"Oh my God!" said Kasey. "Do you think he's another one of these cockroach mech things? I'll bet he is. He talked just like Flores did. There are, like, too many similarities for it to be a coincidence."

"Wait, you actually know about another one of these things?" asked General Gershwin.

"Possibly," said Jay. "We should go check it out."

"Damn right," retorted the General. He pulled his radio up to his mouth. "Control, General Gershwin. I want a high-speed transport ready to leave from Buckley AFB in fifteen minutes and a helicopter ready to take us there in five."

"Please," begged Jay. "A Subway. McDonald's. I swear by my ears, I'd eat Taco Bell and not complain. I'm wasting away here."

"There will be provisions stocked on the transport jet," said Gershwin.

"Any chance we can stop by our hotel on the way out of town?" asked Kasey. "We left our bags on the roof, and I need mine."

"I'm sorry, young lady, but that's not an option."

"General," she said in a sweet, little-girl voice. "I *need* it. It's a *girl* thing."

"It is? *Ow!*" Jay got an elbow in his ribs for that one.

The General got very red in the face. "I don't have time for this. We're about to go to war with these aliens."

"You've already been at war with them," said Dr. Tenenbaum. "You just didn't know it. Who knows how long they've had their agents here on Earth? It could have been years. Decades. Maybe even longer. Do you know how fast cockroaches can breed?"

"How are you going to fight against an army that numbers in the billions?" asked Jay.

"I still need my bag, and I'm not leaving without it."

"Look, let us go get her bag. We'll meet you at Buckley, wherever that is," said Jay.

"Oh no you don't . . . I'm not letting the two of you out of my sight again," said Gershwin. "We'll take you to your hotel ourselves."

Five minutes later, the small group packed into a helicopter and headed back toward the airport hotels.

"You won't need to land or anything," said Kasey. "I can totally fly out and back in. That way you can just circle around while I go get my stuff. Thanks for being such a doll about it, General."

Gershwin made an impatient noise deep in his throat, just loud enough that they could hear it over the thundering rotors.

In a few minutes they circled over the block of hotels and one of the soldiers rolled back the side door, filling the cabin with wind.

"I'll be right back," said Kasey with a dazzling smile. She leaped into the outside air, arms over her head like an Olympic diver. She unfolded her wings and pulled out of her swan dive, gliding toward the hotel roof.

"Likewise," said Jay, and headed for the door.

"Hey, where are you going?" yelled the General.

"I've got a bag too. It's, um, a *boy* thing."

Jay jumped out, missing General Gershwin's furious rant at him. He wasn't sure why Kasey insisted upon returning to the hotel roof, but he didn't want to be left out of any big plans.

He bounded off the parking lot, by sheer coincidence startling the same tourist couple he had the previous night with a cheerful "Evenin', folks."

He judged his angle and made a perfect two-footed landing on the rooftop, interrupting a couple making out in the hot tub. The woman shrieked and ducked into the water to hide herself. The man yelped as his partner's weight shifted onto an uncomfortable part of his anatomy.

"Uh . . . hi," said Jay, floundering for words. He didn't remember a hot tub being on the roof when they'd changed up there before. "I'm, uh, with the hotel. Is your, um, room to your satisfaction?"

"*Jackrabbit!* "

Jay looked over to see Kasey looking down at him from the next level up. He'd misjudged after all and landed on the fifth floor rooftop instead of the sixth.

At least he'd missed the pool.

"*D'oh!* " He smacked his forehead, then turned back to the terrified couple. "Anyway, on behalf of the hotel, we hope you enjoy your stay. Um . . . carry on."

He jumped up to the next level.

"Don't say a word," he grumbled as Kasey retrieved her bag. "What did you really need from here?"

"I told you and everyone else, I need my bag. If we're going to head back to San Francisco now, I'd kind of like to have my cell phone, my purse with my I.D. and my bank card and stuff, and, you know, my house keys."

Jay's mouth dropped open. He hadn't expected anything as obvious as the truth. "I'm kind of new to the whole secret identity thing, I guess."

She stepped over and kissed him. "That's why I'm here, to think of things you forget. And to make you, like, forget things you think you ought to remember."

He spent a moment trying to work this out, then shrugged and gathered up his own bag. Out of habit, he checked his cell phone: seven messages, all from Bunny. "Poor guy has to be worried sick about us," he said aloud. He texted a reply: *Im ok vry busy will call u soon. go team jackrabbit!!!*

"Bunny? He's a sweetheart. Everyone should have a best friend like him," said Kasey. "Do you have everything? We're not going to be back."

Jay nodded.

"I need a minute to call my folks and let them know what's going on. Aren't you going to call your mom?"

Jay shuddered. From the time, his mom's plane should already have landed in San Francisco. He'd been dreading the inevitable confrontation with her. "I'll get around to it," he said.

Kasey poked him. "She's your mom. She, like, loves you. And she'd want to know if you were going to be in some kind of danger."

"I'm in high school. I'm always in some kind of danger. Although it's usually from football players. And occasionally, uh, band geeks."

"You know what I mean. Call your mom."

He punched keys.

"Jay? My plane just landed. Any chance you can pick me up?"

"Hi, Mom. No, I'd say that's pretty unlikely right now."

"Are we still on for dinner and movies tonight?"

"Mom . . . listen . . . something's kind of come up."

"Jay, you didn't make a date tonight, did you?"

"No, Mom. It's not that. It's bigger. A lot bigger."

There was a pause, and his mom's tone changed. "Jay, what's the matter?"

"Mom, I can't tell you just yet. I need you to trust me one time, okay? Please?"

"Are you in some kind of trouble? Do you need help?"

"No, Mom. But someone else needs my help, and it's the kind of call I can't ignore."

She paused again. "I trust you, Jay. Do what's right."

"I will, Mom. I promise. I'll have Bunny call you and explain what's going on. And, um, I love you."

"I love you too, Jay. Be careful, whatever you're doing. Call me if you need me."

Jay hung up. It had gone far better than he'd expected. He sent off one more text to Bunny. *Plz tell my mom whats up with me as jackrabbit saving the world.*

Kasey finished her call and smiled at him. "Maybe you should try calling your, um, your ex?"

Jay slapped his own forehead. He had a feeling that the more time he spent around Kasey, the sorer his head was going to be. For a no-longer Creepy White Chick, she had ideas coming out faster than he could think. "Good point." He dialed. Shari's phone rang four times, then went to voice mail. He gritted his teeth; he hated leaving messages, but desperate times called for desperate measures. "Um, hi . . . it's Jay. Listen, I just wanted to tell you to, um, watch yourself around Mark. You know, in case he happens to be an advance scout for an invading alien race of super-intelligent cockroaches instead of himself. But I'm sure you'd notice if he was. Talk to you later." He winced and hung up. "Sorry. That probably could have gone better."

"You didn't just say that, did you?"

He hung his head. "I get stage fright with answering machines and go all to pieces. Look at it like this . . ." he paused, trying to figure out a good way to rationalize his boneheaded message. "If I'm right, maybe she'll stay away from him and be safe. If I'm wrong, then she's safe anyway because he's just a butt cheese instead of a reanimated tool for the roaches."

"But you're not bitter about it," said Kasey, pointing to the rooftop.

"Not at all." Jay looked down to where he'd picked a hole in the surface through the roofing tar and gravel. "Oops. Hope that doesn't leak."

"Jay, it'll be fine, okay? I promise."

"I hope you're right."

She grinned. "Of course I'm right. I'm a girl."

Jay made himself keep a straight face. He knew that to giggle could mean his death, and he'd have no end of trouble in the afterlife trying to explain to Leporidus the circumstances that caused him to lose his Herald. "Guess we're finished here."

"All right, Mr. Jackrabbit, let's go save the world."

"After you, Ms. Bluebird."

Fourteen

Jay was nervous about bouncing up into the flying helicopter. He didn't want to overshoot the entry and wind up getting his ears chopped off by the rotor. Kasey promised she'd watch him and keep him from going too high. True to her word, she slowed up as he rose toward the 'copter door, ready to block his progress with her body if needed. Fortunately for all involved, he timed his leap well enough to land on the floor of the cabin as easily as if he'd stepped onto it from an adjacent platform.

He reached out and pulled Kasey inside. She folded her wings and sat down in a seat as the soldier manning the door shut it. "Thanks so much, General Gershwin. I really needed that."

General Gershwin didn't reply; he was listening to his headphones with a look of intense concentration on his face, which registered the expression of a twelve-year-old who's carved his first Halloween pumpkin only to discover a squirrel eating the face out of it.

"What's the matter?" asked Jay over the roar of the engine. He'd never been in a helicopter before, and it was easily as loud as a concert he'd been to once featuring a funk metal band called A Week's Worth of Jane. His ears had rung for three days after that show, and they were ringing now. Kasey handed him a set of headphones and pulled her helmet back to wear a set herself. Jay fussed with his, forgetting for a moment that he couldn't put them on over his costume ears. The wire-frame appendages behaved so much like they were part of his body that he forgot they were decorative.

"It's the alien Ship," shouted the General. "Multiple radar signatures leaving it. It's launched dozens of objects. We don't know whether they're missiles or something else. Space Command has just declared an emergency. We could be minutes away from launching a tactical strike."

"Tactical?" asked Kasey.

"Nuclear," said Jay. "We might be about to get front row seats to World War III. And I'm all out of popcorn." His stomach twisted, reminding him that he still hadn't had anything substantial to eat. "Oh, popcorn. Sweet, fluffy, buttery nuggets of crunchy joy. I'd even take a bag of tasteless microwaveable crap right now."

"We're returning to Just Cause Command Center," said the General. "This trip to California is on hold, maybe indefinitely."

The return trip to Just Cause headquarters was much faster than the journey outward had been. The pilot didn't spare a drop of fuel, opening the throttle wide and tilting the chopper far forward to maximize forward momentum. The brightly-lit helipad outside the main Just Cause building rushed up at them and Jay and Kasey got their first taste of a combat-level landing, which felt to them more like a controlled crash than anything else. The landing gear compressed with the impact, jarring everyone's teeth.

Jay and Kasey staggered out, shaken up in spite of their parahuman abilities. General Gershwin seemed unfazed and hurried into the building, both listening to and shouting into his radio. They rushed into the Command Center, where the activity level had surpassed frenzy and chaos some time ago.

"How many signals, and do you have projected targets yet?" called the General as he took up a post on the raised floor where he could oversee the entire operation.

"The last estimate is a hundred and ninety-two distinct marks. Most of them are still too high to project destination targets, but they're definitely performing controlled descents, sir," reported the General's second-in-command.

"Do you have a size estimate?"

"Best data puts them at about twenty tons apiece, sir."

"They could be missiles, then," said the General. "Has the President authorized a return strike yet?"

"Not yet, sir."

At that moment all the network channels switched to the Emergency Broadcast System.

Kasey pressed against Jay and he put his arm around her, watching as the attention signal ended and the President's face filled the screen. He looked tense and uncertain. Unable to provide a reasonable political spin on the situation, he merely reported the launch of the bogeys from the Ship and informed everyone that he had mobilized the entire range of the United States Military to defend the country against a potential attack or invasion, and urged other world leaders to do the same. He pleaded for Americans to remain calm, to stay in their homes until the crisis was over, and to follow the directions of their local governments and FEMA offices. "We will prevail, and God bless us all," were his final words before he signed off.

"Sir, I have pictures from our satellites standing by," called an officer.

"Put them up," ordered General Gershwin.

The main screen began repeating a slideshow of the objects as they emerged from the Ship and fanned out across Earth orbits. Each had a hemispherical nose cone, which one specialist theorized was a heat shield to protect the payload from re-entry. Behind each cone was an object that had an uncanny resemblance to a humanoid with its arms over its head, as if it were grasping the shield.

"What are those?" asked Kasey. "They look like people."

"Oh, my," said Jay. "Giant evil space robots! Kill all humans! We're doomed . . . doomed . . ."

A red border appeared around all the monitor screens in the command center. General Gershwin's jaw dropped. "Good Lord, this is it," he whispered. "The President has authorized a nuclear response."

"Still no response from either the Ship or any individual signals, sir. We're now tracking over t-two hundred and sixty signatures." The officer's eyes were deeply hollowed and he looked terrified.

Jay was stunned. The idea of a nuclear war had seemed unthinkable for his life, something that only happened in the movies. "Can . . . can you hit something that size with a nuke?" he asked the General.

"Not with an ICBM," said the General, his face drawn and pale. "But we have plenty of smaller, independently-targeted warheads at our disposal. If we can hit them high enough in the atmosphere, we might not do too much damage to our own infrastructure. Major, are any of our birds in the air yet?" This last was directed to his assistant.

The Major was trying to balance two telephones at the same time. "Uh, no. Sir, there seem to be some problems with some launch systems."

"Problems?" asked the General. "Exactly what kind of problems?"

"It sounds like . . . widespread failures of launch and delivery systems throughout the network, sir."

"*Widespread failures?* What the hell does that mean? How many missiles are underway?"

Jay looked at Kasey. The seed of an idea was pushing its way through the gravel of his mind, straining to reach daylight like a bean sprout in an elementary school science experiment.

"Roughly . . . none, sir."

General Gershwin sat back in one of the observer chairs, looking less like a powerful soldier than a defeated old man. "We're defenseless."

Jay snapped his fingers. "Roaches. It's got to be them. Somehow they got into launch systems and disabled them."

"All over the country? The world? That's insane," countered the General. "It would take millions . . . *billions* of them."

"Well, aren't there that many cockroaches worldwide?" asked Kasey. "I've seen stories on them on Animal Planet that'll curl your toes just thinking about them. There could be a billion of them just living in New York City. And they're mostly so small, they can get into just about anything. If they have some kind of goal or mission driving them, I bet they could easily get into all the missile launch computers or something and chew through wires and stuff."

"Or causing blackouts and shit, too!" said Jay. Kasey poked him. "Sorry. Blackouts and *stuff*. Superheroes don't say *shit*." Kasey poked him again. "Ow. Shit. Sorry!"

"This is crazy," said the General. "Major, how long do we have before the descending bogeys reach the ground?"

The Major paused, accumulating answers himself. "Say twenty minutes, sir. And we should have course extrapolations in five. We'll have some warning of target destinations at least."

"Right." General Gershwin stood up. "I'm going to go question our resident cockroach expert. Inform me of any new developments."

The Major acknowledged the order. Jay and Kasey hurried after the General.

"General," said Jay. "What do we do now?"

"We'll have to engage them with conventional forces. Assuming that they haven't somehow managed to prevent those from functioning as well," said General Gershwin.

Kasey stamped her foot in petulance. "This doesn't make any sense. They're just insects, right? And they want to take over the world? Well, what would they do with it? I mean, like, they'll just want it to stay as dirty and full of garbage as it is now so they have places to eat. They could have just snuck down from space and just moved in and we'd never have been the wiser."

"Sure, what's another few billion roaches between friends?" asked Jay.

As they walked into the lab where Dr. Tenenbaum had moved her operation, Kasey said. "And what do we have that roaches need, anyway?"

"Thumbs, for one." Dr. Tenenbaum looked up from her microscope. "I've discovered something interesting about this roach."

"Make it fast," said the General. "I've got a war to run."

"All right," said the Doctor. "Genetically, this is a one-hundred-percent normal Madagascar Hissing Cockroach. But it's got some kind of parasites, and I think they're artificial."

"Pretend for a moment that I known nothing about cockroaches or parasites or alien technology and try to explain it in terms I can understand," said Gershwin.

Dr. Tenenbaum's smile became pained. "I am. The parasites are adding new tissue onto and inside of the roach. I think they built its brain, and they've strengthened its legs and reshaped its feet to allow it to grasp items. It's like I'm watching it mutate into something else before my very eyes."

Jay wrinkled his nose. "Nanotechnology? Building a better roach through science?"

"Something like that," said Dr. Tenenbaum. "I think eventually this roach would be able to manipulate tiny tools, given enough time and mutation, but working on this scale is awfully inefficient. If they built that Ship up there, I bet it would have taken them millions of years."

"Ohhh . . ." whispered Kasey. "No wonder they want to take us over, then. We're really good at, like, building all kinds of things."

"This is beginning to make sense," said Jay. "The Space Roaches must have dropped some of these nano bugs onto the Earth awhile ago, and they've been waiting while enough of our own roaches get transformed to perform whatever tasks they needed done in preparation for their arrival. I bet somewhere there's a roach factory churning out these things by the thousands, with a direct radio link to the Ship."

"I see," said the General. "So we find the factory and destroy it?"

Kasey laughed. "Oh, no, that's a silly idea." The General's ears turned red but he remained silent. "We could look forever and never find it. Or them, since it's logical there would be a lot of them all over the world. We'd need to, like, do two things. First we have to find a way to kill off all the enhanced roaches, like a virus or something. Then we have to find a way to destroy all the nano-thingies so they can't make any more. Once we've done that, we can drive away the Space Roaches. Maybe we could, like, let them have Mars or something. They are originally from here after all, right? From Earth. It wouldn't be very neighborly of us to just kick them back to wherever they've been for the past few gazillion years."

"You want a truce with them? They're attacking us!" shouted the General.

"Take it easy, your Generalship, sir. You're going to burst something," said Jay. "Nobody's offering them anything right now. I happen to think Bluebird had a couple really good ideas with the virus and the, um, nanovirus."

Dr. Tenenbaum nodded. "I think I could work up something that would affect the mutant roaches without harming the remainder of our indigenous population."

"Why does that matter?" groused the General. "Kill them all and let God sort them out."

"Actually, that would be the God of Roaches," said Kasey. "And he's why we're in this mess in the first place."

"We can't just commit genocide on an entire race," said Dr. Tenenbaum. "Despite what you may believe, cockroaches are mostly harmless to humanity and form an essential part of ecosystems worldwide."

"Even though they're icky?" asked Jay.

"Even the icky ones," said the Doctor. "I'd really need more sample organisms to work with. Any chance we can find another, um, donor?"

General Gershwin looked at Jay. "It sounds like we may be taking a trip to San Francisco after all, assuming we survive the first wave of the attack."

"What do you mean, survive?" asked Jay.

The General's face was grim. "Two of the alien bogeys are heading here."

Fifteen

"They're descending upon major cities all over the developed world," said the General's aide, Major Escobar, in his impromptu briefing. "We have some clear images shot by recon jets, sir. They can't get very close before their guidance systems break down. Based on the design of the incoming ships, we believe them to be landing vessels and not missiles. They have employed deceleration, implying their intent is not a catastrophic impact."

"I'll give 'em a catastrophic impact." Jay tapped his foot with impatience.

The images Major Escobar displayed showed fifty-foot-tall insectoid robots, with six limbs and antennae that crackled and glowed with energy. Their hemispherical heat shields had either been discarded or burned away during re-entry. The robots now descended with wings that cupped like parachutes emerging from underneath an armored carapace.

"So we can't get close to them and we can't shoot at them." General Gershwin poked at the screen as if he could crush the bug-like robots. "What's left, harsh language?"

"Shit, yeah!" said Jay with enthusiasm.

Kasey elbowed him, hitting the same spot for the fourth or fifth time that day. "Language," she said.

"Sorry, *mom*." He rubbed his ribs. "Actually, why don't you let me and Bluebird go after them when they land? I'd like to see a roach make my equipment fail." He stopped, considering. "Well, maybe not that, but still, we're probably the best chance you have right now unless you want to go after fifty-foot robots with sticks and stones."

"And what do you think you can do that's so much better?" asked the General.

"I can jump real high," said Jay.

"I can fly," said Kasey.

General Gershwin buried his head in his hands. "Dear God, It's a good thing we'll probably all wind up dead when this is over. I'll never be able to explain all this to the President."

"Cheer up, General." Jay grinned. "Want to rub my lucky rabbits' feet?"

Major Escobar made a herculean effort to keep from guffawing and nearly succeeded.

"Go," said General Gershwin. "And good luck. We'll provide what support we can."

"Thanks, your Generalship, sir. You won't be sorry," said Jay.

"I'm already sorry. Get out of here."

Jay and Kasey hurried up to the roof of the main Just Cause building. Numerous soldiers watched the skies, scanning with binoculars, radar scopes, and naked eyes, looking for the first sign of the incoming robots.

"What do you suppose they're going to do?" asked Jay.

Kasey shrugged. "It seems kind of silly for them to come down and trash the place they want to rule. And if they were going to really attack, they'd send more than, like, a couple hundred Giant Evil Space Robots, don't you? I bet they're carrying lots more of the super-smart cockroaches, but the ones who evolved naturally, not the ones they're making here. I think this is an invasion force."

Jay slapped his forehead. How were they going to fight thousands of cockroaches at a time? "We've got to make it dangerous for them to get out of the robots," he said, thinking aloud. "Like surrounding them with toxins or something."

"Well, don't you catch roaches by, like, putting something sticky down and then they get stuck when they run across it?" asked Kasey.

A soldier turned from his post. "Yeah, my grandpappy used to do that back in Alabama. He'd catch 'em in the slaughterhouse by puttin' some bait in the middle of a puddle of resin."

"And that worked?" asked Jay.

"Oh yeah. Then to amuse everyone, he'd set fire to it and watch 'em cook."

"Gross." Kasey touched the back of her hand to her mouth for a moment.

"Of course, he ended up burnin' down the slaughterhouse. Died in the fire." The soldier contemplated his own fingernails.

"Right," said Jay. "What we really need is a way to destroy the whole robot thing quickly and, um, *hotly.*"

"We don't even need to do that much," said Kasey. "All we have to do is open it up and pour in some bug killer or fuel and burn it or something. If we can get to the crew before they can leave the ship, it doesn't matter if we destroy the robot right away."

"Bogies incoming! Five o'clock, seventy-five degrees inclination!" called another soldier.

Jay and Kasey gazed hard into the dark sky before the soldier next to them cleared his throat in an embarrassed sort of way and turned them to face the correct direction.

Two bright stars were descending fast, leaving a faint glowing trail of ionized air in their wake. Spotlights struggled to pick them out and weapons elevated to track them. The soldier manning the radar scanner was aghast. "Why are they coming here?"

Sparks shot from the radar set as the robots drew closer. Other electronic equipment suffered a similar fate as whatever method the space bugs used to disrupt it came into range.

"Mr., uh, Jackrabbit?" called another soldier. "General Gershwin reports alien ships landing elsewhere and discharging, um, insects. He suggests we retreat to more secure facilities."

"No time," said Jay. "Okay, listen up." The soldiers came to attention, much to his surprise and pleasure.

"We have to defend this building no matter what." Kasey stepped forward and Jay could feel that she turned on her special ability to charm and convince. "There's a scientist in here who might be able to stop all this. We can't let her work be compromised. Use whatever you have to, your guns, fire, or your feet, but *keep this building secure.*"

"I could have said that," whispered Jay in her ear.

"Yes, but I said it better. Look at them. They'd, like, do anything for us."

The soldiers gripped their weapons with firm resolve, even knowing that they might fail if they'd been somehow sabotaged by local sympathetic roaches.

"Here they come!" shouted one.

"Hold your fire until we give the word." Jay leaped into the air. Kasey flew after him, her wings flapping in the nighttime breeze.

As he reached the zenith of an arc, Jay realized a fifty-foot-tall robotic insect was a *lot* bigger in person than on a monitor screen. Its body was long and shaped like a flattened egg. Six limbs protruded from the torso, layered with mechanical muscles and ending in grasping talons. The head was a featureless spheroid polished to mirror brightness that seemed to reflect any available light into the eyes of the watcher. Energy crackled between the long antennae extending from the head. The armored carapace had split up the middle to release wings that assisted the robot in a controlled descent, like a parachute.

A dizzying wave of heat struck J.J, radiating from the robots. He didn't know whether it was from their rapid descent through the atmosphere or a side effect of whatever power source they used, but it was really freakin' hot. "Watch out, they're smokin' hot, and not like you," he warned Kasey. She nodded and banked to avoid one of the limbs that reached out for her.

Jay touched down upon the edge of the Command Center's roof and paused as the two robots crashed down onto the parking lot, cracking the pavement and sinking a foot or two into the ground below. Their wings folded behind their armored carapaces and then they stood motionless.

"Your . . . attention." The voice had a different tone and timbre than that of the Supreme Leader, but the inflections were identical. "This facility is . . . under our control. You . . . are to surrender."

"Let 'em have it, guys!" Jay ducked and Kasey spiraled up and away to safety so the troops would have an unobstructed field of fire.

What followed was a disappointing lack of fire from the soldiers.

"It's no good, sir. Weapons are inoperable," said one.

"Crap in a hat," said Jay. "All right, then. Fisticuffs it is." He stood up and started prancing and dancing around at the edge of the rooftop, his fists held in the classical boxing pose. "Come on, who wants some? Who wants a piece of the Jackrabbit? I'll cavort and frolic until you guys can't see straight."

Kasey swerved around, unnoticed by the robots, and dove toward the hangars where Just Cause kept its supersonic transport jet. Jay saw her go out of the corner of his eye and grinned. She had some kind of plan, and that was awesome, because he didn't have a damn thing except his big mouth and matching feet going for him. He bounded back and forth, trying to be the center of attention. After all, that was his specialty.

"Come on, you stupid roach-built kludges . . . I can do this all day. Come get me. I'll *moiderize* ya!"

The two robots' heads turned slightly inward, as if they looked at each other in confusion. Then the energy crackling around their antennae intensified.

"Uh oh," said Jay. "Exit stage *up*."

He sprang high into the air as the robots cut loose with matching crimson energy blasts. The corner of the building disappeared, flashing into ash and vapor.

Jay flew higher than he'd planned. His nerves had made him over-jump. He spent several long, dangerous seconds in mid-air, wondering if he'd get shot down like a clay pigeon, but the robots didn't fire. Maybe his sudden vertical disappearance had confused them. He bounced back to the ground between them. One of them lunged downward with a clawed arm, but it moved so slow that he had no trouble evading it. Instead, he grabbed the arm as it retracted, using it for leverage, and swung up to perch on the upper torso of one robot.

"Ow! Hot! Tag, you're it!" he shouted, and kicked off hard from the armored plastron. The robots fired again, barely missing as he twisted his body around in the air.

Kasey returned from the hangar, carrying a ten-gallon fuel can in each hand as if they were no heavier than Gucci purses.

Jay bounced up next to her. "Are those full?"

"Yes," she said as he dropped.

"I think I'm in love with you."

"No you're not," she said. "You're rebounding."

Jay snorted and dodged another blast from the robots that carved a steaming furrow in the grassy field. "Bounding, maybe. So what's the plan?"

"Plan?" She sounded scandalized. "Knock a hole in them so we can, like, drop this stuff inside. Duh."

"Uh, they're sort of armored," said Jay. "And they've got laser guns too."

"But we're superheroes and Heralds." Kasey smiled at him. "We've got the power of the gods on our side." She shrieked as the robots fired a blast at her for good measure.

"Laser guns might still trump that," muttered Jay, and along with that wry observation, an idea formed. "Hey, draw their fire for a minute, okay?"

"You want me to *what?*"

Nevertheless, Kasey, swooped down low, giving the robots a fast-moving target. Jay watched as the robots' antennae glowed. Just before he estimated they would fire, he jumped up onto one robot's shoulders. The head was about the size of an over inflated beach ball. He wrapped his arms around it and pushed with his powerful legs. The head swung around as the antennae fired, nearly cooking Jay from the sudden blast of intense heat.

The blast went straight into the head of the other robot; it exploded into hot shreds of metal. The headless robot swayed momentarily but didn't fall. Like its designers, it seemed perfectly capable of continuing to function without its head. Jay whooped his success and leaped away, feeling the residual heat as a hot blast of energy scorched the air where he'd just been.

Jay dropped down next to a startled soldier. "Hi there, handsome. Got a cigarette?"

The soldier handed him one.

Jay broke it in half and tossed it away. "Filthy habit. Got another?"

"Hey!"

"Okay then, just your lighter." Jay took the lighter from the affronted man and jumped down next to a tree. He planted a heavy kick against a lower branch, which splintered off the trunk. The dry wood only took a moment to catch flame.

Behind him, Kasey swung around and emptied one of the fuel containers into the sparking neck of the headless robot. It reached up with its topmost pincers, trying to yank her from the sky, but it only managed to catch a few feathers. "Now would be good," she called.

Jay leaped up, flipped over another energy blast, and jammed the flaming brand into the headless robot's neck-hole. Flame spurted outward and the entire machine shivered like it had been struck.

With the great creaking sounds one might expect to hear from a falling tree, the burning robot toppled to the ground, spilling flaming fuel and cooked roaches from the hole in its neck. Soldiers rushed forward with spray cans of roach killer, dousing any of the insects they found still moving. Others eschewed such tactics to get personal with their heavy combat boots instead.

The second robot unfolded new devices from its middle set of arms, resembling snaking cable whips. They lashed out, curving as if guided by unseen hands, seeking to corral Jay and Kasey. Kasey easily kept out of reach, but was forced to dodge shot after shot from the robot's antennae.

Jay misjudged his body position and the end of a cable snapped across his chest, slicing through his costume and into his pectorals, leaving a bright trail of blood in its wake. He yelped and crashed down on the roof of a parked car in the lot, crushing it in. His entire chest burned, and he was afraid to look down for fear he'd see his muscles laid open to the bone.

"Jay!" cried Kasey in horror, arching her back to avoid a beam from the robot. Later, he'd say something to her in private about her using his real name in public, but at the moment all he could think of was the pain.

The robot's servomotors whirred and it took a step toward him. Then it took another. Kasey dropped down to the ground next to the car. "Come on, let's get you out of here before it steps on you. Hey, you're healing," she said in surprise.

"Could have fooled me. Son of a bitch, that hurts." Jay struggled to extricate himself from the wreckage of the car. The pain lessened, replaced by a maddening itch that made him want to grab a piece of ragged metal from the car's roof just to scratch with.

"Come on, Jackrabbit, move it. Move your ass already!" Kasey yelled at him. The robot was nearly on top of them. The cables whipped downward. Jay and Kasey just got clear as the lashes sliced through the car's roof, cutting it like soft cheese.

"Go, get clear. Stay split up." Jay waved at Kasey, who nodded and took to the air.

The robot continued its ponderous pursuit of him as he limped across the ground, still sore but feeling stronger with every step. It took shot after shot at Kasey, which he found maddening. Wasn't he good enough to require all its attention? He could feel his flesh knitting itself back together; blood no longer welled out from the healing cut. Spence was going to be pissed at the state of his costume. Then an idea occurred to him. "Bluebird, get ready!"

"Get ready for what?" she yelled back.

He bounded over to the soldiers performing cleanup on the other robot. He wondered for a moment why the second robot chose to ignore them. Perhaps it didn't consider them enough of a threat when it had active parahumans in the combat zone. The two soldiers sticking blocks of soft explosives along the fallen robot's flank might change them to active threats, and Jay didn't want them to be any more at risk.

"Don't use up all your boom sticks," said Jay. "I'll have another target for you in a second. Let me borrow these." He reached out and yanked two grenades from a nearby soldier's vest.

"Hey, those are incendiaries!" cried the man.

"Oh, well, I guess I'd better be careful then." Jay calculated angles of attack in his mind. The robot charged at him and the soldiers scattered. "Keep your heads down." He looked up at the approaching machine with interest. "And speaking of heads . . ."

He jumped as hard as he could toward the nearby Just Cause building, flipping forward to land against the wall feet first. It cracked under the force of his impact and several nearby windows shattered. His legs contracted and he flung himself upward like a bunnyman-shaped bullet, twisting about in mid-air to lead with his feet.

He struck the robot's head right between where its eyes would have been if it were humanoid. With a crack of overstressed metal, the head snapped off its mount to crash to the ground. His momentum carried him past the robot, but Kasey had been paying attention and waited, hovering. She snapped her wings out to their fullest extension and grabbed onto his ankles as he flew past. She used herself as a fulcrum and swung him around like a trapeze artist, sending him back in the direction he'd come.

He bit the fuses out of the grenades and dropped them into the ragged hole he'd created when severing the thing's head. They clattered downward out of sight.

As Jay dropped down next to the soldiers, the robot blew itself apart in a fiery explosion. Action movie directors had nothing on him. It would only have been better if he'd managed it in slow motion and had time to walk away from the explosion.

"Nice job, Jackrabbit," called Kasey from overhead. She waved and did a loop-the-loop.

Jay saluted back. "Couldn't have done it without you, Blue-babe."

"Why don't you two go get a room?" said a soldier.

"We just might. Or a hutch. Or a nest," said Jackrabbit. "We're flexible like that." He looked back at the destruction he'd wrought upon the alien robot. He grinned and struck a pose against the backdrop of flaming wreckage. "You know, sometimes I amaze even myself."

Sixteen

"Our worst fears have come to pass," said General Gershwin to Jay and Kasey. "It's an invasion force. Communications have been spotty, but we've suffered over fifty landings just in the United States and Canada alone. The targets have been major metropolitan areas, and this is the only site where the landers were destroyed before discharging the ground troops."

"San Francisco?" asked Jay.

"We have a confirmed landing there."

"What are the roaches doing once they land?" Kasey chewed on a thumbnail.

"As far as we can tell, they're going to ground and disappearing."

"Not for long, I expect," said Dr. Tenenbaum. "I'm certain that they're dispersing more of the nanomachines to affect earthly roach populations. Listen, if I'm going to build you this designer virus, I'm going to need a larger representative sample than our single captive. I'm also going to need a large group of assistants and better-equipped labs than this."

"Just Cause facilities are state-of-the-art!" protested one of the civilian staffers.

Dr. Tenenbaum snorted. "Please. Working here is like trying to make fire by banging rocks together."

"Give us a list of what exactly you need and we'll make it happen. We're going to take you to the most secure facility we can." Major Escobar handed Dr. Tenenbaum an iPad and encouraged her to make a list.

Jay's eyes widened. "You mean . . . *Area 51?*" he said.

Major Escobar snorted in derision. "Area 51 is a red herring. We've leaked story after story about the place. It keeps the conspiracy buffs happy and focused on it while the real work goes on in other places."

"Oh? What is it really?" asked Kasey.

General Gershwin frowned. "We really oughtn't to be giving away state secrets, but these are extreme circumstances. You'll have to sign a non-disclosure agreement and we'll issue you security clearance before you can go to Area 8719."

"Oooh, that sounds exciting," said Jay.

"Area 51 is a research facility for fluid transmission methodology." Jay couldn't detect any dishonesty in Major Escobar. Either the man was telling the truth or he played a lot of poker.

"No shit?"

"Well, hardly any," said the Major.

"What's fluid trans . . . whatever you said?" asked Kasey.

"Plumbing," said Jay. "And I think the Major here wants a turn in the bunny suit since he's making the jokes."

"Yes, about that suit . . ." The General eyed the large gash stained with Jay's blood. "You've got a spare to change into?"

Jay shrugged. "I might. I'll have to stop back by my, uh, headquarters. The *Rabbit Hole*. It's a secret."

Dr. Tenenbaum returned the iPad to Major Escobar. "That should be everything and everyone I need."

He looked over the list. "Hey, some of this stuff is classified. How do you even know about it?"

Dr. Tenenbaum smiled. "I had a useful assistant. That is, until she turned out to be a walking dead woman full of mutated cockroaches."

"If I had a dollar for every time that's happened," began Jay.

"You'd have a dollar," said Dr. Tenenbaum. "Everyone saw that one coming a mile away."

"She's onto me," Jay whispered.

"Make that list happen, Major," said the General. "Get that transport jet at Buckley ready to fly. Have the crew run complete diagnostics and I want a complement of exterminators on board. We can't risk letting the Doctor here fall into enemy hands I want you to accompany her to Area 8719. Come get her once preparations are ready."

The Major gave a smart saluted. "Yes sir." He rushed out of the Command Center.

"As for you two," said the General. "I'm dispatching you to San Francisco to find and collect additional specimens for Doctor Tenenbaum. You'll fly in Just Cause's transport jet, as it's the fastest thing available and you have the furthest to go. Once you've acquired sufficient specimens . . . how many would that be, Doctor?"

"As many as possible. I think twenty would be an absolute minimum."

General Gershwin resumed his orders. "Once you've acquired a minimum of twenty mutated cockroach specimens, you will be brought to Area 8719 to deliver them for research. At that time, we will debrief and plan the next phase of this war."

"But where is Area 8719?" asked Dr. Tenenbaum.

"What's the furthest place north you can think of?" asked the General.

"Santa's Workshop!" exclaimed Jay with glee. "What do I win?"

General Gershwin put his face in his palm.

Soldiers escorted Jay and Kasey to the hangar where they boarded the Just Cause supersonic transport jet, the *Rita*. It was a wide-bodied jet with swiveling jet nozzles, allowing it to hover or even fly backward. Jay surveyed the spacious cabin with its comfortable seating and smiled. "First Class, General? You shouldn't have. Is there an in-flight movie?"

They were barely on board before the pilot sealed up the hatch and taxied out onto the tarmac. The engines increased in volume and pitch to a scream, and the *Rita* launched into the pre-dawn sky.

"Hey, General, how come the President hasn't locked down the country? Shouldn't we be under martial law now? Tanks rolling through the streets and stuff?" asked Jay.

"Most of our armor isn't functioning, thanks to cockroach-caused damage," said the General. "It's damn near impossible to fight an enemy like this. We're trying to put on a show for our international opponents that we're not quite as bad off as we seem to be. Voluntary curfews are about the extent of what we can manage right now. Do you have any idea how hard it is to police the entire United States with our current armed forces?"

"Nope," said Jay. "And I'm pretty glad of that."

"I expect that the President really wants to keep people from, you know, panicking and stuff," said Kasey. "If he starts up martial law, people are going to know things are going bad. At least with just voluntary curfews, people will think that things are a little serious but the government's handling it. Right, General?"

"Very good, young lady."

Kasey leaned back and smiled. "*Some* of us pay attention in class."

The General advised Kasey and Jay to catch some sleep on the flight, as it might be the only chance they'd have in the next day or two. He shut his own eyes and his breathing became regular and measured within moments.

"That's amazing," said Kasey. "Sometimes it takes me hours to fall asleep."

"I guess when you're in the military, you have to take your sleep when you can get it," said Jay. "Since we have a minute, will you look at my chest?"

Kasey giggled. "Seems only fair, as much as you ogle mine, handsome."

"Is there any sign of the wound?" Jay held apart the flaps of his costume so Kasey could look more closely. She examined him by running her fingers across his dark skin to detect any irregularities. "I can't tell that you were ever hurt. That's got to be another power you have, and, like, a very good one to know about."

As she was bent down, examining his chest, Jay noticed a large burn down the back of Kasey's costume with her fair skin showing underneath. "Hey, what's this?" He traced it with a finger.

She blushed. "I zigged when I should have zagged. I caught a glancing blast from the robot's laser."

"Are you all right?"

"I think so. It doesn't hurt or anything. I figure I probably healed just like you did."

Jay put his arm around her. "I guess we're both pretty lucky. I wonder how bad an injury we can heal from?"

She shuddered. "I hope we don't find out. Did you hear the General say where Area 8719 is? Brrr . . . I hope Spence can make us cold-weather versions of our costumes."

"That's a good idea. I ought to shoot Bunny a call. I wonder if this jet has an air-phone or something?"

Kasey smiled. "That's not necessary. They're superheroes. I bet they're allowed to use their cell phones here." She dug into her bag and withdrew her phone. "Where's yours?"

"Oh, it's, um, unreliable in the air."

"You forgot your charger, didn't you?"

"Yes. It's sitting on my bedside table at home. You know how it is. You're given superpowers, then a costume, then you're charged with defending the Earth from invading cockroaches from outer space. You forget small details like cell phone chargers."

"Dial away." Kasey snuggled up against him and yawned. "Just keep it down. I'm sleepy and I need a nap."

"A nap does sound nice," said Jay, yawning as well.

"So does a toasted cheese sandwich." Kasey said in a sleepy voice.

Jay's stomach rumbled, reminding him how long it had been since he'd been outside of any food. He'd make a thorough investigation of the *Rita*'s galley supplies before he slept. Even the top-tier superheroes of Just Cause wouldn't fly off into battle without snacks readily available.

Bunny answered on the second ring with an uncertain "Hello?"

"Bunny, it's Jay."

"You bastard! Do you know how worried I've been about you?" Bunny's shriek could have blown the speaker on Kasey's pink phone.

"Uh, no . . ." said Jay.

"It's been hell, here. Absolute hell, Jay. We watched you on the news and I swear every time I saw you jump I was scared to death that you would come down in pieces. Pieces!" Bunny was ramping up like he was trying for an Oscar.

"Bunny," said Jay, but there was no interrupting his friend's tirade.

"And then the giant robot landed here and absolutely flooded the streets with cockroaches. They're all gone now. Underground, I bet. It makes me so oogie I'm afraid to even let one of my feet touch the floor for fear a roach will run over it."

"That's . . ."

"And I haven't heard one word from you since you left town, and the only news I've had has been on CNN, and you know how they are about covering things. Jay, I thought you might have died out there.

You'd better be calling me to say you're coming home or I swear I will be such a bitch to you that you'll never forgive yourself!"

"Bunny, shut up a minute." Jay rolled his eyes. His friend could be overly dramatic at times, but at least his heart was in the right place. "Yes, we're both all right and on our way back to San Fran. We're a little beat up and could use some of Spence's magic to repair our outfits but otherwise we're fine."

"Thank God for that," said Bunny.

"Did you talk to my mom?"

"That poor woman. Yes, I did. She's a little upset to learn that her seventeen-year-old son is going to have to save the entire world."

"How did she take it?"

"Better than I expected. She was only on her second cocktail when I showed up with my patented Bunny Stressbuster Care Package. You know, floral bubble bath, chocolate-dipped strawberries, and a DVD of *Beaches*. We talked for awhile. Cried for awhile. Then we made a shrine to you and your Rabbit God."

"You what?"

"A shrine, Jay honey. With a stuffed rabbit doll and candles and fresh, leafy greens and everything."

Jay palmed his face. "Where is she now?"

"I told her to stay at home in case you needed to reach her there."

"Thanks, Bunny. Things are moving pretty fast right now. Tell her I'll try to call if I get a chance. Will you guys have time to patch up mine and Kasey's costumes?"

"I'll tell Spence to fire up his sewing machine. But Jay, honey, what happened out there?"

"We beat the robots, and captured a prisoner," said Jay. "And we're coming to try and capture some more. Listen, this is really important. I need you to do something for me."

"Anything for you, Jay honey."

"I need you to find Shari and her new boyfriend and tail them. And be inconspicuous about it."

"That self-serving bitch? Why?"

"Just do it, Bunny. It's important. It could be the key in winning this war. But be careful, and don't let anyone see you. Try to, you know, dress down a little. Less like yourself and more like, well, me."

"I'll try to be a little more butch." Bunny made his voice gruffer with less of a lisp. "Ahem. How's this? Man enough for you?"

"That's fine, Bunny. Just find them and follow them. If they split up, follow the guy. I'll call you when we get into town."

"Roger that. Ten-four, good buddy," growled Bunny. "You can count on me."

Jay shook his head and hung up the phone. Bunny made for an enthusiastic sidekick. He just hoped his friend would take his warning to heart and be careful.

Kasey was already asleep. He extricated himself from her and commenced rummaging through storage lockers, looking for something to assuage his hunger.

Interlude 2: Gods' Home

"Oh, I've fallen, and I can't get up!" Sialia tumbled down into the clearing in the forest, favoring one wing as if it were injured.

The two gigantic cockroach guards standing over Anurus, the Frog God, looked at each other.

"Oh, help, please! Someone help! How shall I ever save myself?" cried Sialia, limping in a small circle on the grass. "Here I am, just a tender and tasty morsel, stranded and unable to escape."

The two guards unlimbered their swords—irregular blades with odd angles and spikes protruding at unusual angles—and approached her.

Behind them, Leporidus sneaked out from the high grasses and started to untie his friend.

"What are you doing?" whispered Anurus.

"Saving you, stupid." Leporidus gnawed through a stubborn knot with his sharp teeth.

"I can't believe they're falling for the oldest trick in the book." Anurus struggled to get free.

Leporidus released the final rope and his friend hopped down to the ground. "Old tricks are my specialty."

"I thought that was inspiration," said Anurus.

"That too. We've got a hidey hole back beyond the tree line in the oldest part of the forest. When I give the word, make for it."

Anurus stared at him, wide-eyed. "What are you going to do?"

"Break a Rule," said Leporidus over his shoulder. "Like I am right now."

"What?"

"I'm releasing you. I'm directly interfering with another god's business."

"But . . . Blattodeus is already interfering. He's making a move to take over Gods' Home. Isn't that direct interference?" asked Anurus.

"Listen," said Leporidus with a sigh. "The Rules may or may not apply to him because he's not a human god. I'm not going to argue the semantics with him or his soldiers. But I am a human god, and the Rules do apply to me. Run!"

Anurus leaped forward as if he'd been shot from a gun, hopping like mad for the cover of the trees. The cockroach soldiers spun around at the sound of Leporidus' cry. In that moment of distraction, Sialia flew away, scolding at them as she fluttered toward the trees herself. The soldiers raised their swords and charged at Leporidus.

Leporidus had felt his power reserves increasing. The shrine created by Jay's mother and friend, which they'd done more to support Jay than for any other reason, was like a breath of fresh air. It had been more than a thousand years since anyone had worshipped the Rabbit God, and he was feeling dangerous and powerful because of it. He didn't know from where the giant cockroach soldiers had come. He didn't know if they were mortal, or demigods, or some kind of classification hitherto unknown. Whatever they were, they couldn't be called gods by any stretch of the imagination, and this was the Rule that Leporidus was about to break.

Gods were proscribed from using their divine power against mortals. It had happened only eight times throughout all of recorded history. Four times, the gods in question were heavily censured by the Council of Elder Gods, who were responsible for the inquiries of Rule transgressions. Twice, the offenders had been cast out of Gods' Home, never to return. One rule-breaker was sentenced to death and the vengeance of the gods upon him was swift and furious.

One was acquitted.

Twelve and a half percent chance, thought Leporidus. He'd counted worse odds. He'd learned a phrase from mortals that he hoped would found the cornerstone of his defense, should his actions be discovered to violate the Rules: *Extenuating circumstances.*

Lovely people, mortals; always inventing new ways to excuse themselves.

Leporidus shut his eyes and drew upon the vast well of divine power. Any god could access it at any time; it existed solely for their use or went lacking. He heard the soldiers raising their swords to strike and opened his eyes and spoke one of the Awful Words.

The two monstrous cockroach soldiers turned to dust and blew away on the sudden chill wind that sprang up in the clearing.

Leporidus was as angry as a rabbit could ever get. Gods' Home . . . this was *his* home, and he was going to take it back no matter what the cost.

Seventeen

"Look at this mess." Spence fingered the slice across the Jackrabbit costume. "I can't believe I just made this for you, and you already tore it. And what is this, blood? Do you have *any* idea how hard it is to get these stains out?" He sighed with the weariness of Atlas.

"You know, that happened while I was wearing it," said Jay. "You're lucky I'm here so you can bitch at me about my carelessness instead of carrying on over my closed casket."

Spence brushed his fingers through his hair. "I'm sorry, Jay. It's been a very stressful couple of days since you left, what with the invasion and the bugs and everything. Look at me, I've got dark circles under my eyes! Wrinkles! I look old! Do you have any idea what it's like to look old when you're only, uh, sixteen?"

"You coy bitch," said Bunny as he walked in the front door. "You haven't been sixteen for two years now." He juggled a cup and paper sack between hands so he could close the door with one foot.

Kasey returned from the bathroom, wearing one of Spence's kimono bathrobes and toweling off her wet hair. "Thank you so much, Spence. I feel almost human again. Oh, hello Bunny. I thought you were supposed to be following Jay's ex. Spence, you have the most darling fixtures in that Japanese bath thingie. I've got to know where you found them." She turned to Jay. "They're little kittens and puppies. Absolutely precious."

"She's right. How come you're here, Bunny?"

Bunny showed off his carefully-whitened teeth in a magnificent smile. "I know, I'll just be here a minute. They're not far away. They went to a movie at the Palisades." He handed Spence a bag and a steaming cup. "Pesto and provolone bagel sandwich and a café Americano, dear."

"I forgive you for calling me a coy bitch, but only because I am," said Spence with a laugh.

"So, uh, this is your secret headquarters, is it?" asked General Gershwin from a chair in the corner. He sat ramrod straight, his hat resting on his knee.

Bunny gasped. He hadn't seen the officer when he came in. "Another rooster in the henhouse, Spence?"

"Of course not. He came with them." Spence smelled his coffee, eyes shut, and sighed in contentment. "You are an angel, Bunny."

"Relax, General," said Jay. "You're not going to turn gay just by being here. Besides, Don't Ask Don't Tell is over. You've probably got gay guys in your command."

General Gershwin blushed to the roots of his hair. "No, it's not that . . . it's just that I'm still wrapping my mind around the concept that your headquarters is the basement of a dance studio." He squeezed his temples. "But I'm an open-minded man. I have to be, working so closely with parahumans as I have. Carry on."

"Half your problem is the fit of your uniform, you know," said Spence. "Your pants ride too low and you're always hitching them up. Your shirt bunches in the wrong places when you move and accentuates instead of hides your, um, paunch. Those shoes are atrocious, and so is your hair. If you want to impress Mrs. General when this is all over, you'll let me fix you up right." His smile at Gershwin was devoid of any deviousness.

"My . . . hair?" Gershwin's hand brushed fitfully across his scalp, dislodging some of the straggling hairs that crisscrossed his pate.

"Spence, not to put any priorities on you or anything, but can you fix our costumes or not?"

"Not right away. But fortunately for you, I made two extra copies of each of your costumes from my original designs. I'll just finish them up for you right quick and you'll have yours by the time you're out of the shower."

Jay felt relieved. "Spence, you're amazing."

Spence grinned. "I know."

Bunny hugged Jay and Kasey quickly, then gave General Gershwin a firm handshake. "I'm glad you're all right. I was so worried all I've done the past two days is eat. I'm sure I've gained five pounds. I'll have to do grand *jetés* for days to work off all these calories. Lovely to meet you, General. Take good care of my friends. I'm off to play super spy once more."

"Keep your phone handy," said Jay. "We'll be ready to move soon."

"Jay, I'd like to start making preparations to receive our potential prisoner," said General Gershwin. Jay and Kasey had agreed it was better to keep on Gershwin's good side, and to cooperate with him in every way possible. He'd been appalled to learn they were still in high school, but recognized that they were his best available assets. "Can the two of you outline what you need from me?"

"Before my shower?" said Jay. "Seriously, I'm reeking over here."

"How do you intend to catch the suspect?" The General seemed unimpressed by Jay's odor.

"Oh, I figured I'd drop down alongside him, grab him, and jump away. Easy as pie."

"But you'll need to put him into a sealed container of some sort," said Kasey, leaning back and putting her hands behind her head in thought. The view was enough to make Jay momentarily lose track of his thoughts. "Otherwise all the bugs will just run away. We should have something like a big bucket that we can drop him into. Maybe if it was something held by a helicopter? Then we could remove him from the area quickly before any other bugs could respond. But we'll need someone who can check to make sure he's really, um, infested. Otherwise, we've made this whole trip for nothing and grabbed an innocent citizen to boot."

"Grabbing an innocent citizen is the least of my problems," said General Gershwin. "We can always explain it away as a Homeland Security operation. If we're wrong, we'll give him an apology and a fruit basket or something."

Kasey was stunned. "I can't believe how callous you are about, like, trampling civil rights, General!"

General Gershwin leveled his gaze at her, unblinking and intense. "We are at war. Officially, I might add. Congress voted approval two hours ago. And in wartime, certain rights may be suspended in favor of national security. Now if you want to argue them with me, I'll be glad to debate with you and your entire high school debating club at length and then some . . . once this crisis has ended."

Kasey folded her arms across her chest with a *hmph*. "After this is over, I'm going to take a long vacation somewhere tropical. Mexico, maybe. Acapulco."

"Sounds lovely. The Mrs. and I might even join you," said the General. "But for now, I think I know what kind of setup you're going to need. I can have an Army doctor standing by in a container, ready to check your patient. We can use a firefighting copter and bucket rig—that shouldn't raise suspicion from any of the bugs."

"Why not?" asked Spence around a mouthful of pins.

"It's California, dude. There's *always* a fire *somewhere,*" said Jay.

"We'll adapt the bucket into a vessel that can be sealed," continued the General. "And with luck, we should have enough bugs to keep Dr. Tenenbaum happy by nightfall."

"Good," said Jay. "I'm going to hit the shower."

Two hours later, Kasey and Jay fit themselves into their replacement costumes. While Jay had showered, a soldier stopped by the studio to drop off two state-of-the-art radios for Jay and Kasey. Spence took a few minutes integrating the throat mikes and ear buds into each costume, stringing the main unit into the small of the back for each of them. "Are you sure I can't fit you with a tail?" he said to Jay. "It would help to hide the receiver back here. It simply destroys the lines of the suit. Bah."

Jay shook his head. "No tail. I've still got my pride, you know. Save stuff like that for Bunny."

Spence cackled. "Oh, I will. Count on that."

The radios were dual-channel, changed by touching a switch on the ear bud. The first channel was a dedicated connection between Jay and Kasey. The second was a general military channel, facilitated by an operator, that would be used by all parts of the operation.

"Your mission, should you choose to accept it," said Jay and received yet another elbow in the ribs from Kasey. "Ow! You've hit the same place every single time! Why isn't it healing?"

"Because I'm in the right," said Kasey as they headed up the stairwell to an overcast San Francisco afternoon.

The space cockroaches' Supreme Leader had addressed the world while Jay dried himself off. The others had turned up the television loud enough so he could hear. The humanoid, who by now they suspected was just a vessel for more roaches, gloated over the ease with which his troops had captured all major military installations and that the world was now helpless to resist. He'd gone on in this vein for awhile in the best grade-Z-movie-villain rhetoric before getting down to his demands. The long and short of it was that all industry was going to switch to producing machines designed by the invaders, and all other people were going to work in support of those industries. The human race was going to live, albeit enslaved, to build a great mechanized army and new starships for the roaches. Earth would be Point Zero for the conquest of the galaxy.

Jay was surprised to still see so many people out on the streets, considering the world was in the grasp of the invading roaches. He supposed that to the typical man on the street, it didn't matter so much who was signing his checks so long as he had a job to go to and three square meals during the day. A lot of folks waved and cheered at him and Kasey as they bounced or flew past. He grinned and waved back. As the only parahumans remaining on Earth, he realized that a lot of people were placing their hopes on them.

He promised himself he wouldn't disappoint them.

He waved to Kasey to take a break and they both stopped on the roof of a department store.

"What's up?" she asked. "Why not use the radios?"

"A couple reasons," he said. "Where do you think the other parahumans are?"

She shrugged. "They could be anywhere. I doubt they're on the Ship up there, though. I'll bet this has something to do with the roach god."

"What do you mean?"

"Suppose he somehow made every parahuman disappear? Or took them somewhere?"

"Do you think he really had the power for that?"

Kasey shrugged. "I've read the Bible. God—that is, the Christian version—performed some pretty amazing feats in that. Gods in other religions are supposed to be just as puissant."

"Hey, no fair using big words, Ms. AP English! But then that leaves the mystery of why we're still here and they're not."

"There's no mystery," said Kasey. "It's obvoius that we're not parahumans."

"But . . ."

"Silly boy. I bet even now our genes would test as us being without any parahuman influences at all. Our powers are divine in origin. Being completely of human stock made us immune to whatever power took the others. No wonder our gods chose us to be Heralds instead of existing parahumans."

Jay tweaked his rabbit ears. "That's brilliant."

She winked at him. "I know. What was the other reason you wanted to talk?"

"It's about my ex. Shari."

"What about her?"

"Look, we were going out before this guy came back into her life."

"I know. I was kind of stalking you, remember?"

"Well, I just want you to know that I'm over her."

"Are you?"

"Uh, yeah."

Kasey said nothing.

"I mean it. Once this is all over and we're back in school and everything, I want you to be my girlfriend. Not her." Jay felt like he was talking around a mouthful of marbles. Why was it so difficult to just share how he felt? He needed to be channeling Bunny, who had no filter when it came to emoting.

"What if we go back to the way we were? What if our powers and everything go away and then we're just back to normal? You the only black kid who can't sink a basketball and me, the Creepy White Girl?"

Jay put his hands on his hips. "I wish I'd never said that to you. But yes, even if we go back to the way we were before. I don't want anyone else. You rock, Kasey, and I want to keep you in my life. And I hope you feel the same way."

"I do, Jay. We make a good team."

Jay grinned. "So we're cool."

"Yes, we're cool. And as far as Shari goes . . ." Kasey stood up on her tiptoes and kissed him. "I could punch her lights out before you grab the dude," she whispered. "She'd never know what hit her."

Eighteen

"Hey there, all you G.I. Joes and Janes out there in Ricearoni-land, this here's the Big Bunny Bopper, broadcasting from the top of the Sheraton Palace Hotel. You all got your ears on?" Jay tweaked his own ears while Kasey grabbed her belly to keep from cracking up on the air.

"Operator. Go ahead." The derisive voice belonged to a young woman with a Southern accent.

"Can you connect me to a cell phone?"

"Number, please."

"Okay, Ernestine . . ." Jay gave her Bunny's cell phone number. "Tell him his shoes are lousy. It'll be hilarious."

The operator was unfazed. "One ringy-dingy . . . asshole."

General Gershwin's impatient and harried voice broke in on the frequency. "Could we all please try to show a little more professionalism here? This is supposed to be a military operation."

"Ten-four, good buddy," said Jay.

There was a pause as the connection completed, then Jay heard ringing.

"Hello?"

"Bunny, it's me."

"Jay honey! I was wondering when I'd hear from you. You would not believe the way this bitch just cut me off. Seriously, it's like we're in L.A. or something."

"Not now, Bunny. Where are Shari and, uh . . ."

"Mark," said Kasey.

"Oh, hi Kasey," bubbled Bunny. "The lovely couple is currently walking along Fulton heading for Golden Gate Park."

Jay figured out distances in his head. "I think we can be there in about ten minutes. Stay on the line and tell us if they change heading at all. And if I tell you to bug out, you make like a housewife at a two-for-one Tupperware sale and hit the ground running."

"The park is a good locale for the snatch-and-grab," said General Gershwin. "Lower risk of civilian casualties. I have spotters moving into the area now. Follow the targets and prepare to strike on my command."

Jay and Kasey covered the distance to the park in just a few minutes. The downside to the open space was a lack of tall buildings on which to perch, Jay discovered. He and Kasey took cover near some trees, trying to keep a low profile despite their costumes.

"I'm a little scared." Kasey peeked through the leaves at the path.

They heard shy giggling from behind them and turned. Two young Asian women in matching uniforms were pointing and blushing. One of them held a camera.

Kasey rolled her eyes at Jay, who grinned. "Ladies," he said. "We're doing some superhero business here. You might want to be on your way home, you know? Home?"

"Please . . ." said the one with the camera, holding it out to Kasey. "Will you?"

"We don't have time for this," she growled from behind her visor.

"It's all right," said Jay. "One picture, then you ladies had best skedaddle."

The girls squealed with delight and pushed the camera at Kasey. Jay found himself sandwiched between them. He jumped as a soft hand caressed his ass. Kasey sighed, raised the camera, and snapped a picture. The girls shrieked and bowed to both the heroes before taking their camera and running off, both talking in rapid-fire Japanese.

"What is it with you?" asked Kasey.

"It's the ears. Chicks dig the ears."

A new voice broke over their headsets. "Targets have entered the park from the West."

"Bunny, you still there?" asked Jay.

"Oh my, yes. This is so exciting!"

"Take a hike, buddy. It's not safe for you to hang around. This is superhero work now."

"Jay honey, you couldn't pay me to miss this. I want to see you in action."

"Dammit, Bunny!"

"He's hung up," reported the operator.

They heard the distant sound of an approaching helicopter and knew the moment was almost upon them.

"There they are." Kasey pointed at the couple strolling along the path. "Look at them walking along like it's nothing." She sniffed. "I hate them already."

"ETA on the copter ninety seconds," said General Gershwin. "Everyone stand by. All units report in." Several people checked in from their vantage points around the area.

"Crap in a hat, there's Bunny!" Jay he recognized his friend further up the path. He started to get up from behind the cover but Kasey dragged him back down.

"Are you nuts?" she said. "We show our hand too soon and this is all for nothing."

Jay fumed, willing Bunny to sashay his ass anywhere else. But apparently all the gods to whom he appealed were otherwise occupied with their own problems, for Bunny still walked along, blithely unaware of the impending operation.

They watched as the chopper, bright red with a large, heavy lidded drum swinging beneath it, swung around the buildings at the far end of the park. It leveled out, cruising low and slow on final approach.

Kasey touched Jay's arm. "I'll get Bunny to safety. He'll be fine. I promise."

Jay nodded. "I know you will. Good luck, darlin'." He planted a careful kiss under her visor. Her lips tasted of raspberry lip gloss.

"This is General Gershwin," came the voice. "Jackrabbit and Bluebird, you may act at will. All other units stand by to provide support as required."

"Copy that, Roger Roger, this is Jackrabbit, over and out. Up, up, and away, over." Jay hurled himself skyward, clearing the trees. He heard the rustle as Kasey snapped out her wings and fluttered out from behind cover, flapping for the strolling couple.

Suddenly uncounted roaches swarmed out from the grass, trees, and storm drains, racing toward Shari and Mark. Jay's eyes widened as he realized his landing spot was covered with a living carpet of swarming bugs. Mark reached into his pants and withdrew a shiny weapon identical to the one Dr. Tenenbaum's assistant had wielded.

"It's a trap!" cried Kasey.

"Abort the mission," said the General. "I won't risk losing the two of you the way we lost the others."

"Negative, General." Jay winced as he crunched down onto the roaches below. "Not when we're this close." He lashed out with one foot and sent Mark's weapon spinning away. Feathers brushed his arm as Kasey flew past at top speed, grabbing Shari and carrying her away. "Excuse me, is that your face hitting my foot?" asked Jay. He booted the Mark-thing in the face, perhaps harder than appropriate but certainly enough to be satisfying. "Yep, looks like it."

"Foolish . . . human . . ." said Mark as cockroaches flowed to him, shielding his body with thousands of their own. "We . . . expected you."

"Oh yeah?" Jay grinned. "Bet you didn't expect this." He swung his leg like a punter, catching the Mark-thing's crotch in the sweet spot of the kick.

Sympathetic gasps of pain overloaded the comm channel as Mark flew through the air some thirty feet into a duck pond.

"Boy, I'll bet that would have hurt if you'd still been alive." Jay sprang after Mark.

He splashed into the water where the Mark-thing floundered and grabbed him by his shirt. Showing surprising strength, the infested creature broke Jay's grasp on him and struck him hard and fast across the jaw.

"Didn't hurt," said Jay. Mark hit him again and sent him sprawling in the water. Jay shook his head to clear it. "That was a good one."

"Jackrabbit!" screamed Kasey. He spun to see her struggling with Shari.

Shari held one of the alien weapons and was attempting to point it at him. As he watched, a roach leaked from her mouth. He forgot everything for a moment as he realized she was only a vessel for more of the super-intelligent insects.

The Mark-thing swung a heavy tree-limb at him, catching him unawares. The blow snapped his ribs and Jay tumbled and bounced across the turf, yelping as the broken ends sandpapered together. Shari fired her weapon and part of the duck pond flashed into steam. Then she flung Kasey away and swung around to blast her into ashes.

"Don't you dare, you bitch!"

Out of nowhere, Bunny ran forward and leaped onto Shari's back, pounding ineffectually at the woman's arms. The beam sizzled past Kasey, who fluttered up into the air where she could dodge in three dimensions instead of only two.

"Backup is on its way. Thirty seconds," said the General into their headsets.

Jay grunted and got to his feet, feeling his ribs already knitting back together. "Keep them away, General. This area's compromised. Tell that chopper pilot to swing around once more. I'm going to fulfill the mission. Just as soon as I save my, uh, sidekick."

Jay backflipped over a blast from Shari's laser and landed behind her and Bunny, who was shrieking like a furious girl scout. He wrapped his arms around Bunny and whispered in his ear, "Let go." Then he sprang up and back, lifting Bunny clear of the fracas.

Bunny was in outstanding physical shape—he had to be for his job as a dance instructor—but the brief combat left him weak and shaky and he sank to the ground as Jay set him down. "Thanks, Jay honey. She's stronger than she looks."

Jay stuck a finger in his friend's face. "I ought to kick your ass for getting in the middle of this. But I'm kind of busy, so can we just sort of consider that I did and that you're terribly sorry about the whole thing?"

Bunny nodded and waved for him to get back to the fight. "Oh my Lord, I need a Fresca and a massage." He fanned himself with his hands.

Jay saw troops approaching from every direction on foot, wielding long rifles that looked like refugees from a Western movie. Realizing the roaches' ability to interfere with higher technology, the General had seen to it his men were outfitted with low-tech weapons and gear.

Kasey dove between two trees, avoiding a blast from Shari's laser pistol. The foliage dissolved into ashes and smoke. Jay saw the Mark-thing running toward the pistol he'd lost earlier. "Oh, no you didn't." He sprang for it in a long, powerful leap, stretching himself out flat.

Jay bowled into Mark just as the other closed his grasp on the weapon, sending them both sprawling.

The two boys struggled for the weapon, pitting brute strength against brute strength, cunning moves against cunning moves, and sheer bloody-mindedness against pure instinct. Finally in a move of desperation, Jay head-butted his opponent so hard he saw stars. The impact crushed Mark's skull and would have been instantly fatal, were he not already dead. His limbs twitched, giving Jay the chance to wrestle away the gun. Kasey shrieked a warning and he spun around to see Shari drawing a bead on a group of advancing soldiers.

He leaped out of the pool, raising the gun in both hands, calculating distances and angles with the same uncanny accuracy he used when jumping. The gun had a simple firing stud which he depressed as he drifted through the air, seemingly in slow motion. The beam lanced out to strike Shari high between her shoulders. Jay knew it went against most codes of honor to shoot an opponent in the back, but he knew he couldn't have done it if he'd had to see her face. He reminded himself that she wasn't alive any longer. The aliens had seen to that. Destroying her body wasn't any different than demolishing the giant robots had been back in Denver.

Shari transformed into a column of fire and smoke that dissipated in a few seconds, leaving only a greasy black stain on the grass where she'd stood. Despite trying to convince himself that all he'd done was destroy a suit of armor, Jay knew the image would haunt him forever. He spun around and leveled the weapon at the Mark-thing as it approached him.

"You . . . can kill me . . . but it . . . changes nothing," said the creature with some satisfaction, talking with difficulty through a broken jaw and crushed face.

"Who said anything about killing you?"

Kasey appeared behind the monstrosity, swinging the same tree limb it had used previously with strength belied in someone of her build. The heavy branch connected at the creature's knees, shattering them. It pitched forward to scrabble at the bank of the duck pond.

"You're already dead," said Jay.

Nineteen

It was a long, long flight north.

Jay, Kasey, and the General traveled aboard a military jet along with a small army of technicians, etymologists, exterminators, and a cargo case full of prisoners and corpses. The accommodations in the jet could be called Spartan if one wanted to insult Spartans. He and Kasey huddled against a hull spar, wrapped in a heavy wool blanket to insulate them against the cold air.

They'd managed to extract twenty-nine live cockroaches from the carcass that had been Mark, and salvaged an additional fourteen dead ones. Dr. Tenenbaum would be pleased; her report explained she had already made significant strides toward isolating a possible killing agent.

"Are you all right?" Kasey whispered in Jay's ear.

Jay knew he'd been quiet on the voyage out. He was still trying to sort out all his thoughts and emotions about Shari and losing her for a second time, and by his own hand. On one hand, he knew that she'd already been dead when he shot her, that she'd probably been murdered by Mark between the time he'd seen them in the restaurant and the fight in the park.

On the other hand, it was hard for him to keep reminding himself that he wasn't a killer and that he was trying to work more or less along the path set for him by his god.

"More or less," he admitted. "I'm in kind of a weird place right now."

Kasey raised an eyebrow. "You're wearing a bunny suit, cuddling with a girl wearing a bluebird outfit, sitting in the back of a plane carrying a cargo of, like, super-intelligent cockroaches to a secret military installation so that a scientist can create a virus to wipe out the advance scouts of an alien invasion so we can save the world." She paused to take a breath. "I'd say *weird* hardly begins to describe it."

Jay laughed. "You're right about that." His humor faded as quickly as it had arisen. "I just wish there'd been some other way."

Kasey squeezed him a little tighter, mindful of his ribs, which were sore but healing. "You did everything you could. Nobody got hurt. Not even Bunny."

"Thank the gods for that," said Jay, chuckling. "That stupid, brave bastard. If he'd broken a nail or something, I'd never hear the end of it. *Jay honey, remember that time I took on a supervillain to save your life?*" He imitated Bunny's inflection perfectly, much to Kasey's amusement.

"He really cares about you, you know."

"Well, yeah, he better. We've been best friends since second grade."

"And you care about him too, you big softie."

"Yeah I do. He's been really great about this whole thing. If I was gay, we'd probably be married."

"You haven't ever . . ."

"What? Oh, no," said Jay. "That's never been an issue between him and me. He likes his candy with a hard center. I like mine soft. We're both just fine with that."

"You're an amazing guy. A lot of straight dudes couldn't keep such a strong friendship with a gay friend."

Jay leaned a bit further back and put his hands behind his head. "Yeah, sometimes I amaze even myself. Hard though that can be."

Kasey laid her head on his chest. "I'll refrain from smacking you for that, since you've been recently injured and all. But once this is all over, you're fair game."

"Hey, I already gave at the office," said Jay.

"Oh, I know." Kasey turned her head and winked at him. "We might have to find out how much later."

"Huh?"

This time Jay got the elbow in his ribs.

"Could you be any more dense? Seriously?"

"Well, it kind of sounded to me like you're offering to . . . ohhh!" Jay's ears stood up straight as he realized what she might have been suggesting.

"I know you're in a weird place right now and I don't want to, like, pressure you."

"You're not. I'm not feeling any pressure right now. I've only got the entire world to save." Jay smiled down at her. "You help me forget that for a few minutes at a time. That's a good thing."

"I've been thinking about what we should do about that." Kasey squinted at her visor and rubbed away a stray spot that marred it.

"About that?"

Kasey made an exasperated noise. "Saving the world, duh! Aren't you paying attention?"

"I hang on your every word," he said. "Do go on."

"Well . . . Let's assume that the virus works and we shut down the cockroaches on Earth. What's to stop the ones in the Ship from just sending more?"

"Uh . . . us?"

"You're damn right, *us*." Kasey patted Jay's abs.

"So you're saying we're going to have to go there."

"Yeah, I think we will. And we'll have to bring something to convince them to leave or be destroyed."

"Kasey, there's nothing to jump on in space. And there's no air to fly through. That kind of eliminates any kind of advantages given to us by our respective gods, don't you think?"

Kasey waved her hand impatiently. "Details. We wouldn't have been selected as Heralds if the Rabbit God—I can't remember his name except *Leo*, and I know that's not right—and Sialia didn't think we were, like, up to the task."

"So what you're saying is that the two of us will have to somehow get onto that Ship without being shot down or something, and bring an ultimate weapon with us that will convince the space roaches to leave Earth alone for good."

"Yeah, that sounds about right."

Jay raised his hand and his voice. "Stewardess, I think I'll take that cocktail now."

General Gershwin ambled over to look down at the two of them. "Do I need to ask for a hand check from you two kids?"

Jay dug one of his hands out from underneath the blanket and saluted. "No, your Generalship, sir. All hands are present and accounted for, sir. We were just discussing our strategy and ensuing victory celebration."

"Let's not get ahead of ourselves, shall we?" The General stamped his feet and blew out a breath of frosty air. The jet's cabin was pressurized but not-well insulated against the arctic temperatures outside. "We should be landing within the next half an hour. Once we get inside somewhere heated, we'll have a discussion about where to go from here. In the meantime, get your thoughts in order because you're going to be presenting your plan to the President."

"Which one?" asked Jay, canny as ever.

"Ours," said the General. "And the man who's making it possible for you to even be here right now by Executive Order. Area 8719 is Top Secret, and the fact that you are even permitted to know of its existence speaks of how desperate the President is."

"Well, as long as we're discussing desperate moves and Top Secret clearances and all that," said Jay. "Got any super-secret stealth spaceships lying around that we could borrow? I promise we'll be home before curfew." He nodded at Kasey. "Her dad gets really *pissed* if we're out late. He thinks I have impure intentions towards her." He winked at the General. "I have—*ow*— no such thing." He rubbed his side where Kasey had elbowed it.

"We'll see," said the General, and returned to his seat.

The flight continued. Jay and Kasey dozed a lot, getting what rest they could before they'd be once more called upon to fight on behalf of the entire world. When not sleeping, they talked and picked at some ration packs, which Jay pronounced *barely fit for human consumption.*

Jay decided the biggest problem with traveling on military aircraft was the lack of windows to press his nose against while trying to see scenery outside. It made the whole landing-on-an-icy-runway somewhat of a letdown. He could feel the temperature plummeting as the pilot taxied the jet into an insulated hangar.

"Let's go, you two," said General Gershwin.

Spence hadn't had enough time to make them winter versions of their costumes, although he'd promised to do just that with his next bout of spare time. The benefit to their skin-tight costumes was how easily other clothing fit over them. Jay had Eskimo-style mukluk boots over his feet, a heavy wool overcoat that ran from neck to ankles, and a San Francisco 49ers stocking hat perched jauntily between his upraised rabbit ears. He'd set off the whole ensemble with a matching gold-and-red striped scarf. "I feel like a Gryffindor reject," he said.

Kasey also had a long coat, boots, and scarf, but hers were all snowy white. She eschewed a hat in favor of her helmet with its visor. They both knew that they wouldn't be out in the elements for more than a minute or two—the General had assured them both that Area 8719 was underground, insulated, and heated—but the idea of arctic cold was hard to shake off.

They hustled through the icy hangar. Everything that wasn't directly heated had a sheen of frost on it, and the floor was treacherous and slick. Jay sniffled and immediately regretted it. "Don't you hate it when your snot freezes?" he said. "I still have my summer fur. It's times like this that make me want to be firmly in favor of global warming." He dodged Kasey's elbow, shot her a brilliant victory grin, then slipped on the ice and wound up sprawled on the ground.

"Quit fooling around," said Kasey. "Let's get inside and warm up. I can't feel anything below my neck."

"Really?" asked Jay, interested. "Can you feel this?"

She elbowed him. This time she didn't miss.

They had to pass through an airlock contraption to enter Area 8719. Jay had to yawn to make his ears pop. "That's funny," he said.

"It's due to the nature of the research going on here," said a female officer who met them on the far side of the airlock. "Pressure differentials here are designed to contain airborne contaminants in the event of an accident. I'm Major Finch, commander of this facility. Welcome to Area 8719." She saluted and General Gershwin returned it.

"We've brought additional samples for Dr. Tenenbaum," said the General. "My men are bringing them in now."

"Lieutenant . . . " A clean-cut young man snapped to attention at Finch's command. "Escort the General's men to Dr. Tenenbaum's lab and make sure she has any and all the help she needs for her work."

"Major Finch, may I introduce Jackrabbit and Bluebird," said the General. "They are here by special request of the President."

Jay snapped his heels together, bowing out his legs and saluting. "Sergeant Jackrabbit reporting for duty, Ma'am."

Major Finch raised an eyebrow.

"He's just that way, Major," said Kasey. "Don't mind him. He's, like, harmless."

"No I'm not," said Jay. "I'm, like, *fierce*."

General Gershwin rolled his eyes skyward in a *why me, God?* look.

"If you'll follow me please, sir, I'll escort you and your party to our conference room before we debrief the President."

They moved deeper into the complex, which ran to plain concrete walls painted over with whatever cream color the government overpaid for that particular week. Fluorescent lights hummed overhead, giving the corridors a pale glow that made everyone look ill.

"Cozy," whispered Jay to Kasey. "A few pictures on the walls, some tasteful curtains, and this place would be very homey."

Twenty

An hour later, when they were finished briefing the President on the situation, Jay felt that they hadn't accomplished much more than to confuse the leader of the free world. The President was furious about the invasion and the loss of American parahumans, and seemed stumped by his inability to fight a war with an opponent that he couldn't single out in a crowd.

Jay and Kasey, on the other hand, had learned a tremendous amount about the gritty world of *black ops* and the real purpose behind Area 8719. The research facility specialized in biological and viral weapons, something which Jay thought had been outlawed by some treaty, which his history teacher had mentioned just the month before.

"I feel filthy just having set foot in this place. God, I can't believe my own government is, like, developing such horrible things!" Kasey stamped her foot once she'd learned the true purpose to Area 8719.

"We can debate the right and wrong of it later," said Dr. Tenenbaum. "But the simple fact is this facility has the right kind of supplies and raw materials for me to quickly synthesize the virus we need. They have huge tanks full of blank viral colonies, ready to be imprinted with the genetic code to strike a target. It's fascinating from a scientific standpoint."

"How is the research progressing, Doctor?" asked General Gershwin, trying to keep the briefing on the matter of Earth's liberation.

"Quickly." The young woman adjusted her glasses. "Thanks to the additional samples you brought me, we've been able to confirm my initial development. At the rate we're progressing, I believe we can have an effective weapon against these mutated roaches within twenty-four hours."

"So fast?" said Jay. "You must drink a lot of coffee."

Dr. Tenenbaum winked at him. "When I die, they ain't gonna cremate me, they're gonna percolate me." She tapped her pen on the table for emphasis. "This place is amazing. They've done ninety-five percent of the work for me already. All I really had to do was present the samples of the target and they can tailor the virus to fit it exactly."

"Will it affect any other roaches?" asked Kasey.

"Not as far as I can tell. The mutagen alters the super-roach's DNA enough that it can be considered a distinct species. I haven't had a chance to investigate breeding, but I suspect that super-roaches cannot cross-breed with non-mutated roaches."

"Please." Jay held up his hand in protest. "We just ate. Could we maybe not talk about roaches having sex?"

"Suit yourself, Rabbitman," said Dr. Tenenbaum. "But it's a fascinating subject."

"How about dispersing it?" asked Jay. "We can't drop a bug-bomb on every infested city and installation around the world." He paused and looked at General Gershwin. "Um, right?"

The General's face reddened. "We have a delivery system capable of blanketing the entirety of the North American continent with this virus in twelve hours. From there, we project it will vector around the world within forty-eight hours, reaching over ninety-nine percent of the affected areas."

Jay's mouth dropped open in shock. "Dude, what were you planning to do with this facility? I don't even have a joke about this."

"That information is not necessary within the scope of this briefing," said Major Finch. "I believe we've sufficiently addressed the super-roach problem. That leaves the issue of a nanovirus to eliminate the machines building new super-roaches and a method of delivering the virus to the Ship."

A nameless man, who was teleconferencing from an undisclosed location into the briefing, reported, "The NSA has developed a carrier wave signal based on the specifications we received yesterday. We believe a wide-scale transmission will disrupt the nanomachines sufficiently to prevent them from mutating any further roaches. Our initial tests have shown great promise."

Kasey shook her head. "You guys are scaring me. You must, like, sit around waiting for bad things to happen so you can bring out all your nastiest toys."

"Regardless of what you may think, Bluebird, we are in the business of protecting lives. It's one of the thankless tasks of being the world's policeman—we have to develop the tools and weapons that others cannot or will not and be willing to use them in the hour of direst need." General Gershwin rubbed his hand through his short gray hair. "You may not believe this, but the government has contingency plans in place for nearly everything up to and including alien attack and invasion. We have cabals of people whose jobs are to think up the worst and most unlikely things that could happen and then to develop solutions for them."

"Well, it's still a wonder that any of you can sleep at night," Kasey said, pouting.

"The final issue we're going to tackle is a way of taking the battle to the Ship itself," said the General. "Obviously they're going to react badly with the sudden failure of their ground troops and support systems. We can't shoot it down because of its ability to disable guidance systems. At this point we're reduced to throwing a big dumb rock at it, and we just don't have the capability to build the platform for that quickly."

"A shuttle or rocket launch would be easy to detect," pointed out Major Finch. "We need something like a stealth fighter that can fly into space and then launch some kind of ballistic projectile at the target—something that will travel without motive power."

"It can't contain a warhead," said the General. "Even an impact warhead of sufficient size to destroy the Ship would have to be nuclear, and that requires electronics."

The NSA agent cleared his throat. "We can get you into space. We have a radar-invisible vessel capable of that journey, called *Daedalus*. It should achieve the closest possible approach to the Ship."

An idea occurred to Jay and he leaped to his feet.

"Something wrong, Jackrabbit?" asked the General.

"Uh, no. It's just . . . listen, can Bluebird and I have a few minutes in a private room? I think we should try to reach our, uh, *benefactors*." The General had suggested they avoid broaching the idea that there were lots of gods floating around somewhere creating Heralds and other nonsense. Jay and Kasey had argued until the General pointed out how it would sound to them if they were outsiders. They'd grudgingly agreed to keep quiet about the gods.

The NSA agent was quick as a whip and pounced on the innocuous statement. "Your benefactors? Explain yourself, please."

General Gershwin held up his hand. "It's all right, on my authority." He turned to Major Finch. "Major, is there a chapel in this facility?"

"Yes, sir," said the surprised woman.

"Would that be sufficient for your needs, Jackrabbit?"

Jay shrugged. "Any port in a storm, I guess. We could do worse than to get *that* particular wrong number." He motioned to Kasey. "Come on, let's go make a call."

Major Finch herself escorted the two heroes to the small chapel tucked away in one corner of the base—an amenity for the more devout among the employees whose tours of duty ran six months at a stretch. "You're not going to do anything *weird* in here, are you?" she asked.

"Not unless you have any goats handy for sacrifice," said Jay.

"No!"

"Well all right, then. Nothing weird. At least, nothing that will leave a stain."

The Major sighed and left, looking doubtful.

"All right, here we are," said Kasey. "What is it you want to do?"

"I've got this idea," said Jay, "but I wanted to run it past you first before bringing it up in the meeting."

"All right," she said. "Shoot."

"They say that only a ballistic projectile could get to the Ship, and then it wouldn't be any good because a warhead would be detected. What if that projectile was *me?*" asked Jay.

"What do you mean?"

"A jump," said Jay. "A great leap of faith, from that *Daedalus* thingie to the alien Ship."

"That's crazy!" shouted Kasey, oblivious to the fact she raised her voice in a place of worship. "We're talking, like, zillions of miles here! You can't jump that far!"

"It's in orbit. If I launch myself along the right trajectory, I can intercept the Ship. It might take awhile, but I think I could do it. And I could bring along a supply of the virus. Then all I'd have to do is get on board and then I have leverage on them."

"And how would you go about getting onto their Ship?" Kasey folded her arms, looking pissed off.

"I'd, uh, knock on the hull until someone let me in," said Jay. "Look, they'd want to know who I was and how I got there. Even if they want to take me prisoner, they still have to bring me on board."

"Us," said Kasey.

"Us?"

"They have to bring *us* on board. Because if you think for one second I'm letting you do some crazy stunt like this by yourself, you've got another thing coming. You'll need someone to, like, cover your back when you get to the Ship."

Jay smiled. "I figured you might say something like that, and I appreciate it, but this is something I should only risk myself over."

Kasey was having none of it. "Absolutely not. If you go, we both go. What if something goes wrong? What if your spacesuit fails, or you miss the Ship on your jump? Or what if the roaches don't bring you on board? No way will I let you try that yourself. Maybe the other Heralds long ago got to die as martyrs, but you're my boyfriend, and you don't get that option. Either we both go or nothing. I'm not getting left behind. Sorry, not going to happen."

Jay shrugged. "Suit yourself." He started to turn away but Kasey put her hand on his arm.

"And don't get any funny ideas about pretending to cave in to my demands and then punching me out and leaving without me, either."

"The idea never crossed my mind."

"Liar."

"It always works in the movies," he said, grumbling.

"Now what was that line about contacting our benefactors? Do you want to try and pray to our gods for guidance?"

Jay shrugged. He'd never been religious despite his mother's strict Baptist upbringing. Until meeting Leporidus, he'd always characterized himself as more or less a disinterested agnostic. Now he felt like he really needed some sort of spiritual guidance, and speaking directly to the god who named him a Herald seemed like the best way to gain it. "Sure, I guess," he said at last. "But I don't really have any idea what to do."

"Do what I do," said Kasey. "Bow your head and close your eyes . . ."

"And here you come with a big surprise . . ." said Jay.

"Stop that," hissed Kasey. "This is serious."

"Right, right."

"Concentrate with all your heart on Leo . . . Lepo . . . your Rabbit God, however you pronounce his name, like I will on Sialia. Focus on needing their guidance. And do it like you *mean* it; like it's the most important thing in the entire world."

"Okay," said Jay.

For several long minutes, they knelt there in the chapel, praying to their gods. Jay concentrated so hard, he felt beads of sweat break out on his face, soaking into the soft under layer of his mask. He was about to give up when he sensed a *presence*, right on the edge of his awareness. He zeroed in on that presence, like a moth drawing closer to a light bulb. He breathed life into it, nourishing it with his faith as if blowing on a spark to make it flare into a flame.

He realized the presence was not Leporidus. It was . . . it was . . . the Frog God. He couldn't remember the deity's name. He knew it was *An*-something. *Anus.* No, that wasn't it; something longer than that and less assy. *Anubis.* No, wasn't that an Egyptian god? *Aneurysm.* Closer.

Anurus!

Jay opened his eyes to see a luminescent image of the God of Frogs floating in the air above him. He elbowed Kasey and she looked up and saw him too.

"Anurus? Is that you?"

"It's me," said the frog. "Or at least an aspect of me. This is the best I can manage at the moment."

"Why? What's going on? And where are Leporidus and Sialia?" asked Kasey.

"They are at war with Blattodeus and his troops in Gods' Home," said Anurus. "They fight for the freedom of all Gods just as you fight for the freedom of mortals."

"So they're busy then," said Jay. "Listen, is there any way you can . . . take a message or I could leave a voice mail or something? We really need to talk to them."

"Alas, I cannot interrupt them. They risk their very godhood by battling among their brethren."

"Stupid rule," Jay said with a shrug. "All right, maybe you can help us directly." He outlined the basic ideas of their plan and finished with a "What do you think?"

Anurus paused, considering. "I think you're both crazy," he said at last. "But it seems a valid course of action to me." He paused once more. "I really like the idea of jumping across miles of space. Jumping is kind of my thing too."

"Look, if you get a chance to, let Leporidus and Sialia know what we're up against. If they can, maybe they can give us a little divine intervention on our behalf." Jay realized that might be seen as begging instead of praying. "And we'd be happy to help them in their own battle."

"Oh, absolutely!" said Kasey.

"Sadly, no mortal may travel to Gods' Home."

"All right then. If Leporidus can help me, I promise I'll preach his gospel to anyone who'll listen."

Anurus's eyes bulged. "He has no gospel."

"Aha!" cried Jay. "Then I'll write it for him! I can get so much extra credit for that!"

Anurus nodded. "I shall inform him. I cannot do aught else save to offer my blessing in your task ahead."

"We'll take whatever we can get," said Kasey.

Anurus seemed at a loss. Perhaps he wasn't used to giving out lots of blessings. "Uh . . . may your fleet be swift, your legs strong, and your tongue ever sticky as you leap between lily pads on the river of life."

Jay grinned. "Ribbit."

Interlude 3: Gods' Home

Leporidus fought through layer after layer of Blattodeus' insect guards, leaving a trail of ashes and greasy smoke in his wake. Sialia aided where she was able, but she didn't have the naked rage within her that the Rabbit God held. He truly loved humans, and the way Blattodeus had come in from beyond the stars to abuse his favorite people had him as steaming mad as a rabbit could get.

None of the other denizens of Gods' Home were anywhere to be found. Leporidus was certain they had all been rounded up and were being held somewhere on the grounds. It was strange to see places normally teeming with the divine abandoned but for overturned chairs and spilled drinks. He paused by Poseidon's tub, taken aback by the sight of the powerful god's trident lying unattended at the bottom of the pool.

He sent Sialia to scout around the main facility. He wanted to know where Blattodeus held the rest of the gods. He sat thinking in Poseidon's throne, nosing at the trident's handle as if it could inspire him to some new heroism. Sialia returned in a short while with news.

"It looks like most of the others are held in the sub-basement under heavy guard," she said.

"How heavy?"

"Hundreds. Thousands. I can't tell for sure. There are far more than should be even possible."

Leporidus hung his head. "I can't fight an entire army. Especially when I don't even know if the others will support me if freed. I've broken Rule after Rule, Sialia. I'll be fortunate if they don't lop off my ears and tail and pin them over the front entrance before casting me out of Gods' Home."

"There's more," she said.

"Of course there is."

"A penthouse suite is under guard."

"A suite?" asked Leporidus. "How many guards are we talking, here?"

Sialia clicked her beak. "A lot for a single suite."

"Interesting. Where's Blattodeus?"

"He's in the back offices, surrounded by dolls."

"Dolls?"

"Like mortal children play with. I don't understand it."

Leporidus hopped off the throne. "I want to see this. Show me."

The two gods went around to the rear of the main building. Sialia showed Leporidus ledges upon which he could crawl on his belly, digging his claws into mortar for purchase. Normally, as a god, a fall wouldn't injure more than his pride, but so many Rules seemed to have been suspended that he wasn't going to take any chances. He leaped across intervening gaps, stretching his body out to its fullest to catch the edges. Once he nearly slipped, but Sialia dug her claws painfully into his back and, flapping her wings madly, pulled him back onto the ledge.

At last, they came to the window sill where they could peek in upon Blattodeus. Pushing his ears back, flat against his neck and back, Leporidus glanced around the corner of the window.

Blattodeus stood amidst a roomful of small dolls, as Sialia had described. Each was but a few inches tall. Many were colored brightly, vibrantly, with incredible attention to detail. Leporidus leaned back, confused. Why dolls, of all things? He looked again, taking a few dangerous seconds to examine those closest to the window. There was something about them; something familiar.

They were figurines of Earth's parahumans.

Or were they?

Leporidus' breath caught in his chest as he realized they weren't dolls; they were mortals . . . *imprisoned in Gods' Home!*

The First Rule stated *no mortal may ever set foot in Gods' Home.* And Blattodeus had violated the most important sanctity of the dimension of the divine. He had used his own power to steal away Earth's parahumans and brought them here like a jealous collector.

Leporidus was appalled. There was no word in his lexicon for such depravity. Nearly overcome by his horror, he swooned and Sialia had to prop him up to keep him from falling a hundred feet to the courtyard below.

"What is it?" she asked.

"A Prime violation." Prime violations were against the Cardinal Rules—the twenty-seven considered Unbreakable by all the gods.

"So what do we do about it?" she asked.

"Let's see who's up in the penthouse suite," said Leporidus. "Think you're up to using enough divine power to lift me up to the deck?"

Sialia nodded. She grasped the loose fur on his back in her claws and he felt himself lifted from the window sill, light as a feather. She circled upward, climbing toward the top of the great hotel, hundreds of feet above. Finally she lit on the railing of the deck and sank onto a perch, her chest heaving with effort.

Leporidus peeked through the sliding glass door. A naked god lay frozen on his bed, paralyzed in the act of flinging the covers off. Leporidus recognized the man's muscular physique and ruddy skin. He twitched his whiskers in amusement. No wonder there were so many guards here.

He called upon the power of the divine once more, dissolving the bonds which held the man fast. Another transgression of the Rules, but perhaps one that might tilt the tide of the battle in their favor at last. The red-skinned man began to move, completing his original motion in extreme slow motion, as if he was moving through Zzzbzzz the Bee God's honey. Satisfied that he'd accomplished something of great importance, Leporidus went someplace else, found a cockroach guard, and surrendered.

At first, Leporidus feared that the guards were simply going to slay him with their razor sharp swords. Then it occurred to him that maybe they couldn't because they weren't gods themselves, while he was. That didn't stop them from kicking him around like a furry football, and by the time they finished amusing themselves with him, Leporidus hurt all over, which was an entirely new and unpleasant sensation. Nevertheless, all was going according to his half-baked plan. Shortly, a handful of Blattodeus' guards brought a cheerful Rabbit God before their master.

"There . . . you are," said the Roach God. "You have . . . slain many . . . of my people."

Leporidus shrugged. "Oops."

"I will not . . . tolerate such . . . behavior. Terrible things . . . will be done."

Leporidus indulged in a luxurious scratching behind one ear. "Oh yes indeed they will, Blatty. But not by me. And not by you either."

A heavy impact shook the entire complex. Behind Leporidus a pair of cockroach guards flew across the room to smash into bits. The sound of metal shattering chitin carried through the walls.

Blattodeus' feelers began to quake.

The man Leporidus had freed stepped around the corner. No longer nude, he was resplendent in burnished copper armor and helmet with a proud tassel of scarlet feathers. He bore a round shield spattered and stained with the ichor of uncounted foes. In his right hand he held a spear sharp enough to split atoms. He breathed like a locomotive and a bit of foam was visible at the corners of his mouth.

"May I present to you Ares, the God of War." Leporidus sat up on his haunches and waved his forepaws. "He is the Original Bad Ass. And you are in so much trouble."

Ares bellowed his challenge and charged.

Twenty-One

The *Daedalus* was an honest-to-the-gods flying saucer.

It wasn't quite round—more of a teardrop shape flattened through the middle like an egg yolk. It cruised only a few meters over the ice and snow like a shadow, moving in complete silence. Jay giggled like a toddler when he saw it. He and Kasey agreed to brave the freezing wind and frigid temperatures to watch the *Daedalus'* arrival. It was painted in a radar-absorbing matte black that ate up all available light and obscured surface details until it was nearly upon them.

As it passed overhead, Jay became light-headed and dizzy, with the unusual feeling that he might fall *up*. "Duuude," he said, moved to the extreme of male emotional response. The feeling vanished as it continued past them toward the hangar, extending tripedal landing gear.

"What was that?" asked Kasey.

"Antigravity," said General Gershwin. "We've had it since the '40s."

"No way!" Jay was beside himself. "Are you guys responsible for all the UFOs people have been seeing over the years?"

"Some of them," said the General. "Unfortunately, we can't lay claim to all of them, which has always been troubling to me. Nevertheless, let's get inside the hangar and get the two of you ready for your trip."

"When I was a kid, I totally wanted to be an astronaut," said Jay as they hurried back into the comparative warmth of the hangar.

"Every kid wants to be an astronaut," said Kasey. "You could always talk to Mrs. Postlethwaite and see if she can get you onto the right career path."

"That wouldn't do any good."

"Why not? She's a great guidance counselor. She's totally helped me figure out how to, like, get a career working with animals where I don't have to be a vet."

"It's not her."

"Well, what's the problem, then?"

Jay showed her a toothy grin. "I have problems with authority." His ears twitched as if for emphasis.

The *Daedalus* was larger than Jay expected it to be. The dark black coating made it difficult to estimate size at any kind of distance, which he was certain was an intentional feature. It had nearly the same width as the wingspan of the military jet in which they'd traveled, but seemed much larger due to its saucer-like cross section. The crest of the flattened hemisphere sat nearly twenty feet off the floor. Jay could see numerous panels and hardpoints on the underside of the saucer.

"What do you use this for, General?" he asked. "Scaring inbred farmers and buzzing conspiracy theorists?"

"The *Daedalus'* missions are classified," said General Gershwin. "As in, you don't need to know."

"But I *wanna.*"

A hatch opened on the saucer's underside and a ladder unfolded from it, followed by two crisp, clean-cut young pilots. Jay was surprised to see they were both women with short haircuts; the fair-skinned brunette wore a pixie-style 'do while the one Jay thought of as the Nubian princess had hers shaved down to almost bare scalp. They were both short and slight, almost swimming in their oversized flight suits. Jay grinned and stood a little taller.

"Behave," whispered Kasey.

The two pilots saluted General Gershwin. "Captain Micki Van Zant and First Lieutenant Regina Cox, reporting as ordered, sir."

"At ease, officers," said the General. "I'm General Artemis Gershwin."

Jay and Kasey looked at each other with raised eyebrows. *Artemis?*

"These two heroes are Jackrabbit and Bluebird, your passengers in the upcoming mission. I'm sure you'd both like a few minutes to refresh yourselves. Major Finch will show you to the ready room. We'll convene in the conference room for mission briefing at 0945."

The two Air Force officers saluted and followed Major Finch into the recesses of Area 8719. Jay and Kasey watched them go. "They're so, like, tiny," said Kasey.

"Since the early days of Project *Daedalus*, space and weight has been a consideration," said the General as they also headed back into the base. "The Air Force determined that women would be better pilots for those reasons. Now that many of the early problems with weight have been overcome, the tradition remains."

"Artemis? Really?" asked Jay, holding back giggles.

The General broke his strict military demeanor for the only time they had seen since knowing him. "Shut up."

Fifteen minutes later, they met the pilots in the conference room. Both women had showered and changed into duty uniforms and were nursing cups of coffee. They stood at attention as the General walked in but he waved them to sit back down. "We're not going to have a lot of time for protocol right now," he said. "Major?"

Major Finch stepped forward and turned on the large flat-screen monitor. It showed a map of the world. "We've loaded every ADD with Dr. Tenenbaum's viral toxin. The NSA is standing by to transmit the signal wave that should disable the nanomachines."

"What's an ADD?" asked Kasey.

"Automatic Dispersal Device," said Major Finch. "Fancy name for a terrain-following missile."

"You're going to fire *missiles* at the rest of the country?" asked Jay.

Major Finch fixed him with a gimlet stare. "It's an efficient way to deliver a chemical weapon over an area. It sprays the compound starting at a predetermined distance from detonation, flying in a complete circle, then breaks up non-explosively to disperse the remaining agent. Each of these should have sufficient amount of the virus to affect a major metropolitan area. From such hubs as New York, Los Angeles, Miami, and Seattle the virus will vector outward around the world within forty-eight hours."

Jay leaned forward, his elbows on the table, resting his chin on his clasped hands. "I hope Dr. Tenenbaum has all her genes lined up right or this could be the shortest offensive of all time, with all apologies to Lando Calrissian for that one."

"Who?" whispered Kasey.

"Most important character in the *Star Wars* movies."

General Gershwin cleared his throat and stood. "Your mission is to fly the *Daedalus* into an orbital path that intersects that of the invaders' Ship. At a predetermined distance, you will orient the ship so its airlock points directly along the orbital path. Jackrabbit and Bluebird, armed with modules of the virus, will exit the *Daedalus* on a ballistic course to intercept the Ship."

The two pilots glanced at each other with matching mystified expressions. Captain Van Zant raised a finger. "Your pardon, sir, but we're a *taxi* service?"

"We don't have any other way of getting these two into space quickly and quietly," said the General. "It is not safe for *any* vessel to approach the alien

Ship, and we cannot risk losing the *Daedalus*. Your orders stand, Captain."

"Yes sir."

General Gershwin pinched the bridge of his nose, a gesture Jay recognized as someone trying to forestall an inevitable headache. "Once Jackrabbit and Bluebird have reached the Ship, you will remain in orbit for twenty-four hours, until recalled by Space Command, or until contacted by either of the two heroes, whichever comes first. Then you will return to your point of origin to await further orders. See to whatever preparations you need to make to the *Daedalus* for launch, then assist Jackrabbit and Bluebird with the fitting of their spacesuits." He saluted. "Dismissed."

The two pilots stood, saluted, and departed the conference room.

The enormity of the task they were about to undertake was enough to make even Jay not feel much like talking.

A telephone in the room sounded. Major Finch answered it and spoke briefly before passing it to General Gershwin. He listened carefully, then nodded and spoke two words: "Yes, sir." Jay knew there couldn't be many folks that Gershwin would call *sir*, and suspected that something portentous had just happened.

Gershwin hung up the phone and looked around the room at the others' curious faces.

"You may already be a winner?" asked Jay brightly.

"The President has given the order. We are to commence with Operation Earth Freedom at once."

"Couldn't you have given it a cooler-sounding name, like Angry Firefly or Grandiose Rabbit or something?" asked Jay.

The General ignored him. "The two of you had better get ready for launch. A crew is standing by in the ready room to assist you with your spacesuits."

Jay and Kasey glanced at each other and grinned. Spacesuits. *Sweet!*

Half an hour later, Jay decided that wearing the garb of the astronaut wasn't nearly as cool as it sounded. The suit was bulky, awkward, and didn't bend easily. The backpack unit would have been impossibly hard to carry without his enhanced strength. The technicians explained that each suit was fitted with a state-of-the-art air scrubber that extended the lifespan of their air tanks into twelve hours. Each suit also came with an aerosol sprayer attached to a tank of the anti-roach virus. Dr. Tenenbaum didn't know if it would work against the invader roaches, but it would certainly frighten them once they discovered the effects against their earthbound brethren. To minimize electronic emissions, the suit monitors had been removed and replaced with sophisticated analog equivalents. Their radios would have to be shut off when they reached a certain distance, requiring them to fly the last leg of their journey "blind" to avoid any detection. In short, the technicians did everything they could do to make Jackrabbit and Bluebird invisible for their approach to the alien Ship.

"I feel more like the Stay-Puft Marshmallow Man than Han Solo," said Jay. "Probably look more like him too."

"Is there anything really important that we need to know about wearing these suits?" asked Kasey, muffled underneath her helmet. She'd been forced to remove her own helmet and visor so the spacesuit's helmet could close. Without Spence to provide a suitable alternative, she'd been forced to let her head remain completely unadorned. She made no secret of her jealousy that Jay's cowled head fit neatly under his own suit's helmet with his ears pulled back, making him look like a lop-eared rabbit.

"The manual is bigger than most college textbooks," said the tech making adjustments to her suit's arms and legs. "And you're expected to memorize it. There isn't a whole lot we can tell you without confusing you to no end."

"Just the basics, then," pressed Kasey. "I don't want to get all the way up there and not know what to do."

"All right," said Captain Van Zant. "The short, short version. Don't let it get holed. Protect your faceplate if you think you're going to get hit. Don't take it off unless you intend not to put it back on, because you can't do it without help."

"Don't throw up in it," said First Lieutenant Cox, her teeth brilliant white in her dark face. "You'll suffocate. Not a nice way to die."

"Don't take it off, don't break it, don't throw up. Got it." Jay ticked off the salient points on his fingers.

Numerous roars echoed through the complex as missile after missile launched from bunkers in a nearby glacier. A wall monitor showed the winged silver splinters bursting forth on columns of flame from a deep hole in a thick sheet of ice. An adjacent monitor showed the progress as missiles curved to the south, heading along a hundred different courses.

The timing of the operation was crucial. The NSA would transmit its worldwide signal only minutes before the initial detonations of the viral bombs. The *Daedalus* would launch upon the cessation of the transmission. General Gershwin kept one eye on the clock as Jay and Kasey tried moving around in their suits, then announced that it was time to board and prepare for departure.

The cockpit of the *Daedalus* was small, considering the size of the vessel itself. Jay and Kasey were strapped into their seats, sitting behind the two pilots, closest to the exit in the floor leading to the main cabin and airlock. Jay noted that the cockpit bubble, which appeared opaque from the outside, was transparent from within, and allowed a three-hundred sixty degree view. From his vantage point, he could see the graceful sweep of the top of the ship unobstructed all the way to the oval edge.

"Nice," said Jay. "Why can't all flying be like this?"

A subsonic thrum filled the air as whatever motive power the *Daedalus* used powered up. The ship vibrated and a wave of nausea swept over Jay as the antigravity began to function.

"On second thought . . ." Jay burped, trying to avoid anything worse than air exiting from his stomach.

"Stand by for takeoff," said Captain Van Zant. "Control, this is *Daedalus*. Open the hangar doors."

Ahead of them, the large doors slid aside, tiny bits of ice cracking off the tracks.

The *Daedalus* floated out of the hangar, graceful and serene like a flying manta ray.

"A-grav optimal. Thrusters standing by," said First Lieutenant Cox.

"Reactor engaged, turbines to speed," said Jay and Kasey together.

The two pilots glanced over their shoulders at them.

"I show green across the board," said Cox.

"At your command, General," announced Van Zant.

"Launch," ordered General Gershwin from his vantage point in the monitoring center. "Good luck, and Godspeed."

Captain Van Zant's strict military demeanor vanished as she looked back over her shoulder at Jay and Kasey and winked. "Watch *this*."

Twenty-Two

The journey into orbit was smooth, fascinating, and much faster than Jay would have believed possible. The propulsion system of the *Daedalus* was so quiet that he could hear his blood pounding in his ears with excitement. The ship flew in a traditional orientation, sliding upwards like a stone skipping on the water. If he twisted around in his seat—a difficult proposition considering the bulky spacesuit, he could see the continents shrinking below behind a veil of high clouds as well as the sparkle of sunlight on ocean.

Kasey grew more and more agitated the higher the *Daedalus* climbed. The color left her face after she glanced back once to see the curve of the Earth. Jay reached over to clasp her hand. "Afraid of heights? Kind of funny for a flying hero," he said.

"Those are normal heights. This is, like, crazy. Why am I even here? I can't fly in space! I might as well have stayed back with the General for all the good I'm going to be up here. I can't even feel my wings inside this stupid spacesuit!"

"Babe, your wings are a cloak. How can you feel them?" asked Jay.

"You can feel your ears, can't you?" Kasey asked.

Jay considered. Yes, he was amazed to discover, he actually could feel them, and had unconsciously been thinking of them as part of his body. Just to be sure, he twitched them, and almost yelled in surprise when the tips patted against his back. "Yeah, all right, I can accept that. But you're here for a very important reason."

"What's that?"

"You're the love interest. Every good story should have one." Jay grinned at her. She returned a faint smile.

Van Zant snorted from her seat ahead of them. Cox had left the cockpit to perform standard checks on the airlock before Jay and Kasey had to enter it.

"Have you been flying long, Captain?" asked Kasey.

Ahead, the sky darkened from blue to indigo and at last to black. Stars became visible against the curtain of night.

"I took my first lessons in the Civil Air Patrol when I was seventeen," said the pilot.

"Are we in space now?" asked Jay

Van Zant checked her instruments. "We're at eighty-six kilometers altitude now. The unofficial boundary of space is one hundred kilometers, so we're not quite there yet. However, once we crossed eighty kilometers you officially became astronauts. Congratulations on your remarkable achievement."

Jay grinned; he couldn't help it. "I'm an astronaut. That's sweet." He turned to Kasey. "Hey, you know, if we had kids, and they got teased in school and someone said *yo' momma's an astronaut*, they could say *you're darn right, she is.*"

"You lost me after the *if we had kids* part," said Kasey. "After that I so tuned you out."

"It was just . . . oh, never mind. *Yo' momma* jokes are lost on people who aren't from the 'hood."

Kasey snorted. "I've been to your house, Jackrabbit. Since when are the suburbs *the 'hood*?."

Cox chuckled at that as she floated back into the cockpit; they were now in a microgravity environment. Her skin was several shades darker than Jay's. "Airlock's all set," she said. "Are we there yet?"

"Orbital insertion in four minutes," said Van Zant.

Jay leered at Kasey. "Hey, want to practice some orbital insertion?"

"You may consider yourself elbowed for that."

"Okay. Uh, ow?"

"Are you two seriously going to somehow save the whole world?" asked Van Zant without turning around.

"That's the plan," said Jay, full of pride.

"God help us all."

"Amen to that," added Cox.

"Three . . . two . . . one . . . *mark*." Van Zant worked the controls. The *Daedalus* flipped around and oriented itself so it traveled bottom-first along the orbital path. Jay found himself looking straight up at the Earth hurtling by above his head.

Kasey turned green. "This is a terrible plan. I shouldn't be here."

"Honey, none of us should be here," said Van Zant. "But if you can do something about the war that we are losing, I suggest you do it before I shove you out the airlock myself. Speaking of which, the two of you need to hat up and get ready to fly. We're only ten minutes from maximum safe approach."

Jay squeezed Kasey's hand. "Stick with me, kid. We're going places."

"I wouldn't call tumbling through space *going places*." Kasey followed Jay and Cox down into the main cabin.

Cox did a quick but thorough suit check on each of them, going over tip after tip with them as she circled them.

"I'm never going to remember all this," said Jay. "I'm better suited for jumping and kicking folks in the head."

Cox ignored him and sealed his helmet. "Once you're in space, you can talk without radios by touching helmets together," she said. "You might take comfort in that when you're under enforced radio silence."

"I'd take comfort in, like, my bathrobe and a pint of Jamocha ice cream," said Kasey as Cox sealed her helmet.

"I prefer Cherry Garcia myself," said Cox. "All right, you're ready to go." She sighed. "I wish I could go with you. I've always wanted to space-walk."

"I'll bet this suit would fit you," said Kasey.

Jay steered her into the airlock. "Bluebird, we're going to be just fine."

Kasey's voice was rising in pitch and volume. "We're not going to just be fine. We're jumping out of a freaking *spaceship!* Forget about skydiving . . . we're taking stupidity to a whole new level here!"

Jay touched her helmet with his and spoke in as soothing a tone as he could manage. "Babe, please, you have to settle down. This is how we save the world, you know? But I promise you that I won't let you go, no matter what happens. I know I joke around a lot, and I kind of have to, because, um, it's what my god wants me to do. But right now I'm totally serious."

Kasey hiccuped. "D-don't be. I need you to be f-funny. It helps."

"You want me to be funny on demand? What am I, a tour guide? Uh, then I'm your funny bunny." He paused. "Not funny like Bunny. Funny like . . . uh . . ."

Van Zant called over the speaker. "When the exterior doors open, you do your leap straight through the center of the lock. We'll give you as much of a boost as we can, but then we're on rapid deceleration. You'll have six minutes to make any course corrections, then you shut off your radio and we wait."

"Is she always this bossy?" whispered Jay to Cox.

"She can hear you," said Cox. "And for the record, yes."

"Three minutes," said Van Zant. "Cox, cycle the lock."

"Good luck." Cox shut the door.

The airlock was a small cylindrical chamber, barely eight feet long. Jay twisted around, orienting himself against the interior door so the exterior was over his head. He pulled Kasey around to him. A fine sheen of sweat droplets floated around her face. She looked pale.

He shut off his radio for a moment and touched his helmet to hers. "You okay?" Their suits grew stiffer from internal pressure as the air was sucked out of the lock.

She gulped and nodded, managing a faint smile. "I'm a Herald."

"That's the spirit." Jay flipped his radio back on just in time to hear Cox announce she was opening the exterior door. With a whine that was transmitted through Jay's feet, it rolled back to reveal starry space beyond.

"What should I do?" asked Kasey.

"Face me and wrap your arms and legs around me," Jay said. He took a firm hold of her rear, wishing it wasn't covered by thick, airtight fabric.

He felt weight in his legs as the *Daedalus* accelerated along the orbital path in preparation for giving him a suitable boost.

"Twenty seconds," said Van Zant. "Good luck, you two."

"Why does everyone keep wishing us good luck? They don't think we're going to fail, do they? Hey, you two, you don't think—"

"Launch," said Van Zant.

Jay jumped as hard as he could and the couple flew out of the airlock like a bullet leaving a cannon.

Almost immediately the *Daedalus* fired braking thrusters and the oval vessel fell away from, shrinking to a pinpoint within seconds. Overhead, the great curve of the Earth showed twilight from the sun far behind them.

"Oh God," whispered Kasey. "I'm falling ... I'm falling ..."

"You're fine. We're fine, aren't we, *Daedalus*?"

Van Zant confirmed Jay's off-the-cuff effort. "Nicely done, Jackrabbit. You're exactly on an intercept course.

I show you to reach the Ship in three hours and eleven minutes. Do you have anything to say before we go to silent running?"

"Am I being recorded?" asked Jay. "Oh, of course I am. Okay, I'd just like to say hi to my best friend Bunny and I love you, Mom. Also, reality TV sucks, the 49ers need a better offense, and my buddy Spence made our costumes, so all superheroes ought to check him out. I'm Jackrabbit, and I approved this message."

"Bluebird?" asked Van Zant. "Anything?"

Kasey shook her head inside her helmet, her eyes shut tight.

"She's staying quiet," said Jay. "I think she's trying to keep from throwing up. I'm sure she'd want to say something about making afternoon naps a basic right for employees, the complete ban of pop divas from the movie and television industry, and to use better nacho cheese in the high school cafeteria. Seriously, have you tasted it? It's not cheese. It's not even in cheese's neighborhood. I think it might resemble food, but that's about it."

Kasey relinquished one hand of her death grip on him enough to give him a weak punch in the arm.

"Yes, I'm positive that's what she was going to say," said Jay.

"Duly noted," said Van Zant. "Shut off your radio. We'll wait for twenty-four hours or until we hear you've been successful." The radio clicked off, and Jay realized that he and Kasey were more alone than any other two humans in the history of mankind.

Jay looked up at the Earth overhead, trying to take in the entire amazing sight. Then he became a little overawed and needed to break the tension. "I spy . . . with my little eye . . . something beginning with *A*."

"It's Africa, isn't it?" Kasey didn't open her eyes.

Jay looked at the continent drifting by overhead, inverted from its normal position on maps. "Uh . . . no . . . Really, it's, uh . . ."

Kasey glanced around, then up, then squeezed her eyes shut once more. "It *is* Africa, you big dope!"

"I knew I should have studied harder in Riesling's class. I thought it was Greenland." Jay paused. "It's a long three hours until we reach the Ship. What do you want to talk about?"

"I don't know. I don't care. Just don't make me look."

Jay thought things over for a bit, then sang, "Ninety-nine bottles of beer on the wall . . ."

Twenty-Three

After the first hour, Kasey relaxed enough to open her eyes, although she wouldn't look overhead at the Earth as it eclipsed the Sun. Tiny blotches of light—cities—appeared in the darkness, concentrated along the coasts. Tropical thunderstorms sparkled with occasional lightning like distant sequins.

"There it is," said Jay. Kasey twisted around to follow his pointing finger.

The Ship lay ahead of them, hanging in space and lit up like a Christmas ornament. It had a blocky, ugly design, as if it had been designed solely for functionality, not aesthetics. Superstructures jutted away from the main hull seemingly at random intervals and angles. If it had really been built by superintelligent cockroaches, it must have taken them thousands of years.

"Wow . . ." said Kasey. "It's, like, kind of big, isn't it? I thought with roaches being all, you know, tiny, it might be a small ship."

Jay wondered how the two of them could make any kind of difference in the outcome of the war. "So what's the plan?" he asked.

"Plan?" Kasey sounded pissed. "There's no plan. We haven't yet had a plan since this whole thing started."

"There's no need to be sarcastic. Of course we have a plan," said Jay.

"All right then . . . what's first?"

Jay thought it over. "The first thing to do is to figure out how to land on that Ship without doing my famous impression of a bug hitting a windshield."

"That's an image I so didn't need."

"Relax. I can land on anything."

"I wish I had your confidence."

"So do I. I really had you going there for a minute, didn't I? Truth be told, I'm about to pass *hraka* in my bunny suit." Jay shivered just a bit.

"Well," said Kasey. "I guess the first thing is to change your orientation so you're landing feet-first."

Jay fussed with the little nitrogen jets on his suit until he got himself turned around. In his mind he altered his perception so that he was now dropping toward the Ship from above. "You know," he said after a minute. "We should have called the Guinness Book of Records. Longest jump ever."

"We will when we get back."

"That's the spirit. Listen, I think you're going to have to climb onto my back," said Jay.

"You want me to *what?*"

"I can't flex my legs to land when I'm holding you like this."

"But how am I going to hold onto you?"

"However you can."

Kasey managed to crawl around his body to perch over his backpack. "This isn't going to work. I'll crush your life support when we land."

"Well, whatever we do, it's going to have to be fast. It's hard to tell distances but I think we're going to hit in a minute or two." Jay's voice was tight with tension.

"Can we slow down using the nitrogen jets?"

An idea occurred to Jay. "We'll use them to change our angle of approach. Instead of smacking into the hull, we'll be able to skip along it and stop that way. Gentle as a baby's butt."

"I wish I had some of whatever it is that you're smoking," said Kasey.

"Listen, the next time we jump a bazillion miles onto an alien Ship, we can do it your way."

Jay fired the nitrogen jets in short bursts. Each blast made a small change to their approach angle. Soon, they were keeping pace with the Ship, dropping towards it at only a few feet per second.

All at once, they were upon it. Jay's toes brushed the hull. The spacesuit's magnetic soles clamped down on the hull and then they stopped, swaying uncertainly as their perceptions once again shifted. Kasey stepped down onto the hull. "This is better." She looked up at the Earth. "Now I feel like I'm standing on a deck. What now?"

"I said we'd knock, and that's what we're going to do. Let's find a porthole or a window or something," said Jay.

They began to walk across the surface of the Ship's hull, avoiding unusual protuberances and devices. Eventually they found a rectangular window like a skylight and peeked in.

They saw hundreds of insects zooming back and forth, clinging to textured floor, walls, and ceilings in a corridor. Jay and Kasey looked at each other and shrugged. Jay reached out and tapped on the transparent surface.

All the insects inside froze in their movements. Jay put on his best toothy smile and waved at them.

A minute later, a hole appeared in the hull near Jay and Kasey. They looked at each other, walked across the hull, and climbed into the portal. The exterior door shut behind them and a hissing sound and change in the way their suits fit suggested they were in an airlock. The indicators on their suits showed that oxygen levels outside were rising and soon the pressure matched Earth-normal. As far as they could tell, there was breathable air within the ship. Jay opened his visor a crack and rich smells assailed his nostrils: lubricants, exhaust, organic smells. It was heady and not very pleasant. He went ahead and removed his helmet anyway. It would be easier to deal with whatever came next if his ears weren't all cramped inside it. Kasey did likewise, grimacing at the odors.

The interior door slid open and they found themselves facing a tunnel filled from top to bottom with roaches. The curtain of insects parted and the Supreme Leader stepped through. He still wore the articulated black armor, and up close his face looked even more artificial than ever. "Who are you . . . and what . . . do you want?"

"I'm Jackrabbit, and she's Bluebird, and we've come from Earth to accept your surrender."

Rattling, cockroachy chatter filled the tunnel at a surprising volume level. Jay had the distinct impression they were laughing at him. The Supreme Leader's face never wavered in the least. "I do not . . . comprehend. We have . . . already defeated your world."

"Then you're not really paying attention," said Kasey. "Maybe you've noticed your little nano-thingies aren't working. And maybe your super-roaches down there are dying off by the thousands. And maybe our own weapons and tools and stuff are working again. Did you miss that?"

"It is . . . a temporary setback. There is . . . no way . . . you can win."

Jay rested his hand on the sprayer valve. "Then maybe you noticed these tanks on our backs? Well, the big ones carry our life support. But these little ones carry the same virus your companions below are dying from. All I have to do is release it."

"It will . . . not work. We are . . . different from your . . . Earthly insects."

"Can you be sure of that? Sure, you're separated by, like, millions of years of divergent evolution and . . . oh. Crap, he's probably right," said Kasey.

"It is . . . a moot point. We have . . . already disabled your devices."

Jay looked down to see roaches swarming around his hand and equipment. The damn things were so small and light that he didn't even notice them through the thick spacesuit. "Okay," he said. "What happens now?"

"We must . . . seek guidance. You will . . . accompany us to the . . . Chamber of Communion."

"Communion? You're going to call on your god? We had no idea you were so pious."

"We call . . . upon the only . . . true god. Not the . . . false idols . . . you worship."

"Boy is he in for a disappointment," said Jackrabbit as they followed the Supreme Leader deeper into the bowels of the Ship. Cockroaches flowed all around them in waves of tiny legs and waving feelers. "Dude, our abilities are gifts from those false idols."

"Do not . . . blaspheme within . . . the chamber of communion . . . or your lives . . . are forfeit."

"Whatever," said Kasey. "Listen, if we're going to be talking to your god, maybe we could get out of these suits?" She shrieked as insects swarmed onto her and Jay. In a few seconds of frantic activity, they completely disassembled the military-issue spacesuits, leaving Jay and Kasey only in their costumes.

"Ah," said Jay in disappointment. "That's going to make getting home a little harder."

"The prisoners . . . will not speak. You are . . . profane."

"I'll give you some fucking Samuel L. Jackson-level profanity that'll make whatever you use for ears bleed," grumbled Jay under his breath.

The Chamber of Communion was a large, football-shaped room. Cockroaches swarmed to cover every available inch of space along walls, floor, and ceiling.

Once in place, they sat frozen, antennae pointed at the focus in the center of the chamber.

"These guys make the flag team at school look sloppy," whispered Jay.

"They *are* sloppy, kind of," Kasey whispered back.

"I wouldn't know. I usually just stare at their butts."

Kasey elbowed him.

The Supreme Leader floated into the center of the room and seemingly turned inside out as the roaches within the shell popped out through its skin to completely cover it.

"Ewww!" whispered Kasey.

The roaches that had been within the Supreme Leader drifted away to the walls, leaving nothing remaining in the center of the room except a glow which had no apparent source. A strange whispering sound filled the room—the sound of millions of clicking cockroach voices calling in prayer.

The glow began to solidify into the image of a huge humanoid roach. It waved its highest limbs frantically and hissed incomprehensible sounds. Without any warning, something *bright* happened to it and the image vanished, but not before every roach in the chamber saw their god cleaved in half. They milled about in uncertainty and panic.

"Uh, that looked kind of bad," said Jay. "Maybe we ought to kind of . . . run?"

Kasey grabbed him, outstretched her wings, and launched down the hallway, able to fly easily in the air despite the absence of gravity. Like a furious wave breaking on the shoreline, a million roaches chased after them.

"Where are we going?"

"Away from them," she said. "Every time something like that happens in the movies, things start blowing up and the next thing you know the entire Ship will be gone and we get to float home."

"Where are we going to go? We're on the Ship already! Besides, that's only in the movies."

Flames appeared to fill the corridor ahead of them.

Kasey cupped her wings, braking to a stop. They confronted a column of fire that stretched from floor to ceiling, leaving char marks in its wake. Behind them, the surge of roaches halted the pursuit, uncertain about the apparition.

"I AM THE, UH, LORD YOUR GOD," said a voice.

Jay's jaw dropped open as he recognized Leporidus' tone in the proclamation. "He said he didn't do that," he whispered to Kasey. He turned to the column of flame. "Hey, you said you didn't do that."

"SILENCE, MORTAL."

The roaches reformed the Supreme Leader's body and he stepped forward to confront the column of fire.

"You are not . . . our god."

"YOUR GOD IS DEAD. YOU ARE A PEOPLE WHOSE FAITH IS NO LONGER VALID."

Kasey and Jay looked at each other in surprise. "*Deus ex machina*," said Jay.

"What's that?"

"The God from the Machine," he explained. "Dramatic device. It's when the gods come in to clean up a mess made by us mortals and tie everything up neatly. *And* it's a hackneyed cliché," he said, raising his voice a bit to chastise his God.

"SILENCE, FOOLISH MORTAL," said the column of flame. "I HAVE NOT, UH, NEITHER TIME NOR PATIENCE FOR THEE."

"Without our god . . . we are nothing," said the Supreme Leader. "There is . . . no reason . . . to return to the world . . . of our ancestors."

"PRECISELY," said Leporidus.

"We shall . . . destroy it."

"WAIT, WHAT?"

"Whoa, hold on there a minute." Jay stepped forward and raised his hands. "There's no need to go off half-cocked here. Why do you have to destroy the Earth?"

"We cannot . . . return to our own world. It has been . . . rendered uninhabitable."

"That's a stupid reason to destroy *our* world," said Kasey. "That won't make you feel better about losing your god. People lose their faith all the time. They just find a new source of faith. There's always a reason to continue living, and a reason to continue trying to do good instead of evil."

"Uh, right. What she said." If such a thing were possible, the column of flame burned with a bit of blushing uncertainty.

"We are . . . not evil people."

"Well, no, of course you're not. But destroying a planet on purpose would be, like, an unspeakably evil act. There isn't a god in the entire space-time continuum who could forgive you for that."

Jay nodded with enthusiasm. "She's really smart, fellas. You should listen to her."

"Wouldn't it be better if you started over? Get a fresh start somewhere new? You could build a new life, a new faith, a new world. Maybe then we could all live together in peace and harmony."

Jay sniffed and wiped an exaggerated tear from his eye. "Doesn't it just get you right in the feels? One big love-in." He held out his hands. "Dude, I think we gotta hug."

"But where . . . can we go? Our Ship . . . has no fuel . . . to leave this system. If we . . . do not land soon . . . we will all perish."

The column of flame lowered its voice. "I'm going to get in a lot of trouble for suggesting this, given the current circumstances where I am, but have you considered the possibilities Mars has to offer?"

"No . . . we have not."

"Oh, yeah, Mars is a great place!" Jay grinned. "Wide-open spaces, deep canyons, high mountains . . . uh, rocks and stuff."

"You could go there; your people are pretty crafty. They could, like, over time remake it into a world not unlike the one your ancestors came from," said Kasey.

"You would . . . give us . . . this world freely?"

"In a heartbeat," said Jay. "Not, uh, that we really have any claim over it."

"We must . . . convene." The roaches along with the Supreme Leader flowed out of the corridor back in the direction of the Chamber of Communion.

The column of flame disappeared, leaving only Leporidus the Rabbit God in its place. "Wow," he said. "That was close."

"You sure showed up at the right time," said Jay.

"It was largely luck," said Leporidus. "We managed to overthrow the Roach God before he could completely take over Gods' Home. What a mess. We're going to be straightening it out for millennia. Maybe you guys could start a cult of cleanliness and get us some more janitorially-oriented and housekeeping gods? Hygieia is going to be millennia cleaning things up, and believe me, she'll make everyone miserable telling us about it. *I'm not your mother. Why don't you pick up after yourselves? This is why we can't have nice things.*"

"So what happens now?" asked Kasey.

"Well, that's going to depend on the outcome of the debate down the hall," said Leporidus. "Anurus and Sialia are in the process of returning the Earth's parahumans. We found them being held hostage in Gods' Home. Totally indecent."

"Oh, that's good," said Jay. "So we're not the only ones anymore. What happens if the roaches decide to take our offer?"

"Then you can all go home and live in peace."

"But what if they don't?" asked Kasey.

"Then this ship and all aboard it will be destroyed."

"What?" asked Kasey and Jay together.

"By who?" added Jay.

Leporidus looked away. "By me."

The two humans gasped in shock.

"I cannot permit your world to be destroyed, but in saving it I forfeit everything I am."

"But what about us?" Kasey's eyes were wide. "You'll let us get away first, right?"

"I'm afraid not," answered Leporidus. "It is the duty of every Herald to die in the name of his or her sponsoring god. It has been this way since the Beginning."

Jay considered the option. "Well, I hope the roaches pick life over death, but I guess if it's the difference between the two of us or the whole world, there isn't really any choice, is there?"

Leporidus twitched his whiskers with affection. "That's very mature of you to say so."

"Enough to get us out on a technicality? *There's still hope for the human race* and all that?"

"Sorry, no."

With a whispering of tens of millions of tiny feet, the roaches returned up the hallway. "We have . . . reached a decision," said the Supreme Leader.

"That was fast. You guys don't mess around," said Jay. "So what's it going to be?"

"We shall . . . accept your offer. Go . . . in peace. What . . . is that creature?"

Leporidus looked guilty. He'd forgotten to turn back into a column of fire. "Oh. Crap." He vanished.

Jay asked Kasey, "Did we just give Mars to a bunch of interstellar cockroaches?"

Twenty-Four

"Jay, I swear, if you don't get your head together, I'm going to have to break up with you!"

Jay blinked as every book in his locker tumbled down to the floor. The last one knocked the giant smoothie out of his hand and it fell all over his newly-cleaned Air Griffeys with a muddy-sounding splat. "What?"

Kasey flipped her ponytail. Other kids passed around her like a river flowing around a sturdy rock. In the past she might have hidden in a doorway. Now she was like a primal force of nature, and the rest of the kids could sense it and gave her a wide berth. "You're being a crappy boyfriend. You promised to, like, take me someplace nice for our one week anniversary. You better get your head screwed on straight or else I'm going to have to pin back those ears, Mister."

She winked at him, spun on her heel, and strode down the hall like an icebreaker cutting through the Arctic.

"She totally owned you, dude," said the ginger-headed freshman, still taller than Jay but not nearly as physically imposing anymore.

Jay couldn't believe it. Had it already been a week? Between catching up from a couple of days of missed schoolwork, dealing with General Gershwin's briefings, and trying to decide what superhero team would best fit Jackrabbit's unique personality profile, he'd lost track of his burgeoning relationship with Kasey.

"You suck so hard," said the kid, and loped off to his first class.

Jay blinked again and the freshman was replaced by Mr. Pillsbury. "Look at you, Jones. You miss a couple days of school and suddenly you look like an American Gladiator. You've got to tell me your secret. Come be my power forward and show me how you've achieved your remarkable results."

"What?" managed Jay

"Basketball, bub. You should be tearing it up on the court, leading us to the district championship . . . and State . . . and Nationals!" He wiped a tear away and clapped Jay on the back. "You come see me after school and I'll get you signed up. I bet you've got a vertical leap like nobody would believe." He looked down. "What is that, some kind of algae?"

Jay shook his head to clear it, feeling overwhelmed. He looked down at his feet, which felt like they'd become part of somebody's failed chemistry experiment. The wheatgrass-and-spirulina smoothie was turning his books into a sodden, green mess. Since his transformation into a Herald, he'd found himself growing less and less interested in meat and hungrier for, well, grass.

A tingle on the back of his neck made him look back and there she was. Kasey stood at her locker down the hall, applying blue eyeshadow with the help of the mirror inside her locker door. She saw him watching her, winked, and smiled despite yelling at him a minute earlier. She still wore the headband and conservative dress, but now she wore them with authority and Jay dug her look. He'd even spotted a few other girls who'd traded in their low-rise jeans and half-shirts for longer skirts and cardigans. Maybe Kasey would usher in a new fashion trend among high schoolers. Now she was the Hot White Girl, and he'd become the envy of the entire school.

"Hey, punk, where's your boyfriend?" A couple of football players in their letter jackets stood and surveyed him like he was a tackling dummy. The envy of *most* of the school, amended Jay. "We heard you're getting dumped by that hot chick because you're a shitty boyfriend. Guess you'll have to get your knob slobbed by your—"

A foot encased in a pink Converse hightop interrupted the jock's mocking tone. Jay winced at the meaty thud the shoe made against the jock's face. The football player gasped in surprise, slipped in the spilled smoothie, and wound up face-down in the puddle. "I'm going to kick your gay ass," he roared.

Bunny held his ground and smiled. "Half the school just saw my gay ass knock yours onto the ground. You want them to see it again? Because I'd be happy to give another demonstration, punk."

The jocks looked at each other. "Come on, let's get out of here," said the one who Bunny hadn't knocked down.

The other one stood up, green slime spreading down the front of his letter jacket. "You watch yourself. I can still kick your ass, fag."

Bunny made kissy-lips at him.

The jocks stalked away, shoving underclassmen out of their way.

"Kind of Clint Eastwood, aren't you?" asked Jay

"Is it too much? I was afraid it might be too butch," said Bunny. "But Spence loves it when I talk all tough and everything."

"Yeah, you're great, bro."

"Listen, I've been thinking about taking up capoeira. That's a Brazilian martial art based upon dance. I think I'd be really good at it, and then I can be a better sidekick."

"You're a great sidekick already, Bunny. The best a Jackrabbit could hope for."

"You're so sweet, Jay honey."

"Now, we need to talk about that Playboy bunny costume you're dead-set on wearing."

"It's dashing, isn't it?"

"Bunny, seriously. It's ridiculous."

"It's me, Jay. Totally me. Just like that darling brown bunny suit is totally you."

Jay chuckled. "Yeah, it totally is."

Epilogue: Gods' Home

After a lengthy, detailed inquiry conducted by Apollo and Athena, Leporidus the Rabbit God was exonerated from his misbehavior throughout Gods' Home since his actions kept both the mortal world and the divine lands intact.

As part of the arrangement, it was agreed that the gods would allow the mortals to forget the events surrounding the failed invasion. There would be dreams, and humanity would retain an aversion to cockroaches for the foreseeable future, but the arrival of the Ship, the landings, and the kidnapping of the parahumans would vanish from racial memory. Only those with the most direct involvement would remember anything at all, and those memories would fade over time. More than anything, the gods agreed upon such a course of action out of sheer embarrassment. Their walled garden had been breached, and a great many of them were out of sorts about the whole thing.

"I suppose all's well that ends well," said a cheerful Anurus from his lily pad. Sialia sat perched on a branch above him while Leporidus groomed his fur on the bank of the pool.

"The Heralds have decided to continue their romantic relationship," said Sialia. "What does that make you and me?" She stared at Leporidus with a gimlet eye.

"Friends without benefits?" asked the Rabbit God. "Seriously, what else could we be? We're not even the same species."

"It looks like the Heralds are also going to continue their quest to vanquish evil," said Anurus. "True heroes in every sense of the word." He looked at his friends. "You two chose your Heralds very well."

Leporidus laughed. "Luck of the draw, friend Frog."

Anurus looked confused. "Draw?"

"It's a human expression," said Leporidus. "It has to do with gambling and luck—both friends of mine."

"All right, if you say so," said Anurus. "So what happens now?"

A roar interrupted them. "Leporidus? I want to talk to you!" Ares came stomping up the path, mad enough to spit rivets. "What in the name of Nine Hells have you done to my world, my beautiful Mars, giving it over to a bunch of thrice-damned insects?"

Leporidus leaped up from his resting spot.

"Now, Anurus, we run for our lives."

The three animal gods scattered.

ABOUT THE AUTHOR

 Ian Thomas Healy dabbles in many different genres. He's a ten-time participant and winner of National Novel Writing Month and is also the creator of the *Writing Better Action Through Cinematic Techniques* workshop, which helps writers to improve their action scenes.

When not writing, which is rare, he enjoys watching hockey, reading comic books (and serious books, too), and living in the great state of Colorado, which he shares with his wife, children, house-pets, and approximately five million other people.

Ian is on Twitter as @ianthealy
Ian is on Facebook as Author Ian Thomas Healy
www.ianthealy.com

ABOUT THE COVER ARTIST

Jeff Hebert is the creator of the HeroMachine online character portrait creator. He lives in Durango, Colorado, where he pursues his lifetime dream of drawing super-heroes all day while not wearing pants.